Ian R. MacLeod

This special signed
edition is limited to
750 numbered copies

This is copy

624

JOURNEYS

JOURNEYS

STORIES BY
IAN R. MACLEOD

Subterranean Press 2010

"The Master Miller's Tale" first published in *The Magazine of Fantasy and Science Fiction*, May 2007 © Ian R MacLeod 2007

"Taking Good Care of Myself" first published in *Nature*, May 2006 © Ian R MacLeod 2006

"The English Mutiny" first published in *Asimov's Science Fiction*, October/November 2008 Science Fiction © Ian R MacLeod 2008

"Topping off the Spire" first published as a pamphlet for Novacon, November 2008 © Ian R MacLeod 2008

"Elementals" first published in *Extraordinary Engines*, ed. Nick Gevers © Ian R MacLeod 2008

"The Camping Wainwrights" first published in *Postscripts*, Winter 2008 © Ian R MacLeod 2008

"The Hob Carpet" first published in *Asimov's Science Fiction*, June 2008 © Ian R MacLeod 2008

"On the Sighting of Other Islands" first published in *Celebration*, ed. Ian Whates © Ian R MacLeod 2008

"Second Journey of the Magus" first published online by *Subterranean Online*, 2010 © Ian R MacLeod 2010

First Edition

ISBN
978-1-59606-297-9

Subterranean Press
PO Box 190106
Burton, MI 48519

www.subterraneanpress.com

TABLE OF CONTENTS

The Master Miller's Tale   9

Taking Good Care of Myself   61

The English Mutiny   65

Topping off the Spire   89

Elementals   95

The Camping Wainwrights   131

The Hob Carpet   153

On the Sighting of Other Islands   209

Second Journey of the Magus   213

The MASTER MILLER'S TALE

THERE ARE ONLY ruins left now on Burlish Hill, a rough circle of stones. The track which once curved up from the village of Stagsby in the valley below is little more than an indentation in the grass, and the sails of the mill which once turned there are forgotten. Time has moved on, and lives have moved with it. Only the wind remains.

Once, the Westovers were millers. They belonged to their mill as much as it belonged to them, and Burlish Hill was so strongly associated with their trade that the words *mill* and *hill* grew blurred in the local dialect until the two became the same. Hill was mill and mill was hill, and one or other of the Westovers, either father or son, was in charge of those turning sails, and that was all the people of Stagsby, and all the workers in the surrounding farms and smallholdings, cared to know. The mill itself, with its four sides of sloped, slatted wood, weather-bleached and limed until they were almost paler than its sails, was of the type known as a post mill. Its upper body, shoulders, middle and skirts, turned about a central pivot from a squat, stone lower floor to meet whichever wind prevailed. There was a tower mill at Alford, and there were overshot water mills at Lough and Screamby, but Burlish Mill on Burlish Hill had long served its purpose. You might get better rates further afield, but balanced against that had to be the extra journey time, and the tolls on the roads, and the fact that this was Stagsby, and the Westovers had been the millers here for as long as anyone could remember. Generation on generation, the Westovers re-cemented this relationship by marrying the daughters of the farmers who drove their carts up Burlish Hill, whilst any spare Westovers took to labouring some of the many thousands of acres which the mill surveyed. The Westovers were pale-faced men with sandy hair, plump arms and close-set eyes which, in their near-translucence, seemed to have absorbed something of the sky of their hilltop home. They went bald early—people joked that the winds had blown away their hair—and worked hard, and characteristically saved their breath and said little, and saved their energies for their work.

●

ALTHOUGH IT TOOK him most of his life to know it, Nathan Westover was the last of the master millers on Burlish Hill. Growing up, he never imagined that anything could change. The endless grinding, mumbling sound of the mill in motion was always there, deep within in his bones.

He was set to watch a pulley which was threatening to slip.

"See, how it sits, and that band of metal helps keep it in place..." His mother, who often saw to the lesser workings of the mill, explained. "It's been doing that for longer than I and your father can remember. Now, its getting near the end of its life..." The pulley turned, the flour hissed, the windmill rumbled, and this small roller spun on in its slightly stuttering way. "...and we can't stop the mill from working when we're this busy just to get it fixed. So we need someone to keep watch—well, more than simply watch—over it. I want you to sing to that roller to help keep this pulley turning and in place. Do you understand?"

Nathan nodded, for the windmill was always chanting its spells from somewhere down in its deep-throated, many-rumbling voice, and now his mother took up a small part of the song in her own soft voice, her lips shaping the phrases of a machine vocabulary, and he joined in, and the roller and the pulley's entire mechanism revolved more easily.

Soon, Nathan was performing more and more of these duties. He even learned how to sing some of the larger spells which kept the mill turning, and then grew strong enough to lift a full sack of grain. He worked the winches, damped the grist, swept the chutes, oiled the workings. He loved the elegant way in which the mill always re-balanced itself through weights, lengths, numbers, quantities. Fifteen men to dig a pit thus wide down at school in the village meant nothing to him, but he solved problems which had anything to do with grain, flour, or especially the wind, in his dreams.

Sometimes there were visits from the rotund men who represented the county branch of the Millers' Guild. On these occasions, every-thing about the mill had to be just so—the books up to date, the upper floors brushed and the lower ones waxed and the sails washed and all the ironwork shiny black as new boots—but Nathan soon learned that these men liked the mill to be chocked, braked and disengaged, brought to a total stop. To them, it was a dead thing within a frozen sky, and he began to feel the same contempt for his so-called guild-masters which any self-respecting miller felt.

On the mill's third floor, above the account books with their pots of green and red ink, and set back in a barred recess, leaned a three volume Thesaurus of spells. One quiet day at the end of the spring rush when sails ticked and turned themselves in slow, easy sweeps, his father lifted them down, and blew off a coating of the same pale dust which, no matter how often things were swept and aired, soon settled on everything within the mill.

"This, son…" He cleared his throat. "Well, you already know what these are. One day, these books will be yours. In a way, I suppose they already are…"

The yellowed pages rippled and snickered. Just like the mill itself, they didn't seem capable of remaining entirely still, and were inscribed with the same phonetic code which Nathan saw stamped, carved or engraved on its beams, spars and mechanisms. There were diagrams.

Hand-written annotations. Darker smudges and creases lay where a particularly useful spell had been thumbed many times. Through the mill's hazy light, Nathan breathed it all in. Here were those first phrases his mother had taught him when he tended that pulley, and the longer and more complex melodies which would keep back those four apocalyptic demons of the milling industry, which were: weevils, woodworm, fire and rats. As always with things pertaining to the mill, Nathan felt that he was rediscovering something he already knew.

●

THERE WERE SLACK times and there were busy times. Late August, when the farmers were anxious to get their summer wheat ground and bagged, and when the weather was often cloudless and still, was one of the worst. It was on such late, hot, airless days, with the land spread trembling and brown to every cloudless horizon, and the mill whispering and creaking in dry gasps, that the wind-seller sometimes came to Burlish Hill.

Nathan's father would already be standing and waiting, his arms folded and his fists bunched as he watched a solitary figure emerge from the faded shimmer of the valley. The wind seller was small and dark, and gauntly pale. He wore creaking boots, and was wrapped in a cloak of a shade of grey almost as thunderous as that of the sack he carried over his thin shoulders, within which he bore his collection of winds.

"So this'll be the next one, eh?" He peered forward to study Nathan with eyes which didn't seem to blink, and Nathan found himself frozen and speechless until his father's hand drew him away.

"Just stick to business, wind-seller, shall we?"

It was plain that his father didn't particularly like this man. After all, every miller worth his salt prided himself on making the best of every kind of weather, come storm or calm, glut or shortage. Still, as he unshouldered his sack and tipped out a spill of frayed knots, and especially on a such a hot and hopeless day as this, it was impossible not to want to lean forwards, not to want to breathe and feel and touch.

"Here, try this one…" Spidery fingers rummaged with the hissing, whispering, pile to extract the grey strands of what looked, Nathan thought, exactly like the kind of dirty sheep's wool you saw snagged and fluttering on a bare hedge on the darkest of winter days. "…That's a new, fresh wind from the east. Cut through this summer fug clean as a whistle. Sharp as a lemon, and twice as sweet. Delicate, yes, but good and strong as well. Turn these sails easy as ninepence."

Already, Nathan could taste the wind, feel it writhing and alive. Slowly, reluctantly, his father took the strand in his own hands, and the wind-seller's mouth twitched into something which was neither a smile or a grin. "And this one…Now *this* will really get things going. Tail end of a storm, tail end of night, tail end of winter. Can really feel a bite of frost in there, can't you? Course, she's a bit capricious, but she's strong as well, and cool and fresh…"

It was nothing but some bits of old willow bark, torn loose in a storm and dampened by trembling puddles, but already the windmill's sails gave a yearning creak. Nathan's father might grumble and shake his head, but the haggling which followed all of this conspicuous advertisement was always disappointingly brief. They all knew, had known since before the wind-seller's shape had first untwisted itself from the haze of the valley, that—strange things though they were, the knotted breath of forgotten days—he would have to buy some of these winds.

●

ALTHOUGH NO ONE else believed them, master millers swore they could taste the flavour of the particular wind which from which any batch of flour had been turned. The wind prevails from the east on Burlish Hill, unrolling with a tang of salt and sea-brightness from the blustery North Sea, but no wind is ever the same, and every moment of every day in which it blows is different, and setting the mill to just the right angle to take it was, to Nathan's mind, the greatest skill a master miller possessed. Even as you sang to your mill and anchored it down, it responded and took up the ever-changing moods of the wind in her sails. But the feelings and flavours which came from the wind seller's winds were different again. On dead, dry afternoons when the sky was hard as beaten pewter, Nathan's father would finally give up whatever makeweight task he was performing and grumblingly go to unlock the lean-to at the mill's back to where he kept the wind-seller's winds.

The things looked as ragged now then they had when they fell from the wind-seller's sack—nothing more than dangling bits of old sea-rope, the tangled vines of some dried-up autumn, the tattered remains of long-forgotten washing—but each was knotted using complex magics, and what else were they to do, on such a day as this? Already writhing and snapping around them—a grey presence, half felt, half seen, and straining to be released—was the longed-for presence of some kind of wind. Up in the creaking stillness of the main millstone floor, and with a shine in his eyes which spoke somehow both of expectation and defeat, his father would break apart the knot with his big miller's hands, and, in a shouting rush, the wind that it contained would be released. Instantly, like the opening of an invisible door, the atmosphere within the mill was transformed. Beams creaked in the changed air and the sails swayed, inching at first as the main axle bit the breakwheel and the breakwheel bore down against the wallower which transported the wind's gathering breath down through all the levels of the mill. The further sky, the whole spreading world, might remain trapped in the same airless day. But the dry grass on Burlish Hill shifted and silvered, and the mill signalled to every other hilltop that at least here, here on this of all days, there was enough wind to turn its sails.

The winds themselves were often awkward and capricous things; unseasonably hot and dry, awkwardly damp and grey. They seemed to come, in that they came from anywhere at all, from points of the compass which lay beyond north and south, east or west. Even as Nathan and his father began gladly heaving the contents of all the waiting sacks into the chutes, the atmosphere within the mill on those days remained strange. Looking out though the turning sails, Nathan half-expected to see changed horizons; to find the world re-tilted in some odd and awkward way. Lying in his bunk in the still nights afterwards when the winds had blown themselves out, he pictured the wind-seller wandering the grey countrysides of some land of perpetual autumn, furtively gathering and knotting the lost pickings of a storm with those strange agile fingers, muttering as he did his spells over rags and twigs.

●

THE OTHER CHILDREN at the school down in the village—the sons and daughters of farmers, carpenters, labourers, shopkeepers, who would soon take up or marry into the same trade—had always been an ordinary lot. Perhaps Fiona Smith should have stood out more, as Nathan often reflected afterwards, but she was mostly just one of the girls who happened to sit near the back of class, and seemed, in her languorous demeanour, to be on the verge of some unspecified act of bad behaviour which she could never quite summon the energy to perform. Nevertheless, she could hold her own in a fight and throw an accurate enough stone, at least for a girl. If he'd bothered to think about it, Nathan would have also known that Fiona Smith lived at Stagsby Hall, a structure far bigger and more set-apart than any other in the village, which had a lake beside it which flashed with the changing sky when you looked down at it from Burlish Hill, but he envied no-one the size of their homes; not when he had all of Lincolnshire spread beneath him, and lived in a creaking, turning, breathing mill.

He was surprised at the fuss his parents made when an invitation came for the Westovers and seemingly every other person in Stagsby to attend a party to celebrate Fiona Smith's fourteenth birthday, and at the fussy clothes they found to wear. As they walked on the appointed afternoon towards the open gates of Stagsby Hall, he resented the chafe of his own new collar, the pinch of the boots, and the waste of a decent southerly wind.

It was somewhat interesting, Nathan might have grudgingly admitted, to see such an impressive residence at close hand instead of looking at it from above. Lawns spread green and huge from its many golden windows towards a dark spread of woods, and that lake, which, even down here, reflected the near-cloudless sky in its blue gaze. There were indecently under-dressed statues, and there were pathways which meandered amongst them with a will of their own. Of greater importance, though, to Nathan and most of the other villagers, was the food. There was so much of it! There were jellies and sausages. Cheeses and trifles. Cakes and roast meats. There were lurid cordials, sweet wines and varieties of ale. Sticky fingered, crusty faced, the younger children took quarrelling turns to pin the tail on a blackboard donkey, and those of Nathan's age soon lost their superiority and joined in, whilst the adults clustered in equal excitement around the beer tent. There was also a real donkey, saddled and be-ribboned and ready to be ridden. But the donkey whinnied and galloped as people attempted to catch it, kicking over a food-laden table and sending a mass of trifles, jellies and cakes sliding to the grass in a glistening heap. The adults laughed and the children whooped as the donkey careered off towards the trees, watched by the stiff-faced men and women in tight black suits, whom, Nathan had divined by now, were the servants of Stagsby Hall.

The afternoon—for the villagers, at least—passed in a timeless, happy whirl. Much beer and wine was drunk, and the children's livid cordials seemed equally intoxicating. Trees were climbed; many by those old enough to know better. Stones, and a few of the silver trays, were skimmed across the lake. Then, yet more food was borne out from the house in the shape of an almost impossibly large and many-tiered cake. The huge creation was set down in the shade of one of the largest of the oaks which circled the lawns. Nodding, nudging, murmuring, the villagers clustered around it. The thing was ornamented with scrolls and flowers, pillared like a cathedral, then spired with fourteen candles, each of which the servants now solemnly lit.

An even deeper sigh than that which had signalled the lighting the cake passed through the crowd as Fiona Smith emerged into the space which had formed before it. Nathan hadn't consciously noticed her presence before that moment. Now that he had, though, he was immensely struck by it. He and many of his classmates were already taller and stronger than the parents whose guilds they would soon be joining. Some were already pairing off and *walking the lane together*, as the local phrase went, and even Nathan had noticed that some of the girls were no longer merely girls. But none of them had ever looked anything remotely like Fiona Smith did today.

Although the dress she wore was similar in style to those many of the other women were wearing, it was cut from a substance which made it hard to divine its exact colour, such was its shimmer and blaze. Her thick red hair, which Nathan previously dimly remembered as tied back in a pony tail, fell loose around her shoulders, and also possessed a fiery glow. It was as if an entirely different Fiona Smith had suddenly emerged before this cake, and the candle flames seemed to flare as though drawn by an invisible wind even before she had puffed out her cheeks. Then she blew, and all but one of them flattened and died, and their embers sent up thirteen trails of smoke. Smiling, she reached forward as if to pinch out the last remaining flame. But as she raised her hand from it, the flame still flickered there, held like a blazing needle between her finger and thumb. Then, with a click of her fingers, it was gone. The entire oak tree gave a shudder in the spell's aftermath and a few dry leaves and flakes of bark drifted down, some settling on the cake. The villagers were already wandering back across the lawn, muttering and shaking their heads, as the servants began to slice the object up into spongy yellow slices. They were unimpressed by such unwanted displays of guild magic, and no-one was feeling particularly hungry.

Without understanding quite how it had happened, Nathan found that he and Fiona Smith were standing alone beside the remains of the cake.

"You're from up there, aren't you?" She nodded through the boughs towards the mill. "Bet you'd rather be there now, eh, with the sails turning? Instead of down here watching a good day go to waste."

Although it was something he wouldn't have readily admitted, Nathan found himself nodding. "It was clever," he said, "what you did with that cake."

She laughed. "All those faces, the way they were staring! I felt I had to do something or I'd explode. Tell you what, why don't we go and have a look at your mill?"

Nathan shifted his feet. "I'm not sure. My father doesn't like strangers hanging around working machinery and it's your birthday party and—"

"I suppose you're right. Tell you what, there's some of my stuff I can show you instead."

Dumbly, Nathan followed Fiona Smith up towards the many-windowed house, and then through a studded door. The air inside was close and warm, and there were more rooms than he could count, or anyone could possibly want to live in, although most of the furniture was covered in sheets. It was as if the whole place had been trapped in some hot and dusty snowfall.

"Here." Fiona creaked open a set of double doors. The room beyond had a high blue ceiling, decorated with cherubs and many-pointed stars. "This…" She shook out a huge, crackling coffin of packaging which lay scattered amid many other things on the floor. "*This* is from Father. Ridiculous, isn't it?" A sprawled china corpse stared up at them with dead glass eyes. Nathan had always thought dolls ridiculous, although this one was big and impressive. "At least, I think it's from him. His handwriting's terrible and I can't read the note."

"Your father's not here?"

"Not a chance. He'll be in London at one of his clubs."

"London?"

"It's just another place, you know." Shrugging, Fiona aimed a kick at the doll. "And he's decided I can't stay here at school, either, or even in Stagsby. In fact, I'm sure he'd have decided that long ago if he'd remembered. That's why everyone's here today—and why I'm wearing this stupid dress. It's to remind you of who I'm supposed to be before I get dragged to some ridiculous academy for so-called young ladies."

Fiona crossed the room's considerable space towards the largest of all the sheeted objects which, as she tugged at its dusty coverings, revealed itself to be an enormous bed. Enamelled birds fluttered up from its silken turrets as if struggling to join the room's starry sky. Nathan had seen smaller houses.

"This used to be mother's bedroom. I'd come and just talk to her in here when she was ill from trying to have a son. Of course, it didn't work, so now my father's stuck with a girl for an heir unless he goes and gets married again, which he says will be when Hell freezes."

"All of this will end up as yours?"

Fiona gazed around, hands on hips. "I know what you're thinking, but my father says we're in debt up to our eyeballs. I'm sure that you Westovers have far money than we Smiths, with that mill of yours. My grandfather, now, *he* was the clever one. Had a real business mind. He was a proper master smithy. He was high up in the guild, but he still knew how to work a forge. He used to show me things. How to stoke a furnace, the best spells for the strongest iron…"

"And that trick with the flame?"

Fiona looked at Nathan and smiled. Her eyes were a cool blue-green. He'd never felt such a giddy sense of sharing, not even when he was working hard at the mill. "I'll show you his old room," she murmured.

Up wide, white marble stairways, past more sheeted furniture and shuttered windows, the spaces narrowed. Nathan caught glimpses through windows of the lake, the lawns, Burlish Hill and then the lake again as they climbed a corkscrew of stairs. Cramped and stuffed with books, papers, cabinets, the attic they finally reached was quite unlike the great rooms below. Fiona struggled with a shutter, flinging sunlight in a narrow blaze. Nathan squinted, blinked, and gave a volcanic sneeze.

She laughed. "You're even dustier than this room!"

Standing in this pillar of light, Nathan saw that he was, indeed, surrounded by a nebulous, floating haze. "It's not dust," he muttered. It was a sore point; the children at school often joked about his powdery aura. "It's flour."

"I know." Something fluttered inside his chest as she reached forward to ruffle his hair, and more the haze blurred around him. "But you're a master miller—or you will be. It's part of what you are. Now look."

IAN R. MACLEOD

After swiping a space clear on a sunlit table, Fiona creaked open the spines of books which were far bigger and stranger in their language than the mill's Thesaurus of spells. The same warm fingers which he could still feel tingling across his scalp now travelled amid the symbols and diagrams. Guilds kept their secrets, and he knew she shouldn't be showing him these things, but nevertheless he was drawn.

"This is how you temper iron…This is an annealing spell, of which there are many…" A whisper of pages. "And here, these are the names for fire and flames. Some of them, anyway. For there's always something different every time you charge a furnace, put a spark to a fire, light a candle, even."

Nathan nodded. All of this was strange to him, but he understood enough to realise that flames were like the wind to Fiona Smith, and never stayed the same.

"Not that my father's interested. He likes to joke about how he got through his grandmaster exams just because of the family name. And I'm a woman, so there's no way I can become a smithy…" She grew quiet for a moment, the sunlight steaming in copper glints across her hair as she gazed down at the vortex of flame which filled the page.

"What'll you do instead?"

"I don't know." She looked up at him, fists balled on the table, her face ablaze. "That's the frustrating thing, Nathan. *These* of all times. All the old spells, you know, the stupid traditions, the mumbling and the superstitions and the charms and the antique ways of working, all of that's on the way out. Modern spells aren't about traditional craftsmen—not when you can mine the magic right out of the ground. That's what they're doing now, in places up north like Redhouse and Bracebridge, they're drawing it out of the solid earth almost like they extract coal or salt or tar or saltpetre."

Nathan nodded. He knew such things as mere facts, but he'd never heard anyone speak about them—or, indeed many other things—with such passion.

"I'm lucky. That's what my grandfather used to say. I'm lucky, to be living in this time." She shook her head and chuckled. "The future's all around us, just like the world you must be able to see from up on your hill. And this, now *this*..." She pushed aside the book, and took down a large and complex-looking mechanism from a shelf. "He made this himself as his apprentice piece."

It took up most of the table, and consisted of a variety of ceramic marbles set upon a complex-looking arrangement of arms and gears, all widely spaced around a larger and even brighter central orb which might have been made of silver, gold or some yet more dazzling metal.

"It's an orrery—a model of the universe itself. These are the planets, this is the sun. These tiny beads are the major stars. See..." As she leaned forward, their blaze was reddened and brightened by the fall of her hair. "This is where we are, Nathan. You and I and everyone else, even the Hottentot heathens. This is our planet and it's called Earth..."

Nathan watched as her hands, her hair, fluttered from light to dark amid all this frail and beautiful machinery, and his thoughts, and his lungs and his heart and his stomach, fluttered with them. Although he had no great care for matters of philosophy, he couldn't help feeling that he was witnessing something exotic and forbidden in this strangely God-like view of the universe which Fiona Smith was describing. But it was thrilling as well.

"Now watch."

Leaning down close to the table, afloat in sunlight, she puffed her cheeks and blew just as she had at blown at her birthday cake. But now, smoothly, silently, the planets began to turn.

"You try."

She made a space and Nathan shuffled close. Then, as conscious of the warmth of Fiona's presence beside him as he was of the blaze of the sun, he bent down and he blew.

"It that how it really works?"

She laughed. "You of all people, Nathan, up on that hill, should understand."

Silently, seemingly with a will of its own, in gleam and flash of planets and their wide-flung shadows, the orrery continued to spin. Nathan watched, willing the moment to continue, willing it never to stop. But, slowly, finally, it did. It felt as if some part of his head was still spinning as, dazed, he helped Fiona close the shutter and followed her back down the stairways and along the corridors of her huge house. Everything, the sheeted furniture, the hot air, seemed changed. Outside, even the sun was lower, and redder, and it threw strange, long shadows as it blazed across the lawn. The world, Nathan thought for one giddy moment, really has turned.

●

A SPACE OF desk near the back of the class at the village school lay empty when Nathan and his classmates returned to school, although there was nothing particularly remarkable in that. Soon, they all were leaving, drawn into the lives, trades and responsibilities for which they had always been destined, and Fiona Smith's birthday party, if it was remembered at all, was remembered mostly for the drink and the food.

The windmill up on Burlish Hill turned, and the seasons turned with it. More and more, Nathan was in charge, and he sang to the mill the more complex spells which his father's voice could no longer carry. The only recreation he consciously took was in the choir at church. Opening his lungs to release the sweet, husky tenor which had developed with the stubble on his cheeks, looking up at the peeling saints and stars, it seemed to him that singing to God the Elder and singing to the mill were much the same thing. Instead of calling in at the pub afterwards, or lingering on the green to play football, he hurried straight back up Burlish Hill, scanning the horizon as he did so.

He could always tell exactly how well the mill was grinding, and the type of grain which was being worked, merely from the turn of its sails, but there was a day as he climbed up the hill when something seemed inexplicably wrong. Certainly nothing as serious as a major gear slipping, but the sweep of the sails didn't quite match the sweet feel of the air. He broke into a run, calling to his mother as he climbed up through the stairs and ladders inside the mill. The main sacking floor was engulfed in a grey storm, with flour everywhere, and more and more of it sifting down the chutes. Hunched within these clouds, gasping in wracking breaths, Nathan's father was a weary ghost.

Feeble though he was, the miller resisted Nathan's and his mother's attempts to bear him out into the clear air. He kept muttering that *a miller never leaves his mill*, and struggled to see the rest of the sacks before the wind gave, even though the batch was already ruined. Finally, though, they persuaded him to take to his bed, which lay on a higher floor of the mill, and he lay there for several days, half-conscious and half delirious, calling out spells to his machine which still creaked and turned between periodic, agonising bouts of coughing.

As poor luck would have it, the winds then fell away. It grew hot as well. The skies seemed to slam themselves shut. Much more now for the sake of his father than for the mill itself, Nathan longed for a breeze. He searched for the hidden key to the lean-to, and he found it easily in a tin of nails; just the sort of place he'd never before have thought to look. The few knots left inside the small, close space hung like dried-up bats on their iron hooks, and part of Nathan felt that he had never seen anything so weathered and useless, and part of him already felt the strange, joyous surge of the winds which each clever knot contained. There were no spells in the miller's Thesaurus to tell him how to unbind a trapped wind, nor the sounds that he should make as he did it, but doing so came to him easily as laughing and crying as he stood on the millstone floor. The air changed in a clamour of groans. The mill's sails creaked and bit and turned. At last, there was work to be done, and Nathan got on with doing it with a happier heart. He knew without climbing the ladders that his father's breathing would be easier, now that the mill working properly all around him once again.

Although he was too exhausted to make use of it, Nathan released another wind at twilight purely for the glory of feeling the pull and draught of it through all the mill's leaky slats and floors. More than usually, this one lived up to the wind-seller's tales of bright spring mornings and the shift of grass over cloud-chased hills. When Nathan finally climbed the ladders to see his father, his mother—who had sat all day beside him—was smiling through her tears. He took the old man's hand and felt its hot lightness, and the calluses which years of handling sacks and winches had formed, and the smooth soft gritting of flour which coated every miller's flesh, and he smiled and he cried as well. They sat through the old man's last night together, breathing the moods of the mill, watching the turn of the stars through the hissing swoop of it sails.

●

NATHAN'S MOTHER WENT to live in an old warehouse beside the dunes at Donna Nook, which had once stored southern hops before the channels had silted up. He visited her there on saints' days, taking the early milk wagon and walking the last miles across the salt flats. Although she was wheezy herself now, and easily grew tired, she seemed happy enough there spending her days talking of brighter, breezier hours, and better harvests, to the widows of other millers. In those days, the Guild of Millers still took care of its own, but of course there were no master millers there. Nathan knew, had long known, that a miller never left his mill.

But he was a master miller now—even if the ceremony of his induction which he'd envisaged beneath the golden roof of some great guild chapel had dwindled to a form signed in triplicate—and he gloried in that fact. Heading back from Donna Nook towards Burlish Hill in darkness, he would find his mill waiting for him, ticking, creaking, sighing in its impatience to take hold of the breeze. Often, he sang to it out loud even when no spells were needed. It was only when he was with other people, he sometimes reflected, that he ever felt alone.

The mill was Nathan's now, and that made up for most things, even though there was less and less time for the choir, for all the spells in those whispering books, and every creak and mood and scent and flavour, every seed of corn and every grain of flour it produced, shaped his life. When he rested at all, it was merely to taste the breeze as he stood on top of Burlish Hill. From there, on the clearest of days, you really could see all of Lincolnshire, and gaze down at the huddled roofs of Stagsby, and the rippling windflash of the lake which lay beside the closed and shuttered windows of Stagsby Hall.

Everyone remarked on Nathan Westover's energy in the seasons that followed. Millers were never known to take an easy bargain, but few drove them as hard as he did. Farmers and grain dealers might have gone elsewhere, but here was a miller who worked to whatever deadline you set him, and never let any of the sacks spoil. On nights of full moon, you could look up and see the sails still turning. It seemed as if he never slept, and then he was to be seen early next morning at the grain markets at Alford and Louth, making deals to buy and sell flour on his own account, driving more and more those notoriously hard bargains, clapping backs and shaking hands in ways which earned money, but also respect.

These were good times across the rich farmlands of Lincolnshire. The big cities of the Midlands were spreading, sucking in labour under their blanket of smoke, and that labour—along with the growing middle classes who drew their profit from it, and the higher guildsmen who speculated in shares, bonds and leases—needed to be fed. Borne in on endless carts, and then increasingly drawn along rails by machines powered by that same heat and steam which drove those burgeoning industries, came supplies of every kind, not least of which was flour for cakes, biscuits and bread.

Sometimes, although it seemed less often than in the times of Nathan's childhood, the wind-seller still came to Burlish Hill. In rare hot, windless times, the shimmer of something—at first it could have been nothing more than a mirage twirl of dust—would emerge from the valley, and Nathan wondered as he watched where else this man travelled, and what he did on other, less closed-in days. He always bought a few examples of the wind-seller's produce, although in truth he barely needed them, for he made sure that he made efficient use of all the winds which the sky carried to him, and had little need for such old-fashioned methods of enchantment. The world was changing, just as Fiona Smith had once said it would. Magic was being pumped out from the ground beneath northern cities. You could buy oils and new bearings which were infused with it, which was commonly called aether, and which spilled dark hues in daylight, and shone spectrally in the dark. Nathan was happy enough to use the stuff—at least, if it was for the good of his trade. He knew, or surmised, that the hill itself had once been the source of the power which drove the mill's spells, but perhaps that had been wearing thin, and what else could you do but breathe and work through the seasons which time brought to you, and sing, and wait, and smile, and hope for the best?

Few people ever command anything in this world in the way that Nathan Westover then commanded his mill. He even enjoyed the tasks which most millers hated, and loved filling in the reds and greens of profit and loss on the coldest of nights when the sails hung heavy with ice. Numbers had their own climates, their own magics. Even as the inks froze and his fingers burned with the cold, they whispered to him of how far he had come. He was building up savings in a bank account in Louth—which he was then re-using, re-investing, but still always accumulating, and it sometimes seemed as he stood outside in the bitter air and the night sparkled with motes of frost that the dark shape of the big house twinkled once more with lights.

*I'm sure you Westovers have far more money than we Smiths, with that mill of yours...*Even if it hadn't been true then, it was almost certainly true now, and the rumour was that Grandmistress Fiona Smith would soon be back at her home in Stagsby Hall. Nathan waited. After all, London and all those other far-away cites were merely places, just like Stagsby, and he was too accustomed to the capriciousness of the Lincolnshire weather to be anything other than patient. He even bought himself a suit, which he never wore after the tailor's fitting, although he often took out to admire its cut and shake off its grey coating of dust.

There was an even harder edge to the bargains Nathan drove for the following spring's rye and wheat, an even brisker turn to his mill's sails. Then came another summer, and the larks twirled and sang over the ripening corn, and the skies cleared to a blue so deep and changeless that it scarcely seemed blue at all. Then the weather flattened, and there was no rain, and the heat shrank the lake beside Stagsby Hall, and the corn dried and the dogs panted and even the turning of the mill on Burlish Hill finally slowed until there came an afternoon when everything in the world seemed to have stopped—including Burlish Mill.

Nathan was looking out from the mill's top level when he saw a dark shape emerging from the heat-trembling stillness of the valley below. Certainly not a farmer, for the corn was dying and none of them had anything to bring. Skidding down ropes and ladders, he stood squinting and rubbing the sweat from his eyes as he willed the shape to resolve into a dusty silhouette.

The heat was playing tricks. The body wouldn't stay still, and the movement was too swift. Through the thick, flat air, Nathan caught the brisk rattle of hooves. He waited. A rider on a gleaming, sweating, chestnut horse came up, dismounted, and walked quickly over to him. Female, tall and well-dressed, she took off her riding hat and shook out her red hair.

Smiling at his surprise, Grandmistress Fiona Smith took a step closer, and Nathan saw that, whatever else was different about her, the fiery blue-green gleam in her eyes was unchanged. Then her gaze moved up to the sails above him and her smile widened into a wonder which Nathan had only ever seen on the faces of fellow millers. Still smiling, still looking up, she began to walk around the brown summit of Burlish Hill.

Nathan followed. Fiona Smith was wearing dark riding clothes—boots, a jacket, a long skirt—but they were new and sharply-cut and trimmed with shining edges of silk. This was nothing like the same girl who'd once stood before the candles of that many-tiered cake. Not that he hadn't dreamed, not that he hadn't dared to wonder—but looking at this woman, watching the way she moved, he marvelled at how she'd changed and grown to become something quite unlike the person he'd imagined, yet was still recognisably Fiona Smith...All those ridiculous thoughts, all those years, and yet here, real beyond any sense of reality, she was.

"This is where you keep the winds?" Despite the heat of the day, the air around the stone lean-to had a different edge.

"You know about the wind-seller?"

"I've made a small study of your trade." Fiona shivered. Her eyes flashed. "Why don't you use one now?" Her gaze changed shade as she looked at him. "But that's the old way isn't it?—and no self-respecting miller likes to admit that they can't manage on nature's winds alone. And such winds cost money. That's what I admire about you, Nathan Westover. You're passionate, but you're practical as well. You should hear people talk. Everyone..." She turned beneath the still sails, spreading her arms, encompassing every horizon. "From here to here. They all know exactly who you are."

"But probably not by name."

"The miller of Burlish Hill!" She laughed. "But that's what you are, isn't it? Strange, for a man of such substance to have his life founded on a mere breath of air."

Nathan laughed as well, and felt something loosening like a freed cog inside him. He'd never thought of it like that before, but she was right. "I'd always hoped," he said, "that you'd come here."

"And here I am." She gave what he took to be a curtsey. "And I have a proposal to put to you, Nathan. So why don't you show me inside your mill?"

Nathan would have been speechless, but the mill was the one topic about which he was always capable of talking, and pride soon took over from his shock at Fiona's presence. He could even push aside the thought of how he must appear, with his arms bare and his dungarees still gritty from the dust of a long morning's cleaning, and probably reeking of sweat and linseed oil as well. At least all his hard work meant that his mill was in near-perfect condition. Even if Fiona Smith had been one of the guild inspectors who'd used to come in his father's time, he doubted if she'd have been able to find a single fault. Pristine, perched, as ever, on the edge of turning movement, the mill welcomed them through streams of sunlight into its hot, fragrant floors.

The Master Miller's Tale

"You and I," she murmured as she climbed the last ladder and took his arm to help herself over the lip, "I always used to look up at this mill and wonder if I couldn't become a part of what it does." She was so close to him now that he could feel the quickness of her breath, see how the changed brownness of her skin consisted of the merging of constellations of freckles.

Then they both hunched deliciously close together beside the top-most window, looking down and out at all the world as it was revealed from the combined height of Burlish Hill and Mill. Nathan could feel the warm tickle of Fiona's hair. The world was hazed today, but everything was clear in his head as on the sharpest day as he pointed out the directions of the winds. All Lincolnshire lay before them, and he could feel the soft pressures of her body as she leaned closer. Despite these distractions, he found that talking to her was easy as chanting the simplest spell. When most people looked out from Burlish Hill, they strained for the name of this or that town, a glimpse of the sea, or the tower of Lincoln Cathedral. They saw buildings, places, lives, distances to be travelled, but what Nathan saw and felt was the pull of the sky, the ever-changing moods of the air. And Fiona Smith understood. And she even understood—in fact, already knew—about the demands which different types of grain placed upon a mill. How the millstone had to be geared and levelled differently according to the grist and the weather, and all the complex processes of sifting and sieving, and then of proving and damping, about which even the farmers who produced the stuff, and the bakers who baked it, barely cared. She could have been born to be the wife of a master miller.

Then, as they leaned close, she talked to him of her years away from Stagsby. The school she'd been sent to by her father had been just as dreary as she'd feared, but she'd travelled afterwards, fleeing England and heading south and south, towards warm and dusty lands. Looking out, Nathan could smell the air, feel the spice heat of the lives of those darker-skinned people who, as she put it, slept when they felt like sleeping, and danced when they wanted to dance. He'd never cared much for the idea of travel, for the winds of the world always

29

came to him, but now he understood. The mill was turned fully south, facing across the brown weave of England towards other, more distant, shores. Then, although he hadn't had spoken a single word of a spell, the whole great machine shook, and its gears moved, and the sails swooped in a single, vast turn. It was a sign.

Helping Fiona back down the levels, lifting her fully in his arms, he felt her amazing warmth and lightness. She laughed and her breathing quickened and she pressed herself closer still. Leaning her whole soft pressure of her body against him as they swayed together on the main millstone floor, she planted a long, hot kiss on his lips.

The mill was entirely at rest again when they stumbled outside, but Nathan's head was spinning.

"It's almost a shame to be back here in England," Fiona sighed, fanning her neck as she pushed back her hair. "I hate London, with its traffic and fog and smell. But here, here—being *here*. You know, I'd almost forgotten. But I feel so at home here in Lincolnshire. And you and I, Nathan, we really could be partners, equals. Let me show you…"

Reaching into the pocket of her skirt, she took out something small and round. A coin, a bead, or perhaps merely a pebble. But it had a black aether-glow. Crouching down, she tossed it like a dice onto the brittle brown grass, and the blackness spread. Nathan was reminded of the tumble of the wind-seller's sack of storms, but this was different again, and far more powerful. Grids of fire leapt across the blackness. Dimming even the blaze of the sun, they threw sparks in Fiona's hair. When she looked up at him, that same fire was in her eyes.

"This," she said, "is a map, a plan. It goes far further than you can see from even this hill. Here are the great cities, the ports and towns and industries, of all of England. See, Nathan, see how they blaze! Even you, up here, must use fire. But think what fire really means. Fire means power. The same power you feel when your body grows hot as you move those arms to work all those clever winches, but magnified, multiplied, almost beyond measure. Then imagine all that power, that heat, controlled." The brightness amid the dark mirror which lay spread before them increased. It spilled and moved and pulsed along quivering veins. Nathan felt like God himself looking down on this different world, for he saw every movement and detail as close and intricate as the fine auburn down on Fiona's bared neck as she leaned beside him. There were shimmers of steam, furnace mouths, endless sliding arms of metal. He tasted coal and smoke.

"The world is changing, Nathan, and you and I—we—must change with it. Forget about the old ways, the old songs, the old spells. Already, see here, the arm of the railway is reaching as far as Spalding. Soon it will be here, and here, and here, as well." Fire dripped from her fingers, spilling and spreading between the embers of the towns. "The engines, the rails, will draw everything closer together. People—their trades, their lives."

Nathan blinked. He saw the tiny machines made larger, and enormously powerful, through clever intricacies of iron. But why was she telling him this? He strained to understand.

"I've already had the land down there around Stagsby Hall surveyed. The road itself can easily be widened, and the lake will provide all the water we could ever need—at least, it will when there's a decent drop of rain. And did you know Nottinghamshire's made of nothing but coal? Transportation shouldn't be an obstacle even before we can get a railhead at Stagsby. Right now, the engineers are drawing up the plans for the enginehouse. But they're just *experts*, Nathan, people who work at desks with pens. I need someone who really understands the local markets, and probably knows more than anyone else in this whole county about the grinding of grain. I need someone who has the whole business in his blood."

"You're saying—"

"I'm saying we could work together, down there. We're living at the start of a new age. Forget about the guilds and all the old restrictions, we can make ourselves its kings and queens. As soon as the money is released, straight after the marriage—before, if I get my way—I'll give the order to start digging the steam mill's foundations."

For all that Nathan Westover was a man of business, the conversation was taking a surprising turn. "But what about here, what about this mill?"

"I know, I know, it's a wonderful creation. Of course, it will be months before we can get the steam mill fully commissioned. Even after that, I'm not suggesting that we shut this windmill down immediately. Far from it—I'm sure we'll need it for years to take up the slack and deal with the seasonal rush. But this isn't some dream, Nathan. This isn't about sentiment or imagination. My fiancée's a senior master of the Savants' Guild. He has shares in almost all the major rail companies, and they're developing the latest most powerful magics of steam and iron. Of course, he's old, but he still—"

"What do you mean? You're saying you're *engaged?*"

"Where else do you think I'm getting the money to finance this project?"

Nathan stood up. For all the sun's blaze, the darkness of the map seemed to have spread. Then he started to laugh, taking in great, racking gulps of air. "And you thought—*you* thought that I would give this up? My whole life? Come to work down there..." He raised a trembling hand.

"But what *did* you think, Nathan?" She was standing beside him again now, and far too close. He had to turn away.

"All these years. All these *bloody* years. I've hoped..."

"Hoped what, Nathan?" There was a pause. The light gathered. He sensed a change in her breath. "I wish, I *do* wish, that life could be different. But that isn't how it works, Nathan, and even if it did... Even if it did, can you imagine how much money the sort of the project I'm talking about needs? It's more than you could ever dream of, wealthy though I'm sure you think you are. My husband will get my name and what little of my companionship he still needs when I'm in the city, and I'll get his money and the freedom to live here. It's a fair enough exchange. But as for the rest. As for the rest. It doesn't mean...I *like* you, Nathan, I truly do, and I felt what we both felt inside the mill. And if we *were* together, if we were business partners, and you were the manager of my mill, who knows..." Her hand was upon his shoulder, kneading the flesh, moving towards his neck "Who knows—"

He span around in a blurring rage. "And you imagined that you could have me as your *employee*—working on some infernal machine! You might as well expect me to go to Hell."

"Hell, is it?" Stumbling back, she stooped to snatch up the stone. Its spell swirled around her in a dark vortex of flame in the moment before the map faded. "You think *that* would be Hell?" She grabbed her mare's reins, mounted, and drew the creature about in a wild and angry lunge. It reared, baring its teeth around the bridle. "There's only one infernal machine, Nathan Westover," she shouted, "and we're both on it, and so's everyone else in this world!"

With a dig of her heels, Grandmistress Fiona Smith galloped off down Burlish Hill.

●

THE HEAT FINALLY relented in peals of thunder. Huge skies hurried over Lincolnshire, and what grain there was that year, poor stuff, flattened and wettened, was finally borne up Burlish Hill's puddled track for grinding. If the miller up there seemed even brisker and grumpier in his dealings than he had before, it got little mention, for all the talk was of what was happening down at the big hall. When storms finally blew themselves out, there came a last day of surprising warmth; the last echo of summer cast across the stark horizons of autumn. Sheer luck, although the villagers agreed that the wedding breakfast to which they'd all been invited could scarcely have been bettered. From the few glimpses they'd had of the bride with her flaming hair and pearl-beaded dress, everyone agreed that she made a finest imaginable sight as well. Pity the same couldn't be said of the groom, who looked dried up and old enough to make you shudder at the very thought of him and her… Not that much of that was likely, it was agreed, as the wine and the beer flowed, still less a child. Lights were lit as dusk unfurled. A great machine with a greedy furnace and tooting pipes was set chuffing in the middle of the lawns. It gave out steam and smoke and music, and soon everyone began to dance. Amid all these distractions, few would have bothered to look towards Burlish Hill. Still fewer would have noticed that the sails of the mill still turned.

That winter was a hard one. The land whitened and froze, then rang with the iron wheels of the many carts which headed through the gates of Stagsby Hall to scrawl their marks across the ruined lawns. With the thaw came much work as villagers bent their backs to the digging of what seemed like an endlessly complex trench. Sconces and braziers burned as the work continued long into the nights, and the grandmistress herself was often present, offering the sort of smiles and encouragements for which the men were greedy, although few yet comprehended exactly what the work was for. Still, they agreed as they sat afterwards in the snug and drank their way though the extra money, it might help put Stagsby on the map. It would never have occurred to them that Stagsby had proclaimed itself across all Lincolnshire for centuries by windmill-topped Burlish Hill.

The huge new contrivance itself, part machine and part factory, looked wholly alien as it squatted amid the spring mud at the brown edges of the filthy lake. The opening of it was cause for yet another party at the hall. People were getting blasé about these occasions by now. They commented on the varieties of cake and beer with the air of connoisseurs, and were cheerfully unsurprised when the first turning of the great camwheel failed to occur. Nevertheless, the grandmistress gave a speech up on a podium, and both she and it were more than pretty enough.

Looking down from Burlish Hill through that long winter and into the spring which followed, Nathan absorbed tales and rumours along with the scent of coalsmoke which now drifted on the air. Lights shone now often from the windows of Stagsby Hall, but they were nothing compared to the fume and blaze which glowed beside it. On still days, he heard shouts in odd accents, the toots of whistles, the grumpy huff and turn of a huge and awkward machine, the call of strange spells. The first summer of this new competition, though, went well. Nathan aimed to be as reliable and competitive as ever—in fact, more so. He cut into his savings, reduced his rates, and the crop that year was as good as the previous one had been bad. There was more than enough grist to keep him working night and day, and the winds mostly came when he needed them. Meanwhile, all the machine down in the valley seemed capable of delivering was broken deadlines. If the local farmers took a little of their trade to the new grandmistress, it was more out of curiosity to see the great steambeast at work, and because of her looks, rather than because of the quality of the service she offered. Knowing something of farmers and their nature, Nathan didn't doubt that the novelty would fade. And he was a miller, and there had always be a mill up on Burlish Hill. He was prepared to trust the winds, and the seasons, and be patient.

Nathan was also sanguine about the other changes he noticed in the world. He'd understood long before Grandmistress Smith had laid it out before him on that clever map that one of the main reasons for his success as a miller was the improvement in haulage and communication which the spread of the new steam railways had brought. When a line finally reached as far as the Lincolnshire coast, he was happy to use it to visit his mother at Donna Nook; it saved several hours, and meant he no longer sacrificed an entire day's work. On summer's mornings, the cramped, chattering carriages drawn by those odd new machines were filled with families from the big cities heading for a day out at new resorts. He sometimes even stopped off himself for a stroll along the promenade, although to him the Lincolnshire coast remained essentially a wintry place. This, he thought on a freezing, blustery day when the gaudy new buildings were shuttered and sand gritted the streets, is real weather, brisk and cold and sharp.

The tracks now also ran to the town markets, where the steam and the screech of whistles added to the traditional stink and chaos of the cattle pens, the clamouring baskets of geese and chicken, the shouting and the pipesmoke. There were new animals now, as well. Horses which were too broad and strong and stupid to be called horses, and frighteningly fancy ducks and hens. In this new age of new magic, there were also strange new trades. Still, the tall rooms in which the auctions of grain took place remained places of golden, if bustling, calm. The mass of grain itself was stored in barns or warehouses. All that was here were wicker baskets containing samples, which you could thumbnail the husks off to taste the soft white meat inside. Nathan enjoyed the whole day, and the entire process. He would, he sometimes reflected, have come to these auctions even if he didn't trade himself. He even enjoyed the conversations, which were invariably about the air, the earth, and the crops.

Market day that September in Louth was busy as ever, and the roar of voices and the jostle of shoulders was entirely familiar. Standing towards the back, Nathan was tall enough to see over the caps and heads of the factors and farmers, and still had a voice which the older millers who clustered at the front had lost. Then, as the bidding commenced, he noticed a shift in the usual ebb and flow. There was a surprising swirl of attention near to the auctioneer's desk, and it was centred around a solitary head of flaming red hair.

It was the same at the next auction, and the one after that. Against all tradition, Grandmistress Fiona Smith—a woman, and no member of any of the recognised agricultural guilds—was bidding on her own behalf. Not only that, but she was far better at getting the auctioneer's attention than anyone else in the room. Worst still, the masculine reserve of these country guildsmen meant that they withdrew from bidding against her at prices which were far too low. Essentially, she was getting her grain on the cheap because of how she looked.

Nathan was shocked to discover that seemingly sensible men could act like such fools. If a batch of corn or oats was selling at a price he knew to be ridiculous, he made sure he made a better bid. Sometimes, he pushed things too high, and the red head which absorbed so much of the hall's attention would give a negative shake. Still, grain was grain, and he had the stuff stored at his own expense until he found the time and the energy to have it delivered and ground. He'd always thought of himself as hardworking, but in that season and the ones which followed, he surprised even himself. The mill turned as it had never turned, and there was always something more which needed to be done, and even a decent wind wasn't always enough for him.

On days when there was a moderate easterly, or a keen breeze from the north, Nathan still found himself looking up in frustration at the slow turn of his mill's sails. Finding a wind hanging hooked in his lean-to which made a close enough match to the one which was already blowing was an entirely new skill, although it was one he did his best to learn. Sometimes, on the right days, the whole mill span and thrummed with a speed and a vigour which he'd never witnessed. It was thrilling, and the needs of the many mechanisms dragged the songs from his throat until he was exhausted and hoarse. On other days, though, the winds fought angrily, and the mill's beams creaked and its bearings strained and its sails gave aching moans. Such strains inevitably increased the wear on the mill's components, and the costs and demands of its maintenance soared.

On cold winter nights, when there was now still grain in need or grinding, or flour which somehow had to be dried off before it could be sold, he dragged himself to the desk with its books of spells and accounts at which his father and many other generations Westovers had sat. But the nib trembled, his lungs hurt, and the red and green figures could no longer be persuaded to add up. He'd once never have thought of leaving any job half-completed, but now he staggered off to snatch the few hours sleep with the coloured inks still warring. Then he dreamed of storms of figures, or that the mill was the storm itself, and that the air would never stir again across all of Lincolnshire if he didn't work its sails.

●

NATHAN HAD GOT little enough in reply on the rare occasions when he'd mentioned the wind-seller to his fellow millers. Did the man come to them on those same still, hot days on which he always seemed to visit Nathan? That hardly seemed possible. Was there just one wind-seller, or were there several of their species or guild? And where exactly did he come from—and what essential substance was it, after all, from which his winds were made?

A flat, hot day. The mill groaning and creaking, and Nathan's bones filled with an ache for the time—it seemed only moments ago—when there was always too much grain, and never enough hours in the day to grind it. This summer, though, he'd had to rein in his bidding in order to keep up his repayments to the bank, whilst the carts had borne their grain less regularly, and in smaller amounts, up Burlish Hill. The farmers never looked Nathan directly in the eye or told him what they were doing, but the evidence was down there in the valley, in a pounding haze of noise and heat. Could people really labour in such conditions, when the day itself was already like a furnace? Nathan wiped his face. He hawked and coughed and spat, and worked the bloody phlegm into the dry ground of Burlish Hill with the heel of his boot. Only last week in Gainsborough, he'd been having a bite of lunch at one of the inns beside the market before taking the train which now reached Burwell, only five miles south of Stagsby itself. His bread roll had tasted gritty and sulphurous. He'd spat it out.

A distant engine chuffed across the landscape, trailing its scarf of steam. Somewhere, a whistle blew. Nathan coughed. No grist in need of grinding, but he still had half a mind to unlock the lean-to and take out whatever winds he had left in there, just for the ease they brought to his breathing, and the cool feel of them twisting in his hands...

A grey shimmer was emerging from the valley, and it was too stooped and solitary a figure for his heart to begin to race. Nathan remembered his fear and excitement back in the times when his father had been master of this mill, and every spell had been new, every wind fresh and young. Still, it was good to think that some things didn't change, and he almost smiled at the wind-seller; almost wished him a cheery goodday.

The man flapped his old cloak. He seemed to give a shiver as he studied the hot, dry horizons. "The hardest of all seasons, eh?"

Nathan shrugged. Almost every farmer said something similar to him when they came up here. It was usually a prelude to their explaining how they couldn't afford his normal rate, and it was scarcely in his interest to agree with them. But Nathan found himself nodding. This really *was* the hardest of all seasons.

"I've a hundred remedies…" The wind seller unshouldered his sack, and there they all were displayed: a knotted multitude of rags, but such beautiful things, especially on a day such as this. Storms and airs and breezes hazed about them in a thousand hurrying tints of blue and black and grey. Nathan knew how to drive a bargain, and the Elder knew he wasn't in position for extravagances, but he couldn't help feeling stirred, drawn, excited. And was it his own wheezing breath or that of the mill itself which gave off that needy groan?

Nathan barely heard the wind-seller's patter about his products. He of all people didn't need to be told about the poetry of the skies. He lifted a tarred and bunched handful of a northerly rope that wasn't from the north at all, and felt the bitter bliss of it swirling around him, then the soft twine of a southwesterly blown in from far beyond every southwesterly horizon. Its breath in his face was the laughing warmth of a kiss. He bore them all, great stirring armfuls of them, into his stone lean-to, and hooked them up on their iron hangers, where they stirred and lifted with a need to be let loose. It was sweet work, delicious work, to hold and be taken hold of by this knotted blizzard of winds, and Nathan found that he no longer cared how many he really needed, nor what he could afford. By the time he'd finished, there was nothing left beyond the sack itself, and, had the wind-seller offered it to him, he'd have taken that as well.

Nathan was sweating, gasping. He was possessed by hot spasms, shivers of cold. How much had he actually paid for this glut? He couldn't recall. Neither did he particularly care. But as the wind-seller whistled through thin lips and laid the empty sack of rag across his back, Nathan felt that today he was owed something more.

"Tell me, wind-seller," he asked, although he knew that such questions could only be asked by those who belonged to the same trade or guild, "exactly how is it that your winds are made?"

"It was your father I used to deal with, wasn't it?" The man's cold gaze barely shifted, but it took in all of Nathan, his mill, and his hill. "Although you and he might as well be the same. Same mill, same man, same sacrifices, eh? But it's always slightly behind you, isn't it?—I mean the best of all days, the keenest of winds, the sweetest of grain. It's never quite where you're standing now. And the longer you work, the more you give up, the more time hurries by, the more it seems that the strongest breeze, the whitest clouds, always came yesterday, or the day before."

"You're saying your winds are taken from the past?"

Twisting his neck, the wind-seller gave a shake his head. "Time was, there were no sails up here, no millstone—and no miller, either. But the winds still came, and the sun rose and fell. Back then, people saw things clearer. You, miller, you've merely given up sweat, and years, and the good state of your lungs to keep this mill turning, but for those people it was the seasons and then the sun itself which had to be turned." The wind-seller laughed. It was a harsh sound. "Imagine—the blood which was let, the sacrifices they made, to ensure that spring arrived, that the next dawn came! But the past is gone, miller—used-up. It's as dry and dead as this ground, which has been seeped of all its magic. What we're left with are the husks of our memories. Just like this sky, and this land…"

Nathan watched the wind-seller shape sink down into the valley's haze. Might as well, he reflected, have tried talking to the winds themselves.

●

CONVERSATION AFTER THE markets in Lincolnshire bars always came free and loud. Nathan had never been one to seek out companionship, but now he found that there was some consolation to be had in sharing a glass or two, and then a few complaints, after another pointless day at the auctions. Grandmistress Smith was less of a novelty these days, and she won her bids less easily, for there were other steam mills at Woodhall and Cranwell, and an even newer, bigger, one in construction at South Ormsby. The world was changing within the giddy scope of one generation, and it wasn't just the wind and water millers who were losing out. Elbowed in with them amid the hot jostle of sticky tables in those bars were hand weavers, carters—even smithies: for all that the Smithies Guild was hand-in-glove with the financiers who constructed these new machines, it was the high-ups, the pen pushers, the ones who wore out their fat buttocks by sitting at desks, who made a nice living, and devil take the old ways and local village business founded on decent, traditional skills. It was an odd coalition, both alarming and reassuring, and the talk turned yet more furious as the evenings darkened and business suffered and the drink flowed.

Plans were hatched, then laughingly dismissed as more beer was bought. But the same complaints returned, and with them came the same sense of angry helplessness. Nathan was never a ringleader, but he and everyone else around those tables soon agreed that there were better ways to spend your time and energy than sitting uselessly in a bar. They were *guildsmen*, weren't they? They had their pride. Better to go down fighting. Better still to resist wholeheartedly, and not go down at all.

They met one night at Benniworth. In the morning, the precious furnace which had just been delivered was found transformed into a dented mass of metal as if by a hailstorm of hammerblows. They met again at Little Cawthorpe. A culvert beneath the embankment of the new railway which would bear coal from Nottingham far quicker than the old canals was blown apart, although the damage was far less than might have been expected, considering the amount of explosive which was used. Lincolnshire earth, as any farmer would have attested, was notoriously slow and sticky stuff to move. Something stronger and better was needed, and Nathan brought it with him the next time they met outside Torrington in an owl-hooting wood.

"What you got there, miller?"

Lamplit faces gathered around him, edging and prodding to get a glimpse of the oddly lumpen knot he held in his hand.

"Something alive, is it?"

"Something that'll make them think twice about stealing the living off decent guildsfolk?"

Nathan couldn't bring himself to explain. He merely nodded, and felt the glorious lightness of a wind which had come from a point in the east to be found in no compass. These men didn't really expect to understand. Theirs was a loose alliance, and they remained almost as wary of each others' skills and secrets as of those they were campaigning against.

They called themselves The Men of the Future by now, because that was the opposite of what their wives and neighbours shouted after them, and their target was another mound of earth, although this was far bigger than the railway embankment. Steam mills and their associated machinery were even greedier for water than the watermills they replaced, and a reservoir to supply one such new machine had recently been constructed here in Torrington, taking up good grazing land and creating more aggrieved men. As, shushing each other and stumbling, they came upon it through the moonless dark, the clay bank looked huge. They laid the several caskets at its base. Then they turned towards Nathan.

"Whatever that thing is, might as well use it now, miller."

Nathan nodded, although his movements were slow. The wind which twisted in his hand gave off sharp scent of spring grass. Leaving it in this marshy spot was like destroying a treasured memory. But what else could he do?

They scrambled back through darkness from the hiss and the flare of the fuse. A long wait. The thing seemed to go out. A dull crump, a heavy pause, then came flame and earth in a sour gale, and a white spume of water lit up the dark.

The men cheered, but the rumbling continued, shaking the ground beneath their feet. Some were knocked over, and all were splattered by a rain of hot earth and stone. There was more fire, and then a boiling, roaring wave. They ran, scattered by the power of all the enraged elements which they had unleashed. It was lucky, it was agreed when heads were finally counted as they stood on a nearby rise, that no-one had been buried, burned, drowned or blown away. It looked as if the dam was entirely wrecked. Several fields had certainly been turned into mire. People would have to listen to Men of the Future now.

It was a long walk home. Drenched, muddied, Nathan kept to the edges of the roads although he scarcely expected to encounter any traffic on a night this black, but then he heard a rumble behind him. He turned and saw what seemed to be a basket of fire approaching. Then he saw that it was some kind of wagon, and that it was powered by steam. For all his increasing familiarity with such engines, he'd never heard of one which ran along an ordinary road, and curiosity made him reluctant to hide from sight.

It rumbled past. Big wheels. A big engine. It really did shake the earth. Then it stopped just a few yards past him, spitting and huffing, and a door at its back flung open.

"I'm guessing you're heading the same way that I am, Nathan Westover," a voice called. "Why don't you give your feet a rest?"

Dazed, Nathan stepped out from the edge of the ditch. He climbed in.

"You look as if you've..." Grandmistress Smith' eyes travelled over him.

"It's been a hard season."

"That it has. I'm just back from London, from burying my husband. We'd grown fond of each other, contrary to how people talk, and he was a decent enough man. Neither do I make a habit of picking up men from the roadside on my travels, although I hear that's how the tale is told."

Nathan had heard no such tales, and his chest was proving difficult in the sudden change of air within this hot compartment which was padded with buttoned velvet, and lit from some strange source. The woman who sat opposite was dressed entirely in a shade of black far deeper than that he remembered she had once worn on her sole visit to his mill. No silks or trimmings. Her hair had dimmed as well; trails of grey smoked though it. Only the flame in her eyes was unchanged.

"I suppose," she murmured, "you think we're deadly foes?"

"Isn't that what we are?"

She waved a hand. "Merely competitors, like your fellow millers. And it was never as if—"

"Fellow millers!" Nathan wheezed. He cleared his throat. "There are few enough of us."

"But when you say *us*, Nathan, why must you exclude me? We make the same product. I bid for the same grain in the same halls. And you and I…There's a new science. It's called phrenology, and it allows you to determine a man's—I mean a person's—nature merely from studying the bumps on their head. I've had it done myself, and mine reveal me to be stubborn and obstinate, often far beyond my own good interests." She attempted a smile. "And you…" She reached across the carriage. Her fingers brushed his bald scalp. "You're an easy subject now, Nathan. One hardly needs to be an expert to understand that you're much the same. And I suppose you remember that offer I made…" The steam carriage, which was a clumsy, noisy thing, jolted and jostled. "Of sharing our skills. It could still be done. Of course, I have to employ men from the new guilds to see to the many magics and technicalities of running a steam mill. In all their talk of pressures, recondensing, and strange spells—I can barely understand what they mean even when they're not talking the language of their guilds. Once, I could snap my fingers…" She did so now. There was no flame. "And that mill of yours. The dusty air—anyone can see what it's doing to you. We could still…"

She trailed off. The machine rumbled on through the night, splashing through puddles, trailing spark and flame.

"There's no point, you know," she said eventually as they neared Stagsby. "You can't resist things which have already happened. Those men, the ones who give themselves that stupid name and are causing such damage. They imagine they're playing some game, but it isn't a game. The Enforcers will—"

"That's not what counts—someone has to put up a fight against steam!"

The lines deepened around her eyes. "You're not fighting steam, Nathan. What you're fighting is time itself."

●

MORE THAN THE grain and the flour, more even than the mill, the winds were Nathan's now. Work or no work, whatever the state of the air and the clouds, they encompassed him and the mill. He talked to them in their lean-to, unhooked them, stroked their bruised and swirling atmospheres, drew them out. As the rest of the world beyond his hilltop went on with whatever business it was now engaged in, Nathan's mill turned, and he turned with it. He laughed and he danced. Strident winds from a dark north bit his flesh and froze his heart. Lacy mare's tails of spring kicked and frisked. His winds swirled around him in booming hisses as he sang out the spell which made them unbind, and they took hold of his and the mill's arms. In that moment of joyous release, it seemed to him that he was part of the air as well, and that the horizons had changed. There were glimpses of different Lincolnshires through their prism swirl. He saw the counter-glow of brighter sunsets, the sheen of different moons. It reminded him of some time—impossible, he knew, too ridiculous to recall—when, godlike, he'd looked down on the brightly flowing tapestry of the entire universe, which span like some great machine. He saw the ebb and flow of cities. He saw the coming of flame, and of ice, and the rise of vast mountains pushing aside the oceans. He saw glass towers and the shining movements of swift machines along shimmering high-ways of light. He believed he glimpsed heaven itself in the sunflash of silver wings amid the clouds. The visions faded as the mill took up the strain of the wind, but they never left him entirely. They and the winds returned to him as he lay on his bunk and snatched at flying fragments of impossible sleep. The came to him more quietly then, not with a scream and a screech and a growl, but in a murmur of forests, a sigh of deserts, a sparkle of waves, a soft frou of skirts. They breathed over him, and he breathed with them, and he let them lift him in their fragrant arms. In and out of his dreams, Nathan laughed and danced.

For all the many winds which he'd bought from the wind-seller on his last visit, Nathan knew he'd been less than frugal in their use. Sometimes, on the days of hard sky and mirage earth, he'd look out for that characteristic silhouette climbing up the little-used path from the valley, but the man never came, and part of Nathan already knew that he never would—not because of the indiscreet questions he'd asked, nor for the money he now couldn't afford to give him, but because the man's trade was like that of the millers themselves, and was thus in decline. Why, Nathan had even heard it said that sailors, who were surely the other main market for the produce of the wind-seller's guild, were now installing clever and brassy devices on the decks of their ships which could summon a wind to fill the sails when there was no wind at all. Partly, that sounded like the blurry talk of smoky bar-rooms, but that, as far as Nathan could see, was how so much of the world had become. He still looked out for the wind-seller on those sour days of bad air which seemed to come all too frequently now, but he knew in his heart that a figure would never shape itself out of the smoke and haze of the valley below. Those last purchases, this mar-vellous glut, had been like the rush of flour in the chutes when the hoppers were nearly empty. Soon, all that would be left was dust.

Nathan horded his last winds as a starving man hordes his wither-ing supplies. He toyed with them in his mind, carried them about with him, inspected them, sniffed them, sang to them, got the tang of their currents in his mouth. Still, the moment of their release had to come, and it was all over too quickly. And just how were they made—where were they from? The question might now seem immaterial, but it wouldn't let Nathan go. He studied the knots ever more carefully, not only for their feel and bluster, but also the exact nature of their bond. Of course, he'd always known how to undo them—that came to him as easily as winching a sack of grain—but their tying was something else. His fingers traced the long, wavering pattern, which he realised was always the same, no matter what substance from which the knot was formed. He followed the kinks which were left in the exhausted scraps once the wind had gone. With so few left, and the wind-seller so absent, it even seemed worth trying to see if he couldn't capture a few small winds himself.

Small they were. He was sure that something vital was lacking even if, as the wind-seller himself had once seemed to say to him, that *something* had already been bled from the very ground. Still, and guilty though he felt, Nathan would sometimes desert his mill for a few hours to gather grasses, or wander the hedgerows of the landscapes below in search of strands of sheep's wool, deer pelt, castings of snake's skin: anything, in fact, which could reasonably be knotted, and through which the winds might once have blown. The knots strained his fingers. They hurt at his heart. They blurred before his eyes. Yet, whatever it was which might once have been trapped within them wasn't entirely lost, for when he undid them, they would let out a sigh, the breath of lost season's air. Never sufficient to drive anything as big as his mill, but enough to bring an ease to his breathing on the most difficult nights when his lungs seemed to close up inside him, and to add some flare and spectacle to the conflagrations wrought by the Men of the Future.

Although the wind-seller never came, Burlish Mill had other visitors now. Men with canes and women with extravagant hats, borne almost all the way to Stagsby from the midland cities, first class, would climb Burlish Hill on summer afternoons and smilingly ask what exactly the cost was for a guided tour. He was slightly less brusque with the painter who lumbered all the way up the slope with his boxes, canvases and easel, but all his talk of *setting down for posterity* was off-putting, and Nathan sent him back down as well. Dismissed, too, was the man who lumbered up with a wooden box set with a staring glass eye, within which, bizarrely, he claimed he could trap and frame light itself.

His trips to Donna Nook had grown less regular, and the last occasion he chose to see his mother was the sort of bitter, windy winter's day when he'd have spilled the hoppers with the sacks of grist he knew his mill longed for, had he any left. After the confinement of the train, he'd hoped that the air along the coast would make his breathing easier, but he felt as if he was fighting some new, alien substance as he hunched towards the old hop warehouse, which now had sand sliding in through its lower windows. His mother wasn't up in her little room, and the fire was out. Stumbling, wandering, he finally found her hunched and gazing seaward from the crest of a dune. Her body was dusted, as if by a coating of the finest and lightest of flours, with a layer of frost.

Now, the nights when he did the work of the Men of the Future were his only escape from the needs of the mill. More and more, he came to think of the world beyond Burlish Hill as a dark and moonless place, erupting with hot iron and black mountains of clinker and coal. The Men of the Future had grown better organised, and the targets of their visitations were kept secret from all but a select inner group to which Nathan had no desire to belong. He was happy, although he knew that happy wasn't really the word, simply to meet in some scrap of wood or of heath, and to take the long, silent march towards another citadel of smoke and fire. There were so many of them now, and with so many purposes. Not just weaving and milling, but threshing, road-making and metal-beating: so many new technologies and spells. Sawmills were powered by steam—printing presses, even—and with each threatened trade came a swelling of their ranks. Pale, slim-faced men from far towns, workers with skills which Nathan couldn't even guess at, were taking charge, and they knew far better than their country colleagues how best to destroy a steam-driven machine. It wasn't about sledgehammers or pickaxes, or even explosives. Such brutal treatments were time-consuming, inefficient, and loud. Far better, they murmured in their slurring accents, to use the powers and magics of the devices themselves. Nathan could appreciate the cunning of setting a millstone turning so its two faces tore and clashed themselves apart. Could see, as well, how clever it was to put lime in a cold furnace, or molasses in a water vat, although some of the more arcane skills which these men then started to use, the muttering of short phrases, the leaving of scrolls of symbols which caused machines and furnaces to break apart when they were re-started, seemed too close to mimicking the work of the new steam guilds themselves. But something had to be done, and they were doing it, and these new Men of the Future continued to encourage the use of the small winds Nathan brought himself. Not that they were essential, he understood, to the work in hand, but their ghostly torrents, which lit up these damnable mills and factories with strange, fresh atmospheres, had become something of a signature of their work across Lincolnshire.

The nights when they met were never ordinary. There was always a similar mix of fear and hopeful excitement. They were, Nathan sometimes reflected, like midnight versions of the summer trips which families from the cities took on the railways to the lakes, the hills, the coast. Some Men of the Future even caught the day's last train to get to their next meeting place, then the morning's milk run to head back home again, and here they all were tonight, gathered once again in some typically remote spot, although the distance of travel had been much shorter than usual for Nathan. He even knew the farmer on whose land they were now standing; he'd once been a good source of trade.

Faces down, backs hunched, the Men of the Future shuffled towards their target in wary silence. As ever, the night was moonlessly dark, but to Nathan these were familiar roads. He didn't count himself a fool, and had long anticipated the night when they would head towards Stagsby. A year or two before, he'd have probably left them to get on with their work and returned to his mill, or perhaps even tried to persuade them to wreck a different machine. Not now. When he was heading home through a grey dawn after one conflagration, a passing grain merchant had halted the hairless beasts drawing his wagon to ask the way to Stagsby's Mill. Nathan knew from the scent of the sacks alone that here were several days' work of good barley, and offered the man an uncharacteristically cheery good morning. The merchant stopped him short when he began his directions. He was looking, of course, for the steam mill down in the valley; not that other thing—just a relic, wasn't it?—up on the hill.

Burlish Hill was nothing more than a presence in the darkness as the Men of the Future passed through the village, where no murmurs were made, no lights were shown. Then came a faint gleam of iron as they met the closed gates of Stagsby Mill. But, just as Nathan had witnessed before, one of the thin-faced men at the head of their procession murmured cooingly to the metal, and the metal wilted and the gates swung open.

There was no lawn, no trees, only bricks and mud, now at Stagsby Hall. But Nathan, as he turned and blundered into the men around him, couldn't help remembering, couldn't help trying to look. This was the most dangerous time of their work. One night, there would surely be mantraps, men with guns, regiments of Enforcers, or those poisonously fanged beasts like giant dogs, which were called balehounds. Indeed, many of the Men of the Future, especially those of the old kind, would have relished a fight, and there was a brief flurry when the eyes of some living beast were sighted in the pall of dark. Then came suppressed laughter, the glint of smiles. Nothing more than a donkey, old and mangy, tethered to an iron hoop. Once again, their secrecy seemed to have held.

The Men of the Future reached the doors of the machine itself, which gave as easily as had every other barrier. Inside, there was a warmth and a gleam to the dark. The furnace was still murmuring, kept banked up with enough coal to see it through to next morning without the need to relight. There was living heat, too, in the pipes which Nathan's hands touched. He'd been in enough of such buildings by now for some aspects to seem less strange, but this one, especially when the doors of the furnace were thrown open and light gusted out, stirred deeper thoughts. After all, grain was ground here. Although this place was alien to him, aspects of it—the strew of sacks, the smell of half-fermented husks, the barrels of water with their long-handled scoops for damping down—were entirely familiar. But there was something else as well. Nathan sniffed and touched. He was so absorbed in whatever he was thinking that he crashed his head on a beam and let out a surprised shout. Faces glared. Voices shushed him. Rubbing his bare forehead, he realised what it was. This place was cramped, awkward and messy compared to some of the machines they'd recently targeted. After all, Stagsby Mill had been working down in this valley for almost twenty years, and was getting old.

He watched as the thin men set to their work, quietly shovelling coal into the furnace, stoking up its heat, whilst others of their ilk smirkingly tended to the taps and levers which controlled pressure and heat, murmuring their own secret spells. The heat grew more solid. New energies began to infuse the bricks and irons of the engine house. The main rocker let out a protracted groan. A hiss, a gesture of quick hands, and Nathan was summoned towards the glare of the furnace. The wind which he held in his hands was one of his own best gatherings—just a few looped wisps of seed-headed grass, but it felt soft and sharp as summer sunlight—and he felt sad to release it, much though he knew that it had to be done. Teeth of flame gnashed as he tossed it into the glowing mouth. The furnace gave a deep roar. Coughing and gasping, he was shoved back.

The Men of the Future were in a rush now, but eager and excited as they bustled out. Back in the safety of the cool darkness, they turned and looked, shading their eyes from the open enginehouse door's gathering blaze. There were jeers and moans of disappointment when a shadow blocked the space ahead; some idiot was standing too close and spoiling the show.

"Martin, Arthur, Josh!"

A woman's voice, of all things, although none of them recognised the names she called. When she called them again, and added a few others, along with some hells and goddamits for good measure, it became apparent that she hadn't expected to find herself alone. There was derisory laughter. So much for the hired thugs and the balehounds, although, as Grandmistress Fiona Smith stepped across the puddled mud towards the gaggle of men who hung back in the deeper darkness, it became apparent that she was holding a gun.

"You're trespassing! I warn you—I'll *use* this thing…" The gun was hefted, although it was plainly an old device. "This isn't just filled with swan shot."

The laughter grew louder. This was all simply adding to the show. The grandmistress glanced back when sudden light speared from every aperture of building behind her.

"What exactly have you done to my—"

Then the entire engine house exploded.

Nathan ran, fighting his way through the searing air, the falling bricks and earth. The blaze was incredible—it was like battling against the sun. A figure lay ahead of him, although it shifted and shimmered in a wild dance of flame and smoke. He grabbed it, drew it up, hauling it and himself across the burning earth which seemed to be turning endlessly against him until, finally, he sensed some diminution of the incredible heat. Coughing, gasping, he laid Fiona Smith down on the rubble and mud beside what had once been the lake of Stagsby Hall. The water was scummed now, licked into rainbow colours by the leaping flames at his back, but he fumblingly attempted to scoop some of it over her blackened and embered flesh before he saw that it was already too late. Little flamelets and puffs of smoke played over Fiona Smith's charred body, but the fire was leaving her eyes. He leaned close, hands moving amid the glowing remains of her hair, and in that last flicker of her gaze, there came what might have been a twinge of recognition, then a final gasping shudder of what felt like release, relief. Nathan's hands still twined. Looking down, he saw that his hands had unconsciously drawn a knot in the last unsinged twine of Fiona Smith's glorious red hair.

●

THE CLIMB UPHILL had never been harder. His own flesh was burned. His lungs were clogged and charred with flame and soot. As he finally reached, half-crawled, across the summit, he realised that this was the first time he'd ever ascended Burlish Hill without sensing the moods of its air. Now that he did, hauling himself up and looking around at a world which, but for the fire which still blazed in the valley, lay dark at every point of the compass, he realised that that there wasn't a single breath of wind—not, at least, apart whatever was contained within that last knot of hair he'd cut loose with a glowing claw of metal, and which his fingers now held crabbed in his pocket, and was far too precious to be released.

Nathan coughed. With what little breath he had, he tried to call out to his mill. The sound was nothing: the mere whisper of dead leaves from some long-lost autumn. Impossible that this vast machine should respond to anything so puny, but, somehow, groaningly, massively, yet joyful as ever, it did. The sails began to turn. In a way, Nathan had always believed that the winds came as much from the mill itself as they did from the sky-arched landscape, but he'd never witnessed it happen so clearly as it did on that night. Invisably, far beyond the moon and the stars, clouds uncoiled, horizons opened, and—easy as breathing, easy as dancing, sleeping, and far easier than falling in love—the keen easterly wind which most often prevailed across Burlish Hill, but which was never the same moment by moment, began to blow.

There wasn't a trace of grain in need of grinding, but Nathan still attended to his mill. He released its shackles of winch and brake and pulley to set it turning wildly until the all mechanisms which he'd known and sung to for his entire life became a hot, spinning blur. The sound which the mill made was incredible—as if it was singing every spell in every voice which had ever sang it. He heard his father there within that deep, many-throated, rumble, calling to his mill in the strong, clear tones which he had once possessed, and humming as he worked, and sometimes laughing as he laboured for the sheer joy of his work. And the softer tones of his mother, and all the other mistress millers, was there as well. *See, Nathan, how it sits, and how that band of metal helps keep it in place...Now, its getting near the end of its life...* Nathan Westover heard the sound of that stuttering pulley, and then of his own unbroken voice, which had caused its turning to mend. All the winds of this and every other earth sighed with him, and the mill's sails swooped, and the world revolved, and the sky unravelled, and the stars and the planets span round in dizzy blurs, and the seasons came and went. He saw Fiona Smith, young as she was then, puffing out her cheeks before that huge cake at Stagsby Hall, when the place had still possessed lawns, and its oaks were unfelled. Saw her again at this very mill. *I have a proposal to put to you, Nathan...*Saw her as she was at the assumed, for want of any other sightings, that the miller himself had died inside his mill. The perfunctory official investigations gave people little reason to vary their views. The other theory, which was that the wealthy owners of the latest self-condensing machines had used the so-called Men of the Future as a means of destroying competition, received little credence, and then only amongst those who were in their cups.

Soon, as the wind lifted the ash and bore it westwards, and the rain dissolved the charred wood and the grass re-grew, nothing but a circle of stone was left on Burlish Hill. Nor was the steam mill down in the valley ever reconstructed. Farmers now sold their harvests on wholesale contract to the big new factories, thus giving up their financial independence for what seemed, for a while, to be a good enough price. Stagsby Hall was acquired by one of the leading families of the steam guilds as a country retreat. Soon, its lawns were re-established and the lake was dredged and gleamingly re-filled; the interiors were extravagantly refurbished in the latest style. The ruins of the steam mill were shored up and prettified with vines and shaggy moss. Five years on, and they could have been a bit of old castle; a relic from an entirely different age. But much of this was hearsay. To judge by all the chuffing, huffing modern carriages which came and went that way through the village, parties were frequently held at Stagsby Hall, but they weren't of the sort to which anyone local would ever be invited. You really had to climb up to the top of Burlish Hill to get any real sense of how fine the big house now looked. From up there you could still watch the clouds chase their reflections across the lake, and see the sunflash of its windows, and breathe the shimmer of its trees, but few ever did, apart from stray couples seeking solitude—for what, otherwise, would be the point?

●

WEEVILS, WOODWORM, FIRE and rats are the four apocalyptic demons in a miller's life, and, of these, fire is worst. But, Nathan reflected as, burned and breathless, he looked back up at the river of flame which steamed westwards from Burlish Hill, there were worse things still. At least, he told himself as he walked on, he hadn't left his mill, for there was nothing left to leave.

Following no particular direction, he kept walking until morning, and came across a railway station which he dimly recognised from his journeys as a Man of the Future. He sat and waited there, and took the first train, which bore him all the way to the coast. It was a bright day. Even this early in the summer season, families were camped out on the beach behind coloured windbreaks. Laughing children were bathing in the ocean's freezing shallows, or holding the tethers of snapping kites. Nathan watched and felt the bite of the salt against his face, happy to see that the world still turned and the winds still blew, whether or not there was a mill on Burlish Hill.

The rails went everywhere now. They took you places it was hard to imagine had ever existed before the parallels of iron had found them. Even when the timetables ran out and he discovered himself sitting on an empty platform at a time when he knew that no train would be coming, their shining river still seemed ready to bear him on. He travelled. He journeyed. He leaned out of carriage windows, and looked ahead into the fiery, smoking, sunset, and licked the salt smuts from his lips. Had he the breath left within him, he might have sung to the teeming air.

Another summer was coming, and the fields were ripening across the wide and heavy land. He sat on the steps beside the bridge of a riverside town where a mother and her daughter were feeding the crusts of their sandwiches to the geese and swans. They were both red-haired. Nathan's fingers bunched the knotted lock he still kept in his pocket. He often longed to release it, and to feel the special giving of a final wind-spell. But he remembered the look in the last embers of Fiona's eyes, and he wondered what he truly had trapped there; what, if released, he might be letting go.

North and south, he travelled on through the many nights, and the landscapes which lay around him in the darkness were stitched in flame. Dawn brought rooftops, chimneys, on every horizon. Swallowed in giant buildings, spat out with the litter and the pigeons onto surging streets, he gawped and wandered. He was cursed, bumped into. Leering offers were made in return for money he no longer had. The sky was solidly grey here, and the airs which rushed up to greet him from the chasms of streets were disgustingly scented. This was a place without seasons, or with seasons which were entirely its own. Nathan had grown accustomed to the tides or delays of departures at stations, but here he was lost.

He wandered the darkening city, taking odd turns as he sought out some direction which was neither north nor south, east nor west. Far behind him, the girders of some vast structure were being erected, their black lines gridding the sky, but there were less people here, and those who were became furtive in their glances, or ran away at the sight of him with screams and clatters of clogs. Not a place to be, he thought, for anyone who doesn't have business here. But, more and more, he felt that he did. He almost ran, and the bricks rushed by him, whispering with the echo of his dried-out lungs. Whispered, as well, with the glow of all the spells and talismans which were scrawled across them. Some, he was almost sure, belonged to his own guild. Others, he thought, had the taint of the sea about them. And here were the symbols of men who tended the tallest roofs, and of other guilds of those who worked in high places, and breathed the changing airs as they looked down on a different world.

Wheezing, exhausted, light-headed, he stumbled on. There were gates and walkways. The hidden thrumming of vast machineries ground up through the earth. Dawn, though, brought a different kind of landscape. He was tired beyond exhaustion, and it amazed him that his feet dragged on, that his heart still stuttered, that his lungs raked in some sustenance, but the city had cast itself far behind him—so far that the shifting horizons had smeared it entirely out of memory and existence. Here, puddled and rutted lanes unwound and divided to the lean of empty signposts, bounded by endless hedgerows: fences, gates, railings, snags of string and wire and thorn. And the wind blew everywhere, and from all directions—and the world fluttered with the litter of what seemed like the aftermath of some archetypal storm. Hats and scarves, stray shoes, newspapers, the pages of books, umbrellas, whole lines of washing, the weathered flags of guilds, even the torn sails of ships, fluttered everywhere, or were snatched to tumble in the sky like wild kites.

Nathan's fingers bunched once more around the knot of Fiona's Smith's hair. Here, if anywhere, was the secret of how she might be released. He understood now what all his wanderings had been about, which was to get here, wherever *here* was, and find the spell, the secret, which might unlock that last knot. But he was tired. He was tired beyond believing. Walking, he decided as he leaned against another blank signpost, was an activity he might still just about be able to manage, but he wasn't so sure about breathing, nor sustaining the increasingly weary thud of his heart. But still he pushed on, and the winds, as they came from every and no direction, pushed with him, tearing at his clothing, afflicting him with hot and cold tremors, spiralling around him in moans and whoops. Then he heard another sound—it was a kind of screaming. Although he now had no idea what it was, it drew him on.

Another fence, its slats torn, flapping and rotting, and another gate, which turned itself closed and then open in the wind, although that wasn't where the screaming came from. Nathan had to smile. It was simply an old weathercock, fixed to a fencepost, and turning madly, happily, this way and that in the wind. So familiar, although he'd never stood this close. The one odd thing about it, he realised, as it screamed and turned on its ancient bearings, was that the four angles of the compass which usually projected beneath such devices were entirely absent, even as rusty stubs. Then the gate reopened, and the weathercock screamed and shifted in directions which lay beyond any compass, and the wind also turned, pushing him along the path which lay beyond.

There was a house, although its windows flapped and its slates and chimneys were in disorder, and there was also a garden of sorts. That blurry sense which he'd felt all morning was even stronger here. There were trees which in one moment seemed to be in blossom, but the next were green, then brown, then gold, then torn to the black bones of their branches in sudden flurries of storm. Roses untwined their red lips and then withered. This was a place of many seasons, Nathan reflected as he gasped his way on, although it belonged more to winter than it did to summer, and more to autumn than to spring.

As much as anything, the hunched figure which lay ahead seemed to be shaped out of the ever-changing territories of the air. Not just windy days, or the sudden bluster of summer thunderstorms, but also the hot stillness of afternoons which seemed to be without prospect of any wind at all, at least until you saw something separate itself from the grey shimmer of the world below. The wind seller had his sack laid open beside him. He was gathering the tumbled sticks of a nearby willow which shivered and danced its wild arms. Somewhere inside Nathan's head, that weathercock was still screaming, and with it came a sobbing agony in his lungs. He knew he didn't have the strength left to tell the wind-seller what he wanted, and it was a release and a relief to him when the man simply held out his pale fingers, which looked like stripped willow themselves, and took from him that glorious red tress. As Nathan Westover stumbled and fell into the puddled mud, he saw the wind-seller's hands working not to release Fiona Smith's last breath, but looping her hair again to draw another, final, knot.

Taking Good Care of Myself

THE SOCIAL WORKER came a day or so before I arrived. He was as briskly pleasant as the occasion, which I'd long been dreading, allowed. He was dressed bizarrely, but people from the future always are.

"We'll need to send a few helpful machines back with you," he murmured as he inspected our spare bedroom and the bathroom and then the kitchen, which no doubt looked ridiculously primitive to him. "But nothing that'll get in your way."

Helen was equally reassuring when she came home that evening. "It's a tremendous challenge," she told me. "You always say you like challenges."

"I mean stuff like climbing, hang-gliding, pushing things to the edge, not looking after some senile version of myself."

"Josh." She gave me one of her looks. "You have no choice."

She was right—and there was plenty of space in our nice house. It was as if we'd always planned on doing precisely this, although I hated the very thought.

I arrived a couple of mornings after, flanked by swish-looking machines, although I was just as pale and dithery as I'd feared. The creature I'd eventually become couldn't walk, could barely see, and certainly didn't comprehend what was happening to him. Exactly how long, I wondered (and secretly hoped), can I possibly last like this?

Scampering around our house like chromium shadows, the machines performed many of the more obvious and unpleasant duties, but much was still expected of me. I had to sit and talk, although my elderly self rarely said anything in response, and none of it was coherent. I also had to help myself eat, and wipe away the spilled drool afterwards. I had to hold my own withered hand.

"Do you remember this house—I mean, you must have lived here?"

But I was much too far gone to understand. Not, perhaps, in a vegetative state yet, but stale meat at very best.

Sometimes, I took me out, pretending to push the clever chair which was in fact more than capable of doing everything—except getting rid of this cadaverous ghost—by itself. My work suffered. So did my relationship with Helen. I joined a self-help group. I sat in meeting halls filled with other unfortunates who'd had the care of their future selves foisted on them. We debated in slow circles why our future children, or the intelligences which perhaps governed them, had seen fit to make us do this. Were they punishing us for the mess we'd made of their world? Or were these addled creatures, with their lost minds, their failed memories, their thin grip on this or any other kind of reality, somehow the means of achieving time travel itself? Predictably, various means of killing were discussed, from quiet euthanasia to violent stabbings and clifftop falls. But that was the thing; complain as we might, not one of us ever seemed capable of harming ourselves. Not, anyway, the selves we would eventually become.

I declined. The machines, with a will of their own, grew yet more sophisticated and crouched permanently beside me as I lay immovably in my spare bedroom cradled in steel pipes and crystal insertions. They fed me fresh blood, fresh air. I doubted if this husk I'd become was conscious of any presence other than its own dim existence now, but still I found myself sitting beside me, and talking endlessly about things I couldn't remember afterwards. It was as if I was trapped in a trance, or that part of me was dying as well. I lay entirely naked now under clever sheets which cleaned themselves. Occasionally, inevitably, I would lift them up, and breathe the stale air of my own mortality, and study the thin limbs and puckered flesh of what I would eventually become. The death itself was surprisingly easy. The machines saw to it that there was no pain, and I was there; I made sure I didn't die alone. A faint rattle, a tiny spasm. You're left wondering what all the fuss is about.

After the funeral, which of course I also had to arrange myself, and was far more poorly attended than I might have hoped, and then the scattering of my ashes at the windy lip of one of my favourite climbs, I looked around at my life like a sleeper awakening. Helen had left me, although quietly, without fuss. My house felt empty, but I knew that it was more to do with that old man than with her. I'm back to climbing regularly now. I'm back to freefall and hang-gliding. I find that I enjoy these sports, and many other kinds of dangerous and challenging physical activities, even more. After all, I know they can't kill me, and that the last phase of my life really isn't so very bad. But things have changed, for all that, and I still sometimes find myself sitting alone in my spare bedroom and gazing at the taut sheets of that empty bed, although I and all those future machines have long gone. The sad fact is, I miss myself dreadfully, now that I'm no longer here.

The ENGLISH MUTINY

I WAS THERE. I was fucking there.

I know that's what they say, all of us English anyway, and half the rest of the Empire besides. The fact that people think they can make that claim—tell anyone who'll listen to them how they survived the atrocities and seiges—is supposed to be evidence enough. But I was. I was *there*. Right at the beginning, and way, way earlier than that. I knew Private Sepoy Second Class Johnny Sponson of the Devonshires long before that name meant anything. *More* than knew the guy, the bastard, the sadhu holy monster, the saint—whatever you want to call him. I loved him. I hated him. He saved my fucking life.

Me? I was just a soldier, a squaddie, another sepoy of the Mughal Empire. I really didn't count. Davey Whittings, Sir, Sahib, and where do you want that latrine dug? Always was—just like my Dad and his Dad before him. All took the Resident's rupee and gave their blood. No real sense of what we were, other than targets for enemy cannon. Stand up and salute or drop down and die. Nobody much cared what the difference was, either, least of all us.

But Johnny Sponson was different. Johnny came out of nowhere with stories you wouldn't believe and a way of talking that sounded like he was forever taking the piss. In a way, he was. In a way, he was shitting us all with his tall good looks and his la di da. But he was also deadly earnest.

This was at the start of the Scottish campaign. One of them anyway—rebellious bastards that the Scots are, I know there's been a lot. Never really saw that much of Johnny at first as we marched north through England. But I knew there was this new guy with us who liked the look of his reflection and the sound of his voice. Could hear him sometimes as I lay trying to get some sleep. Holding forth.

But no—no…Already, I'm getting this wrong. The way I'm describing Johnny Sponson, someone like him would never have got as far as being torn apart by Scottish guns. He'd have copped it long before in a parade ground misfire with some sepoy—oops, sorry Sarge, silly me—leaning the wrong way on his musket. Or maybe a garrotte in the night. Anything, really, just to shut the loudmouthed fucker up. But with Johnny, there was always something extra—a tale beyond the tale he was spinning or some new scam to make the halfblood NCOs look like even bigger cunts than they already were. Even then, even before the revolt, mutiny, freedom war, whatever you want to call it, Johnny simply didn't give the tiniest fuck about all the usual military bullshit. He was an original. He was a one-off.

Johnny might have been just a private, a sepoy, lowest of the low, but he'd grown up as Lord-in-waiting on one of the last English estates. Learned to read and fight and fence and dance and talk there, and do all the other things he could do so much better than the rest of us combined. Even I was listening to Johnny's stories by the time we crossed Hadrian's Wall. We all were. And the place he was describing that he'd come from didn't sound much like the England I knew. There were no factories or hovels or beggars. I pictured it as a world of magic—like so-called Mother India or heaven, but somehow different and better still. The landscapes were softer, the skies less huge. I saw green lawns and cosy rooms filled with golden warmth, and the whole thing felt real to me the way they only can when you're marching towards battle and your back aches and your feet hurt. It was a fine place, was Johnny's estate, and all of it was taken from him because some Indian vakil lawyer came up with a scrap of ancient paper which disproved the Sponson family title.

The way Johnny told his story, it span on like those northern roads we had to march. He used words we'd never heard. Words like *right* and *liberty* and *nation*. Words like *reversion*, which was how the Mughal Empire had swallowed up so much of England when the country was rightly ours. Bankrupted, disinherited, thrown out on the streets, Johnny had had no choice but to sign up for the Resident's rupee like the rest of us. And so here he was, marching north behind the elephants with the rest of us Devonshires to fight the savage bloody Scots.

Never seen such mountains before. Never felt such cold. The Scottish peasants, they live in slum hovels that would make a sorry dump like York or Bristol seem lovely as Hydreabad. They reek of burned dung. The women came to our camps at night, offering to let us fuck them for half a loaf of bread. They'd let you do it, as well, before they slipped a dagger into your ribs and scarpered off with the bread. Can't even remember how I got hit exactly. We were on this high, wind-bitten road. Elephants pulling the ordnance ahead. Then a whoosh. Then absolute silence, and I was staring at a pool of my own steaming guts. It seemed easy, just to lie there on the frozen road. I mean, what the hell difference did it make? Private Davey Whittings, second class. Snap your heels, stand up straight lad, salute the flag of Empire and pay good attention to the cleanliness of your gun. Death or glory, just like my Dad always used to say before beating me for something I hadn't done.

But the voice I heard was Private Johnny Sponson's, not my Dad's at all. My Dad's been dead these last fifteen years, and I hope the bastard didn't give the vultures too much bellyache. But I was raving about him—and how my dear Mum had then done the decent thing and walked into a furnace—as Johnny pushed my insides back where they belonged, then lifted me up and tied me to what was left of a wagon. Then, seeing as all the elephants were dead and the bullocks were all shot to mincemeat, he started to haul me himself back along that windy road for…I really don't know how many days, how many miles.

At the end of it, there was this military hospital. I already knew all about military fucking hospitals. If you wanted to live, you avoided such places like the plague. If you wanted to die, it was far better to die on a battlefield. Without Johnny Sponson there, I wouldn't have stood a chance. The whole place was freezing. Wet tents in a lake of mud. Got me through, though, Johnny did. Found me enough blankets to stop me freezing solid. Changed the dressings on my wound, nagged the nurses to give me some of the half-decent food they otherwise saved for themselves. Bastard saved my fucking life. So in a way I was the first of Johnny Sponson's famous miracles, least as far as I know. But Christ wasn't there, and neither was Mohammed or Shakti. Johnny wasn't some ghost or saint or angel like the way you'd hear some people talk. It was just him, and he was just being Johnny, and filling my head with his Johnny Sponson stories. Which was more than enough.

Told me how half the platoon had got killed or injured in that Scottish bombardment. Told me how he'd fluked his way around the cannonfire in the same way he'd fluked his way around most things. Then he'd seen me lying there with half of me insides out and decided I could do with some help. Suppose he could have saved someone else—someone with a far better chance of living than I ever had. Why me? All the time I knew him, I never thought to ask.

Johnny told me many things. How, for example, little England had once been a power to be reckoned with in the world. How this guy called William Hawkins had once sailed all the way around the Horn of Africa to India back in the days when the Mughal Empire didn't even cover all of India let alone Europe, and no one had even dreamed of the Egyptian Canal. How Hawkins arrived in pomp at the court of Jehangir. How, the way things had been back then, he'd been an emissary from equal kingdoms. No, *more* than that, because Hawkins had sailed from England to India, and not the other way around. After that, there'd been trade, of course. Spices and silks, mainly, from India—with English wool and the sort of cheap gewgaws we were already getting so good at manufacturing in return. The stuff became hugely fashionable, so Johnny assured me, which always helps.

So there we were, the English and the Mughals, equal partners, and safely half a world away from each other, and between us lay the Portuguese, who were travelling and trading as well. Then something changed. I was still half in and out of my fever, but I remember Johnny shaking his head. Like, for just this once, he didn't know the answer. *Something*, he kept saying, as if couldn't figure what. Of course, these were difficult times, the sort the priests will still tell you about—when it snowed in England one sunless August and the starving ate the dead, and the Mughals down in India expanded across India looking for food and supplies—looking for allies, as well. They could have turned to England, I suppose. That was what Johnny said, anyway. But the Mughals turned to Portugal instead. A great armada was formed, and we English were defeated, and the Mughal Empire expanded all that way to the northerly fringes of Europe. I know, I know—I remember Johnny clapping his hands and laughing and shaking his head. Bloody ridiculous—England and India united by an Empire, which has since pushed south and west across France and Spain and Prussia, and east from India across all the lands of Araby. Half the world taken as if in some fit of forgetfulness, and who the hell knows why…

So I recovered in that hospital with a scar on my belly and a strange new way of looking at things. Sometimes, it sounded to me as if Johnny was just talking to himself. In a way, I think he was. Practising what he wanted to say in those famous speeches that came not long after. He certainly had a way of talking, did Johnny. So much of the truth's lost now, but Johnny really *was* an educated man. He'd say the words of writers written years ago in English, of all languages—instead of proper Persian or Hindi or Arabic—as if they were fresh as baked bread.

There was this Shakes-something, and I thought at first Johnny meant an Arab prince. I can even remember some. *If it is a sin to covet honour, then I am the most offending soul.* That was one of them.

Learned from his tutors, who taught him about the old ways of England in that fine estate before the Mughals took it away from him like the greedy bloodsucking bastards they are. Not that Johnny would put it so bluntly, but I learned that from him as well—how it wasn't as simple as the Indians being in charge and us English being the servants, the sepoys, the ones who worked the mines and choked on our own blood to keep their palaces warm.

Death. Guns. Spit and blood and polish. How to use a bayonet in the daylight of battle and a garrotte in the dark. That was all I knew before Johnny Sponson came along. I was never that much of a drinker, or a chancer, or a gambler of any kind. Don't stand out—that was the only thing I'd ever learned from my dear-departed Dad, bastard that he was. I spent most of what little spare time I had, and even littler spare thought, on wandering around whatever place I happened to be billeted. Liked to look up at the buildings and over the bridges and stand outside the temples, just studying the scene. Watch the sadhu beggars with their ash-smeared bodies, their thin ribs and twisted and amputated limbs. I was fascinated by the things they did, the way they adorned and painted what was left of themselves, affixed it with hooks and nails and bamboo pins. But what struck me most was the contrast—the beauty of their aspiration to be one with God, and the ugliness of what you actually saw. And the ways they smiled and rocked and moaned and screamed—was that pain, or was it ecstasy? I never really understood.

Those of us Devonshires considered alive enough to be worth saving were put on board this ship which was to take us to our next posting in London. The winter weather was kind to us on that journey south. The cold winds pushed us easily and the sea was smooth, and the sailors were good at turning a blind eye in the way that sailors generally are. We sepoys lay out there on the deck underneath the stars with the sconces burning, and we talked and we danced and we drank. And Johnny, being Johnny, talked and drank and danced most of all.

You remember what that time before the mutiny was like—you remember the rumours? The plans to extend the term of service for us sepoys from fifteen to twenty years? That, and the forced conversion to Islam? Not that we cared much about any kind of religion, but the business of circumcision—that got us as angry as you'd expect. It just needed *something*...I remember Johnny saying as I leaned with him looking out at the ship's white backwash and the wheeling gulls— how the Indians would be nothing without us English, how the whole of their Empire would collapse if someone finally pulled out just one tiniest bit like a house of cards...

There was a lot of other stuff as well. Hopes and plans. What we'd do come the day. And Johnny seemed at the centre of it, to me at least. But where all those rumours came from, whether they were his or someone else's or arose in several different places all at once, I really couldn't tell. But that whole idea that England was waiting for Johnny Sponson—like the people knew him already, or had invented him like something magical in their hour of need...I can't tell you that that was true. But there are many kinds of lies—that's one thing that being around Johnny Sponson taught me. And maybe the lie that there were whole regiments of sepoys just waiting for the appearance of something that had the size and shape and sheer fucking balls of Johnny Sponson...Well, maybe that's the closest lie there is to the truth.

So we ended up down in London, and were billeted in Whitehall barracks, and the air was already full of trouble even before that spring began. Everywhere now, there was talk. So much of it that even the officers—who mostly couldn't speak a word of English to save their lives, as many of them would soon come to regret—caught on. The restrictions, the rules, the regimental bullshit, got ever stupider— and that was saying a lot. The whole wretched city was under curfew, but Johnny and I still got out over the barracks walls. There used to be these bars in London then, down by Charing Cross—the sort where women and men could dance with each other, and you could buy proper drink. Illegal dives, of course. The sweat dripped down the walls, and there was worse on the floor. But that wasn't the point. The point was just to be there—your head filled up with pipesmoke and cheering and music loud enough to make your ears ring.

IAN R. MACLEOD

And afterwards when the booze and the dancing and maybe a few of the girls had finally worn everyone out, Johnny and I and the rest of us sepoys would stagger back through London's curfew darkness. I remember the last time we got out was the night before the Muharram parade when the mutiny began, and how Johnny danced the way even he had never danced before. Tabletops and bar-tops and crashed-over benches held no obstacle—there was already a wildness in his eyes. As if he already knew. And perhaps he did. After all, he was Johnny Sponson.

Johnny and I rolled arm in arm late that night along the ghats beside the Thames. And still he talked. He was saying how the Moslem Mughals were so nice and accommodating to the Hindus, and how the Hindus took everything they could in return. Something about an officer class and a merchant class, and the two getting on with each other nicely, the deal being that every other religion got treated like dogshit as a result. Like the Jews, for example. Or the Romanies. Even the Catholic Portuguese, who'd had centuries to regret helping conquer England for the Mughals. Or us Protestant Christians here in England—although anyone rich enough to afford it turns to Mecca or buys themselves into a caste. Why, Johnny, he could take me along this river, right within these city walls, and show me what was once supposed to have been a great new cathedral—a place called Saint Paul's. A half-built ruin, it was, even though it was started before the Mughals invaded more than two hundred years ago.

I remember how he disentangled himself from my arm and wavered over to a wall in that elegant way he still managed when he was drunk. The guy even *pissed* with a flourish! Never stopped talking, as well. About how this wall was part of something called the English Repository, where much of what used to belong to the lost English kings—the stuff, anyway, that hasn't been melted down and shipped back to India—had been left to rot. Thrones and robes. Great works of literature, too. Shakespeare, Chaucer—men no one in England has heard of now...Nobody came here, except a few mad scholars looking for a hint of English exoticism to spice up their dreary poems. That, and another kind of trade...Johnny was still pissing as he talked. "I believe the mollies frequent the darker aisles. Their customers call them repository girls…" Finally, he hitched himself up, turned around and gave me the wink. "I believe they're quite reasonable. You should try them, Davey."

We wandered on. But, as any soldier will tell you, it's a whole lot easier to get out of barracks than it is to get back in, and Johnny and I were spotted by the sentries just as we were hanging our arses over the top of the wall. Which is how we ended up on punishment duty on next day's famous parade, and perhaps why everything else that happened came about.

It started out as a fine winter morning. People seem to forget that. Muharram, it was, and I remember thinking that this whole pestilential city seemed almost beautiful for once as we troops were mustered beside the Thames at dawn. Even the rancid river looked like velvet. And on it was passing all the traffic of Empire. Red-sailed tugs, and rowboats and barges. I remember how this naval aeropile came pluming by, the huge sphere of its engine turning, and how the sky flickered like spiderwebs with the lines of all the kites, and me thinking that, despite all Johnny said, perhaps this Empire which I'd spent my whole life defending wasn't such a bad thing after all.

Then the parade began. You know how the Indians love a bit of pomp, especially on holy days. And us Devonshires were there to celebrate the great victory we were supposed to have won against the savage Scots. Whatever, it was another fucking parade, and soon the clear skies darkened and it started sleeting, although I suppose it must still have looked some sight just like it always does. Elephants ploughing up Whitehall with those great howdahs swaying on their backs. Nautch girls casting flowers, and the dripping umbrella lines and prayer flags of the crowds who'd quit their sweatshops in Holborn, Clerkenwell and Chelsea for the day. The shining domes of balconies of the Resident's Palace along Downing Street. And camels and oxen and stallions and bagpipes and sitars.

Johnny and I had been given these long-handled shovels. It was our job to follow a cart behind the elephants and scrape up and toss their shit onto the back of it. Punishment duty, like I said, and were lucky not to have got something a whole lot worse. But the crowd thought it was fucking hilarious—sheer bloody musichall, the way we slipped and slid, and I guess that Johnny's dignity was hurt, and he was tired and he was hung-over as well, and maybe that was just one last hurt too many in a life full of hurts.

There was a guy in the crowd who thought me and Johnny scrabbling and falling in the sleet and shit in our best uniforms was even funnier than everyone else. He kept pushing on through the crowds so he could point and laugh some more. I hardly noticed, but Johnny gave this sudden roar and lunged towards him, waving his shit-caked shovel like it was a halberd. Not sure that he actually meant to hit anyone, but he *was* mad, and people started falling over and shouting just to get out of his way, and that spooked the elephants, and the next thing I knew a wave of chaos was spreading along the parade.

Soon, guns were firing. You could tell they were Indian repeaters rather than the slow old muskets which was all us sepoys were trusted with. It didn't feel like a parade any longer—more like some kind of battle, which is the one thing we sepoys know something about. The elephant's bellowing and rampaging added to the chaos. I remember how the whole side of this great gold crusted temple just crumbled when one lunged into it. I remember the way it fell apart, and how the bibis and the priests inside came screaming out, and the freezing English sleet just kept on pouring down. Fucking beautiful, it was.

London was in uproar, and I managed pretty well that day with just my bayonet and my shovel, even if I say so myself. Of course, there was bloodshed, but there was far less than anyone expected, or the tales would have you believe. The Indians—the so-called loyal troops, the camel regiments out of Hydreabad and all the cavalry—they just fired and fell back beyond the city walls. London didn't burn that day—although the temple monkeys got it, and of course the tigers in Hyde Park and anything else that didn't look English. Like I say, there had been rumours of an uprising, and most of the higher caste Indians and the rich merchants and the Resident and all of his staff had left London days or weeks before. The city just fell into our hands.

We were like kids, rampaging after years of being kept locked up. The shops and warehouses were gutted, of course, and so were all the bungalows of Chelsea and the temples of Whitechapel and the palaces of Whitechapel. It was like an army of ants at work in a kitchen, only people were carrying these huge sideboards and settees instead of grains of rice. Everything was spilling out of doors, and we were all dancing and laughing, and most of our gunshots were aimed in the air. Sepoy or Londoner, half-blood or English—on that first day of the uprising it really didn't matter. We were all on the same side.

Didn't see much of Johnny for a while—got myself lost in the cheering crowds. When I did find him it was already late in the afternoon, it was no surprise that the crowds were cheering most loudly around him—waving bits of curtain rod and billhooks and scythes, beating stolen temple drums. This was outside the great temple of Ganesh at Whitefriars, and I suppose most of its treasures must already have been looted, and its priests killed, and there was Johnny clambering high on the tower to speak to us all.

I won't bore you with most of what Johnny said. You either know it already or you don't care, and you get can still the pamphlets the censors haven't destroyed if you know who to tip the wink. It was just… Well, for me, it was simply Johnny being Johnny. Going on the way he always did, only now he had a bigger audience. And some already knew he was the guy who had swung that first shovel which got the whole mutiny started, and the rest would have believed anything he said by then. That day, we all wanted to believe. The stuff he was saying as he clung to the lotus blossom carvings on that tower, to me it was all typical Johnny Sponson—and it was still sleeting, and the stones must have been slippery, and he'd have killed himself if he fell, Stuff about how, contrary to most outward appearances, London *was* a great city, and this whole country was great as well. Not some province of Empire, no, but England, England, in its own right! And he mentioned all the names I'd often heard—names which the other sepoys and the rest of London were soon chanting as well. Elizabeth! Arthur! King Henry the Something! No, no, he was telling us, this shouldn't be the temple of Ganesh. If it was anyone's temple, it should be the temple of Christ, for Christ was an Englishman, and so was God. And if the Indians thought we were rats, well, then we'd make it the temple of Karair Matr, the rat goddess, and we'd swarm all over them and eat out their eyes…! Once Johnny got going, there was nothing could make him stop, and we were all cheering and no one wanted him to. London was some place to be, on that first great day of the English Mutiny.

I found Johnny again some time later down by the ghats where it was fully dark. By then, people had lit many fires—after all, it was freezing and they needed to keep warm. The city glittered with broken things. It looked like a box of spilled jewels. And those who had gathered around him had already sorted themselves in the way that people who sense where power lies always do. Already, he was giving out orders, and all of London was taking them. I had a job to get to him as he sat by this huge bonfire on the padded bench of a broken palanquin surrounded by bodyguards. Nearly got knifed in the process, until Johnny saw who it was and shouted for them to let me through.

"Well, Davey," he said. "Something *has* happened. Birnam Wood has moved, perhaps. Or Hampstead Heath, perhaps…" It was still his old way of talking, and I could tell from his eyes that he was long past being drunk.

"What happens now?"

He smiled at the fire. "That's up to us, isn't it? They that have the power to hurt, and will do none, they rightly do inherit heaven's graces."

Despite the flames, I felt myself going cold. Already, I was starting to hate such nonsense, and all the bloodshed and destruction that I already feared would follow. We've all suffered one way or another, I suppose, Indian and English, no matter what side we took in that mutiny or revolt. The odd thing to me is how little us sepoys, who know as much as anyone about battle, didn't see how it was bound to turn out. Thought we could just march out across England, that everything would fall to us as easily as London did on that first marvellous day.

It even seemed that it was going to happen that way—at least for a while. We got news from Chester about a revolt which had started there several days earlier, and how all the non-English in the city had been slaughtered, which helped explain why the Indian troops in London had been so edgy, and quick to pull out. News from Bath and Derby, as well. Not that I'm much at reading maps, but Johnny used to study them endlessly as his rebel regiments fanned out from London to mop up what then seemed like the flimsy Indian resistance. It really was like dominos or falling cards or some unstoppable tide—all of the fancy descriptions Johnny liked to use when he climbed high on that tower of that temple of Ganesh to speak to us all.

It's a lie to say we didn't have a plan. We were soldiers, we were disciplined—we knew how to fight, and we knew that this whole land was rightly ours. Of course, we needed supplies, and of course we took them, but that's no more than any army does. And as for the other things—well, armies do tend to do some of those, as well. It comes with the trade. But the rumours of bonfires being made of all the raped and mutilated bodies—that's just Indian talk. Bodies don't burn that easily in any case. And Johnny, he never wanted those things to happen, and he flew into towering rages when they did. And all the time the red of Empire was changing on his maps to English green, just as the English winter was warming to spring. We'd hear that yet another town had overthrown its oppressors, or another battalion or whole regiment which had gone over to the rightful English side. Seemed like just a matter of time before this whole country was ours. Seemed like it wouldn't be long before we heard news that the Resident himself had peacefully surrendered to the Zenana Guard who protected his women, and then we could put away our bayonets and guns and garrottes. And after that…After that, everything would be the same as it was before, only better.

But Johnny's dreams were bigger, and we needed those as well. We needed *him*. It's an odd thing, I suppose, that we were happy to kowtow to a high-caste omrah like Johnny Sponson when we were so busy despoiling the estates his likes had come from. But that was how it was, and it was something Johnny played up to. Set himself up in old Saint James Place, he did. Said the place could be defended, if push ever came to shove. Didn't exactly sit on a throne—he was always too busy pacing about and giving orders—but there was certainly a throne in the great hall in which he'd established his command, and its walls and floors were covered with beautiful rugs and many other fine things which had been looted from the Indian palaces across London. Every time he climbed that gold-encrusted tower of the Great Temple of Ganesh, he climbed a little bit higher, and the clothes he wore were that much grander. He spread his arms out to all the thousands who waited below him, and this red velvet robe set with jewels and gold encrustations spread out around him in the wind.

I might have been Johnny's oldest and best friend, but in most ways I was still nothing special. Had no appetite for giving out orders, for a start—got too much of that from my bastard Dad, and all the bullshit NCOs I've served under since. Anyway, there were plenty of others that did. In the new England we thought we were creating, that was one thing that hadn't changed one little bit—people were still telling other people what to do. Still, Johnny looked out for me, just as he always had. I passed messages. I listened. He asked me to be his eyes and ears.

I talked to people. Regiments which had arrived fresh at the capital, or ones which were returning bloodied and exhausted from some campaign. I didn't speak to those who were setting themselves up as captains and majors and generals—even wearing the sashes and badges of the men they'd tortured and killed, they were, by then—but to men like myself, ordinary sepoys, common soldiers, who still had to fight for their lives just like they'd always fought. And they spoke freely. They had no idea that I was any different to them.

That way, and using what I suppose you'd call my soldier's intuition, I started to get a picture of what was happening across England. Sometimes, it seemed to me that I understood things far better than

Johnny's generals, or how they were drawn on his precious maps. The Indians and their loyal regiments had retreated, that was for certain, but they hadn't vanished. They'd mostly drawn back into the major cities we sepoys had laid siege to but still hadn't mustered the forces to attack. They were skulking in the huge new fortresses at Dover, for example, and hiding in the castles and ramparts surrounding Liverpool, Portsmouth and Bristol, which had all been recently enlarged. Basically, the way I saw it, the bastard Indians had made sure they kept control of the main ports apart from London, which they'd given up because they knew its walls were too old to properly defend. Kept, as well, the power of their navy, both merchant and marine, which—uncaring shits that sailors are—had remained loyal to them. For me, it seemed as if the Indians had anticipated our mutiny far better than we sepoys. I even heard about the ships and reinforcements coming from Portugal long before the story was believed.

At first Johnny listened to what I told him, but soon, being Johnny, he listened less and less, and talked more and more. Lord Johnny Sponson of all England just laughed and danced across his plundered carpets and around his gilded logpiles of half-ruined furniture in his great and echoing halls. Johnny did all the things he'd always been good at, and all his new friends and commanders—and mistresses—agreed and applauded and laughed and danced as well. The women, of course, were mad for him. For the ease of his limbs, and who he was, and what he could do for them. And if that look in his eyes, the way he smiled, wasn't quite the same as the Johnny I remembered, who the hell was there but me to care or notice?

Spring turned to summer, and the Indians with all their new supplies and fresh foreign troops pushed out from their fortresses. They defeated us Bewdley and Oxford. They moved back across the Severn and the Thames. The weather turned hot, and food grew short because most of the farms in the area around London where we rebel sepoys were now pinned had been abandoned and no one had thought to harvest the crops. The Indian armies had the repeating rifles which they'd never allowed us sepoys to use. They had proper cannon instead of our antique ceremonial relics. They had fresh elephants, and armoured aeropiles to plough along the captured rivers, and barrels of terrible Greek Fire. Their victories weren't so much defeats as routs—organised destruction, and the revenge they made upon all the thousands of sepoys they captured was terrible. They tied our bodies to their new guns and blasted them to pieces because they thought that we Christian English feared for our souls if we weren't given a proper burial. They pierced us with hooks. They burned us on slow fires of charcoal. They fed us, half-roasted but still alive, to the crows.

It was late August by the time London was fully encircled, and the great sepoy army which Lord Johnny had drawn around him had gathered within its feeble walls. The place was hot and over-crowded. The sewers were shattered. The river stank. The wells had turned. Yet there was still hope. There was still dancing. The severed heads of freshly discovered collaborators and Indians were regularly borne along the streets whilst the Indians generals waited outside the city walls.

I remember I was wandering one morning in the strange place London had become. The temples were emptied, the buildings and bridges were torn. There were no sadhus now, no beggars—or we were all sadhus and beggars. It was hard to tell. A smog of burning hung over the city. It darkened the sky. It shaded out the sun. The streets seemed strangely paved in that odd twilight. I pushed through drifts of sheet music. My boots crunched on the shattered brass shells of pocketwatches looted from a store. Stooping to look at them more closely, I saw there were even a few broken scraps of gold. I remembered walking—it seemed, not so long ago—arm in arm with Johnny close to this same place as we headed back from that bar at Charing Cross. There was no beer now. There was scarcely any water. But ahead of me, although now daubed with fresh layers of slogans, was the wall of the English Repository against which Johnny had pissed.

A movement caught my eye. This city was no longer safe—my hand went straight to my bayonet—but what I saw was a female figure, smallish and seemingly youngish, dressed in a brocaded red sari. The figure beckoned. Although I had no idea what she wanted, I followed.

The entrance to the English Repository had once been grand. Filthy statues which I suppose had once been supposed to represent art, or love, leaned around its collapsing arch. It was dark outside that day, but inside the darkness was far greater. The sort of dark you get that piles up over ages from shadows and mildew and things long left to rot. A few muttonfat candles smoked, and I could see it was just as Johnny had said. Old stuff, once kingly and grand, but now so ruined as to have been ignored even by the rampaging mobs, was piled everywhere. Rain-leaked ceremonial carriages. Beds like the bloated corpses you saw down by the river, their upholstery green and swollen. And books everywhere. Not just on shelves, but piled on the floors and spilling their leaves amid the puddles. It was a damp place, even in the middle of summer. Reeked of piss, as well. The English Repository would barely have smouldered had all the rest of London burned.

The woman in the glittering, once-beautiful sari was still shuffling ahead of me. Beckoning me on, and talking all the while in this cracked voice—saying words which made no sense, but also sounded familiar. Something about the rags of time, and love knowing no season—nonsense really, but pretty, bookish nonsense of a kind I knew only too well. I understood what she was by now, and I saw as we entered some kind of courtyard filled with the dead remains of furniture and rusting suits of armour that there were many others of her kind. They looked like crows—roosting there, and cackling as well. Repository girls, Johnny had called them. What a strange and desolate place to live, I thought—but I let the woman pull me to her, even though she stank as sourly as the city itself.

She was fumbling beneath my trews with black crow fingers. And I could see the rotting spines of the books amid the mushroom shelves behind. Could even read the same names that Johnny had once said to me. Shakes-something. And Chancer—Chaucer? Donne—Dun, Donny, is that how you'd say it? Somebody called Marlow. All the old Johnny bullshit. At least, that was how it seemed to me. And beyond that, leaning against a mossy wall with dead bits of vine growing over it and half the paint peeled and blistered off, there was this huge old painting of some lost great English estate. You could tell that it no longer existed. You could tell that it came from an England which had been plundered and destroyed long ago. I pulled away from her and threw the scraps of gold I'd picked up outside that looted shop as I fled to stop the woman following—although, like everything else in this city, it was worthless. She was shouting after me about how she had a son, a nice boy, for sale as well.

London had stirred itself while I was in the English Repository's darkness. The streets were suddenly rivered with people. They were smashing what hadn't already been destroyed. They were chanting and wailing and pulling at their clothes. Guns were firing into the air—a waste of precious shot. I feared that the Indians had already breached our walls. But I know what a battle feels like, and I realised that this wasn't one, although there was so much noise and confusion that it took me some time to find out what had really happened. Even then, I still didn't believe. Johnny Sponson, Lord Protector of all of England had been out walking this very morning, keeping up morale, touching the ill and the wounded who clamoured to be cured, showing his face to the adoring crowds. I'm sure he thought he was well-protected, but the Indians must have positioned snipers close enough for one of them to pick him out. After all, he'd have made an obvious target, dressed as he now dressed. I grabbed arms and shouted into faces. Was he alive? Was he dead? No one seemed to know for sure.

I pushed on towards Saint James Palace. Try to go any other way, and I'd have been trampled for sure. You've never seen such sights— heard such sounds. And then, of all things, I heard my own name being shouted by the guards who were protecting the palace gates, and hands were all over me and I found myself being lifted up. Yes. Here's the one. Yes, this is Private Sepoy Davey Whittings. No, no, back, back you fucking idiots. This is *him*. I feared for my life, although death and I had long since reached an understanding. But there I was, being hauled over the crowds and shoved through the gates of Saint James Palace by Johnny Sponson's liveried guards, then led through ruined logfalls of gilded furniture which weren't so very different to those in the English Repository. Then a final door banged behind me, and I was standing alone in the great hall of Johnny's throne room.

The place seemed huge and oddly still, emptied of all the usual so-called generals, and fawning and laughing fools. But something big had been set in the middle of it—a tall thing of red curtains and lotus-carved pillars more than large enough to make a room of its own. When I peered inside it, I saw Johnny, and I realised it was some kind of bed. He was half-lying, half sitting, against these cushions, and he was smiling—almost chuckling—and he was wearing his usual cloak and a jewel-studded turban and many chains of office, and his right arm was hooked in a sling. It took me a moment to take in what I was seeing.

"So you're not dead?"

"Is that what they're saying?"

"No one knows for sure."

"And they're all crying, howling out my name?"

"What would you expect?"

He chuckled louder. "Glory," he muttered, "is like a circle of water, which never ceases to enlarge, till by broad spreading it disperses to nothing—haven't you found that to be the truth Davey?"

"You know I don't understand that kind of fucking bollocks. I never did."

"Don't you?" He seemed surprised—almost pained. "Perhaps not."

"Why did you ask for me, Johnny? Why the fuck did you bring me here?"

Part of me wondered if he really had feared that he was dying, and had wanted to see his old pal Davey Whittings for one last time. But then, he didn't look so bad, and so many others were closer to him now—hangers on, women who dressed like princesses and acted like whores, men who smelled like butchers because of the reek of death on their clothes. Old mates of mine, some of them, although you wouldn't have recognised them now. But I was still plain old Davey Whittings, Sir, Sahib, Sepoy Second Class. With all of London wailing his name outside, I wondered if Johnny Sponson hadn't simply wanted to see me just remind himself of how very far he'd come.

He didn't give a straight answer to my question, of course. He never could. He just gave another one of those Johnny chuckles. He just grinned a Johnny grin. And then he started talking about how England had needed someone. Not Johnny Sponson necessarily, but he'd been the one more than anyone else who had felt that need, and had known how to fill it. Said he was like the soil of England, this sceptered Isle, this seat of majesty…all the usual bollocks. It really was like he was giving me his deathbed speech, even though he plainly wasn't dying. Or, more likely, he was doing the same thing that he'd done when he sat beside me in that filthy hospital, and was rehearsing what he was planned to say later to a much bigger audience when he climbed the Great Temple of Ganesh, or perhaps, seeing as he was wounded, got himself hoisted up there on a wooden cross.

I could imagine his words ringing out across the adoring crowds. And I knew that they'd love him all the more now that he'd cheated death itself. And he was right, as well—when he said he gave them the spirit they needed to fight. That they needed him as much as he needed them. Without him, they'd be a rabble or looters and cutthroats—soldiers without orders. And without them…he'd just be plain old Johnny Sponson. The man who'd saved my life. The man I'd once grown to love.

But this different Johnny Sponson seemed pleased, excited, by his brush with a sniper's bullet. He was full of new wildness and strange hope, and odd new theories to add to all of those he already had. How, for example, the reason that the Indians had spread this Empire so far was because of their simple need to survive those dreadful few summers and freezing winters of two hundred and more years ago. How it all would have been different if something strange hadn't fallen out of the skies to darken our world. As ever, he was full of it. Nothing had changed. Part of him was just being more and more of what he already was.

Despite London being surrounded by a far larger and better-equipped army, Johnny was convinced that this wasn't the end of the English Mutiny. And, as he talked of how the Scots had seized the moment to attack beyond Hadrian's Wall and were marching south even now, and how the Lowland Hollanders would soon be breaking the Indian blockade and sailing up the Thames with fresh ships and supplies, he even began to convince me. I could feel it happening—I could see the colours returning to English green on his beloved maps, and I knew that others would believe him even more than I did. But the difference was, I hated the very thought of yet another battle, even if victory was the result. Nor could I understand why I was suddenly on the same side as the fucking Scots seeing as I'd nearly lost my life fighting them. All that would happen if we sepoys were able to break this siege and the Hollanders arrived and the Scots came to our aid was that there would be more destruction, and another year's harvest fallen to neglect as a result. Above all, there would be more deaths. Killing was the only thing that we sepoys were good for, when all was said and done. Try to get us to do anything else and we fucked it up.

I looked around me at this great and empty throne room. Johnny was going on even more now about duty, and about flags, and the need for loyalty, the need to stand up straight before what mattered, and fight for your nation and obey orders and do the right thing, even if the right thing was death. Perhaps the wound in his arm was worse than I'd thought, or perhaps he'd already taken something to help with the pain, or maybe he was simply a little drunk, but he was ranting now—and all of it was stuff I'd heard before. On parade grounds and from the mouths of officers, and back when I was a kid in the hovel we used to call home.

I reached my hand into my pocket, and felt for the loop of wire I still carried there, just like the good soldier I still was. And I opened it out and held it there whilst Johnny was still talking. I think it took him a moment to realise what I was about to do. And even then he didn't exactly seem surprised. After all, part of him was still like me, still a sepoy. He knew death was always waiting around the next corner, especially at the moment when you thought you'd finally left it behind.

"Why...?"

He struggled, but he was wounded—hampered by that sling and his ridiculous clothes—and my movements were quick, and by then I'd had more than enough of Johnny's bullshit talk. Still, it's not a swift death, or an easy one. You need strong hands, a strong will, to use a garrotte. His loosened hands batted against me. His legs spasmed. His faced reddened, then blued. His tongue went out. He leaked piss and blood. His eyes rolled. But I didn't let go. I was a soldier, a sepoy. Death was my job. But in truth, it wasn't the thought of all the fresh battles he'd urge us sepoys to fight which kept me pulling the wire. It wasn't even all the dead bodies and sobbing women and smoking skies and ruined towns that another season's fighting would bring. If the bastard had sounded like anyone towards the end in what he'd been saying, it was like my Dad when he was in his cups. So it wasn't for the glory or for the sake of saving anyone or rescuing London or preserving the Empire that I killed Johnny Sponson. I simply wanted to shut the fucker up.

Someone must have decided that I'd been alone with my supposed best mate in that throne room for a little too long. Perhaps, seeing as they knew what Johnny was like, it had gone a bit quiet, as well. Whatever it was, the guards burst in yelling, and they saw instantly what I had done. Word went out from there quicker than you could ever have imagined—beyond the palace gates and across London, right out over the city walls to the waiting Indian armies with their huge siege engines and repeating guns. Johnny Sponson, Lord of whatever he was lord of, our Prince and our King—private sepoy second class, expert bullshitter, brilliant dancer and secret son of some English Repository whore—was dead. The grief and the chaos was incredible. London burned that night. It was wrecked even before the Indians moved in to occupy it the next morning. Or so I think I've been told.

I'd imagined Johnny's guards would simply kill me. I hadn't counted on the fact that they were sepoys just like I was, and understood that death wasn't something I'd care that much about—that it was like the face of someone you've given up trying to love. They knew, as well, that their own chances of survival and the success of this whole mutiny had vanished with Johnny Sponson's death. They'd probably even seen the bodies of their captured comrades—or, once the Indians had finished, what was left of them.

You can see what Johnny's sepoys did to me yourself. They had a whole night to work at it before the Indians breached the city walls. And work they did. Then they left me there, destroyed as I was, right there in Johnny's throne room, laid beside the body of the man I had killed as flames took hold of the rugs and tapestries and licked up the walls. Perhaps they wanted me to be a signal, a sign, although I doubt if they ever imagined I'd have survived for as long as I have.

As you will long ago have noticed, they left me my mouth and tongue after they'd cut away my legs and retwisted my arms. I miss my vanished sight the more, though, because I'd love to have seen what has been made of this newly rebuilt city on the cold northerly fringes of this great Empire. I'd like to believe it's as beautiful as sometimes, in the right fall of hope or light or darkness, I thought it might become. I can't hear you, either, kind Sir, Sahib, Brahmin, Begum, Fakir, Lord, Lady, but I do not ask for words, or alms. Just touch here on my chest where the white ash is smeared. Tell me it's true that this city has been remade into something beautiful—that I'm propped on the marble steps of a fine new temple, filled with light and mosaic and the very breath of Christ, Mohammed, Brahma—that the skies above teem with kites and flags and spires and muezzin towers and the cries of mullahs and the clamour of bells. Touch me here, where the flesh isn't so burned. Then I'll know. Then I'll understand.

And don't worry about the ash, Sir, Sahib, if your hands are clean or your clothes are smart. It'll wash off easily enough.

TOPPING OFF the SPIRE

●————————————————————→

SWALLOWING HARD AND clutching the swaying rope balustrade, Father Thomas forced himself to re-open his eyes and look up at the spire. It was as bad as he feared. It was worse.

He'd never been so frightened in his entire life. From up here at the edge of the church roof, and although he could barely look down, he was certain he could already see the entire world. The town itself looked tiny. The ground was impossibly remote. Why had the bishop—safe down there with all the other dignitaries—selected him for the privilege of blessing the spire's final capping stone? It had been a long-standing joke amongst Father Thomas's fellow priests that he wouldn't even climb the seminary trees to pick apples, and could never be persuaded to sleep on a top bunk. And now he was expected to climb this high—and then much higher—all on his own.

Late last afternoon, he'd gone to seek strength in the church below. The landscape around the vast building was changing. The workshops and forges and cookhouses already had an abandoned air. He remembered how, in his childhood, he'd been fascinated by all the activity. The fires, the cursing, the creaking winches, the endless chipping of stone. It had been part of the reason, he supposed, that, seeing as he couldn't be a stonemason, he'd decided to become a priest.

The church had been empty and cold when he stepped inside through a creaking inner door. Damp and mould was already at work on some of the lower plastering and paintwork, which had been completed more than fifty years before. The building might finally be finished tomorrow, but everyone understood that the work could never stop if the power within it was to be contained. A few tribute candles burned in the side alters. Looking up at the high, dim roof, telling himself how strong and solid this whole glorious structure was, Father Thomas bowed and crossed himself, and knelt before the great golden fence of the altar.

"Help me, Lord, in the time of my greatest fear—"

In a glowing roar, the whole of the great central atrium was suddenly aswarm with curling swan-necks of light. Thomas choked his murmurings and looked around. Surely all of this wasn't because of him? Pagan manifestations as strong as this had become blessedly rare. Its glow cast the deeds of the apostles in the stained glass windows into vague shadows. It faded the carvings of saints and gargoyles. It shrank the altar to a cave of glittering stone.

Briefly, the entire church threatened to dissolve. The pillars of the central aisle became trees of a forest. Their vaulted boughs swayed amid the starry heavens on the roof. The patterned tiles across the floor became pools of light. His ears roared with the play of sounds which were part wind, part birdsong and part some distant moaning like the howl of wolves. He cried out, half in fear and half in awe of something he knew he should find detestable. These old gods were gone—if gods they had ever been. Their powers had been tamed. What rose from this ground now was something far more real. A literal rock upon which a better and substantial faith could be built.

Then it all settled, and with it the last of the day's light drained from the huge windows. The few remaining candles, caught by the fleeing breath of the emanation, twisted themselves out. Father Thomas found himself kneeling alone in the dark quiet of this nearly completed building. He'd been hoping for was a reprieve—a runner with a message from the Bishop to tell him that the plans for tomorrow's topping off ceremony had been changed, or that someone other than him would be climbing the spire. But everything was set, the Bishop's offices were already closed, and this was no longer a time of miracles.

There'd been barely a breeze when he commenced his climb from the solid earth, but the wind up here was strong enough to tug at his hassock with playful, dreadful hands. The thin wooden structure swayed and wheezed as bigger gusts poured around him. He shuffled along the last walkway of the roof until he was facing the final array of ladders which had been roped together and propped, seemingly with ghastly casualness, against the spire's sheer face. He looked around, dizzily taking in horizons of sky and earth, then all the tiny figures below him, their pinhead faces looking up. His head span. His hands trembled. His legs shook. The first ladder quivered like something alive as he gripped it.

He hated his limbs for moving. Hated these ladders. Hated the whistling wind. Hated the weight of the last capping stone which was roped in a rough harness to his back. He peered up at the gantry sur-rounding the top of the spire, which seemingly consisted of nothing more than two thin planks. Up there, there was no handrail. No ropes, even. He gave a laugh. The whole idea of climbing these last ladders to somehow stand up there unaided was ridiculous. Far better that he simply spend the rest of his life clinging here, halfway up the spire.

He remembered his lessons at the seminary. He remembered the sickening tales of pagan times. How the formless *something* which people had worshipped in these northern lands had risen and wafted, wild as snow in a winter's dream. Hardly the stuff, as Father Thomas had agreed with his tutors, on which any real, sensible and solid faith could be founded. Nor had those ridiculous myths and a few mossy stones set in ragged circles ever been enough to see it properly contained. And so the great work of building churches, not only here but across all of Christendom, had began. And so it continued, stone on stone on stone. Still, even in this advanced age, and just as had happened as he knelt before the alter last night, the older visions sometimes seeped out. At night when he was young, Thomas had peered out of the shutters beside his straw cot, and witnessed a lightness pouring up into the sky like a vast candleflame, and had almost understood the untamed awe which his forefathers must have felt in this sacred place before his Church claimed it. There had been no question then but that Thomas would become a stonemason. He'd wanted nothing more from his life than to help transform that vision into solid, dependable rock. Then his stupid fear of heights had overmastered him from the first dizzy occasion when his father had gently tried to urge him up several ladders to view at close quarters a lintel of which he had been particularly proud. But, just as the bishop had explained when Thomas had confessed his continuing dread of even standing on a stool to get a book from a higher shelf in the seminary library, fear was in itself a sign from the one true God which he must now surmount.

Gritting his teeth to stop them from chattering, he forced himself to go on and up. The wind bit harder and chillier as he climbed the last stretch of ladder, clambering up and out onto the tiny and unprotected gantry, teetering wildly for one terrible moment until he wrapped his grateful arms around the tip of the church's spire. The weathervane turned and flashed above him in the changing sunlight. Keeping one arm and the side of his body pressed against the spire's shingles, he felt in his cassock pocket for the pat of lime mortar he had brought up with him. He could feel the stuff oozing between his fingers and dripping off into the empty space as he scooped it out. Still, he was able to raise his hand sufficiently high to blindly push most of it into the semi-circular space of stone just above his head.

Almost half the job done now. Still hugging the spire, he some-how managed to unhook the ropes from his shoulders and ease the last stone down and around himself so that he held it propped against his pounding chest. The wind roared. The thin planks creaked. But some-how, he felt less afraid. He remembered his father's disappointment, and how his friends had made fun of him—Thomas, who was too scared to even stand atop a tree stump to play king of the castle. They would see him differently now. From so far below, they would never be able to tell how badly his knees shook, his hands trembled, or notice the pallor of his face, as he eased the stone up towards its resting place. But his fear, real though it was, was no longer all-encompassing. He felt as if he was supported by something both stronger and yet more frail than the platform itself, or even the spire; he supposed it was faith. Here he was, standing so high he could see the whole world. He'd be a hero after today—or at least, people would think him less of a fool. Even the bishop might cease berating him for his incompetence. The stone nipped and bruised at his fingers when he pushed it down. As it settled, it made a small grating sound, like the door from somewhere into nowhere closing in its frame. Something closed within Father Thomas as well. He could feel the change. The spire felt different as he took it again in his trembling embrace. More solid, yet diminished. No longer alive.

From far below, he heard the faint cheers, drums and trumpets of the watching crowd. The church was complete. *He'd* completed it. Glancing giddily up at the spinning weathervane, then all the way down towards the massive span of the roof, he saw nothing but heavy stone, mute copper, dead timber, dark lead. The dull earth lumped and dimmed and hazed itself all the way to the horizon. Even the sky above him was empty of everything but clouds and sunlight. For all his fear, he'd imagined he'd been climbing this spire to celebrate something glorious. Now, he realised he'd destroyed it instead. Once, people had been in awe of this sacred place. They had worshipped and made sacrifices and seen visions and told each other stories shaped out of their dreams. Now, all that they would ever see was a building made by the hands of men. The power and the light were finally contained.

For all his seminary training, Father Thomas wondered again about sacrifices. On this of all days, it suddenly seemed odd that one wasn't to be made. In commemoration of what—the old idols of mist and light, or the solidly single deity of books and stone?—he had no idea. But things would be different from now on, of that Father Thomas was sure. This, after all, was what this ceremony of topping off the spire was supposed to celebrate.

He forced himself to glance down one last time, just to get his bearings as to exactly how and where all those terrible zigzag ladders went. As his gaze span past stones and buttresses, arches and lintels, one last trail of lost glory, darker, brighter and more beautiful than any sunset, briefly touched him. Then it was gone. All he saw was desolate stone, empty air.

He gripped the spire. His breath roared in his throat. His blood boomed in his ears. From here, he tried telling himself, it was simply a matter of getting down again. He strove to conjure comforting images of warm fires and mugs of mulled wine back at the seminary. He attempted to see himself moving to let go of this spire and shuffling in reverse off the tiny, creaking plank, shifting himself out and over the terrible precipice to somehow take hold of the first quivering ladder so that he could begin to work his way back down towards the distant ground. The visions tumbled. They wouldn't stay solid. But surely getting down had to be easier than going up? After all, he had the pull of the earth to help him. But he felt impossibly weary.

Blinking away tears, still clinging to the spire as the sound of hymns and wild rejoicings soared up to him on the wind, Father Thomas edged his weakening body backwards and braced himself for the impossible journey ahead.

ELEMENTALS

I CAN'T REMEMBER exactly when it was that my friend James Woolfendon first propounded his theory of elementals. James had an active mind, and an easy way of expressing it. You could always tell when he was there at the club from the crowd which had gathered around him, and from the ring of his high and excitable voice. If it wasn't one theory or idea, it was another. Hypnotism, magnetism, the hollowness of the earth, new varieties of engine governor, the imminence of man-powered flight, and methods of educating orphans—they all came and went. In fact, with James they often swirled together. One day, for example, orphans might be hypnotised. On the next, fallen women placed on the island of Atlantis (once its discovery had been made, which James was sure was imminent). Or perhaps, to save those women from falling, they might be taught to fly instead. So James' theory of elementals, bizarre though it may strike you as now, seemed less surprising to us back then.

James embraced what we thought of as the modern in the late days of the last century as happily as anybody. More, in fact. Nothing escaped the searchlight of his enthusiasm. He made studies of the corpses of criminals in Pentonville Morgue. He climbed the Great Fire Monument to take samples of the city air. He designed new treadmills and restraints for the correction of criminal tendencies. He measured the limbs of foetuses. His townhouse in a square off Grafton Street was filled to the brim with so many wonders that people joked that he must employ a permanent roster of removal men to take things out of the back to make room for the things which were coming into the front.

Not that James lived in chaos. Far from it. If there was one thing which characterised James Woolfendon, at the least the James of then, it was tidy precision and impeccable punctuality. Turn up late for one of the afternoon lectures he gave on his theories and discoveries in a small theatre he favoured off the Strand, and you were likely to receive a withering look and an equally withering put-down. James had no time, as he said often enough, for vagueness or fiddle faddle. If he had a weakness, it was that he had no weakness.

As I've already said, I have no precise recollection of this first mention of his theory of elementals. Mostly likely, it would be have swirled up with many other thoughts and suppositions. Equally likely, it would have been at our club, and probably at that time in the evening when things had started to become enjoyably blurred. Most of the usual crowd would have been there, young gentlemen whose fathers or grandfathers had done well out of the coal beneath their estate, or some gypsum quarry they had inherited from a spinster aunt, or a fortunate freehold of land needed for a main railway station, or, like myself, had done well out of the South American trade. But if we were considering anything at all in those gay times, it would have been whether to call for another cigar from the humidor, or perhaps summon a cab to sample the feminine delights to be found in the meaner streets between Drury Lane and Covent Garden.

Elementals, the way James would have put it, were no new discovery. In fact, they were oldest of all possible phenomena. The Sumerians and Egyptians had recorded their existence—had worshipped them and called them gods, just as the savage Hottentot and wild Blackamoor still did. Elementals, James would have exclaimed over our slurring laughter, were genuine physical entities. Not that they were made of a type of matter which was yet generally understood. But he had proof of their existence. Proof—and this is one phase which I'm sure I do remember—which could bite your finger, or burn your hand.

Relaxed as I and many of my friends would have been, the idea of elementals would have drifted by easily enough. And from there, and however we filled the rest of that particular night, there was less of James Woolfendon to be seen in the next few months. There were no more lectures for us to enjoy at that little theatre. There were few, if any, appearances at the club. The man, we decided, when we talked of him at all, must be abominably busy. Perhaps, we joked, the next time we would see James Woolfendon, he would be perched sporting a pair of wings on top of Saint Paul's, or navigating the Thames by submarine boat. Inasmuch as we'd ever remembered this theory of elementals at all, we'd soon forgotten about it.

●

IT WAS A particularly hot summer's afternoon. I remember that exactly. An afternoon so hot that one spent one's time wishing one could climb out of one's own skin and lie somewhere hidden and cool. I was walking back through the flat heat towards my bachelor apartment from a fine lunch with the vague plan of clearing an incipient headache, when I found that my route had led me along Grafton Street. Even then, I didn't immediately think of James, but, passing the entrance to his square, seeing those tall white houses, I had the idea that I could call in to trouble his servants for some quinine and ice. As to James himself, I suppose I half-entertained the idea that he had gone travelling. He'd visited enough strange places in his time. So the idea that he might be at home on that doldrum afternoon, and actively engaged in some project, wasn't uppermost in my mind.

The house was a smart four story establishment of the sort which are impossible to obtain nowadays unless you belong to the super-rich set. I'd never paid it much thought, but what I noticed on that sweltering afternoon were signs of surprising neglect. Bits of gutter hung awry. The white plaster was peeling from its walls. The windows were dirty. The curtains were poorly drawn. It didn't strike me as odd at that precise moment that a place might deteriorate so rapidly. But odd it certainly was. And the pavement in front of the place was lumpy, and wires of the sort which were soon to become common throughout the city looped towards the house from an ugly succession of tarred poles. The withering look which a lady of the square gave me as she emerged from her own doorway a few houses on said it all. I was already a little concerned about my friend James Woolfendon when I stepped up to press the bell button. My shock was even greater when it was James himself who opened the door.

"Oh, oh—it's you!" He seemed delighted to see me, even though he dressed practically as a workman in rolled up sleeves, moleskin trousers and a stained leather apron. His skin was somehow both flushed and pale. If I'd have passed him in the street, I'd have given him a wide berth, and maybe tossed him a few pennies.

"On this hot day, I..." I looked around, and then back at James, rather lost for words "...just happened to be in the neighbourhood..."

"Well *here* you are." He nodded, then barked a laugh as if the phrase was the funniest thing he'd heard all day. "Perhaps I can show you what I've been working on?"

The house was dim and it was hotter than Hades. It was hard to make anything out at first. But the smell—the smell was extraordinary. Or rather, smells. Every breath, every movement I made, seemed to bring so odd new savour to my nostrils. The smells weren't exactly bad, most of them, anyway, but neither were they the sort of smells you expected to find in a gentleman's city residence, even if that resident was James Woolfendon. There was coal gas, for a start. And hot metal. And a whole variety of dark and singed smells of a kind which I associated dimly with transformers and telegraphs. And there was a wet smell as well—that sense you get when you stand beside any large body of water. And, as an occasional unpleasant counterpoint, there was an unmistakable whiff of the sewer.

"Come, come," before I could make a quick exit, he'd scooped an arm around my shoulder. "I believe I mentioned this work to you when

I last saw you. But things have progressed. Nothing will be the same, not once I have published."

At least there was more light in some of the rooms he led me into, but it gave through dusty windows and rotting lintels onto ever greater chaos. Some sort of explosion seemed to have occurred in his library—such were the numbers of papers and books which lay scattered on every surface and across the floor. Some, I thought, actually seemed to be clinging to the ceiling, fluttering there as if struggling to escape like trapped moths. The next, a bathroom, was so filled with pipes that getting into it would have required the skills of a contortionist. There were endless sounds of hissing, creaking, bubbling, groaning. The whole house was like the pump or engine room of some factory. And there were no servants. No wonder that neighbouring lady had given me such a look. It was as if the services which might have lit, powered and watered, and indeed, flushed, most of this city had all been drawn into this one spot.

"How much power do you need?" I shouted to James. "The bills must be huge."

"Huge at the moment," he said, laughing again. "But not for long. Soon, all of this will be self-sustaining. And not long after, every house in this city will be the same." He laughed even louder when he saw my expression. "This is just a work in progress! Everything will be far more compact once I have filed the patents and worked out a more precise method of controlling elementals."

It was his first mention of the word that day, and I still had no real idea what he meant. James took out a spanner from his torn trouser pocket and began to tap and twist and tighten a variety of outlets and inlets. Between dodging thin jets of water, and odd slips and splashes, he told me more about his theory. As much, in many ways, as I would ever know.

"It must be acknowledged that our pre-Christian ancestors worshipped, and feared, a whole variety of lesser powers." He waved his spanner. "You can imagine the sort of thing. Spirits of the wood. Spirits of the fire. Spirits of the beasts we hunted, or who hunted us.

Spirits, indeed, of what were then thought of as the four elements. Even when our forefathers started ploughing fields and building homes, and churches, we still maintained many of our old beliefs."

I nodded. That much seemed self-evident. Although, as a cultured and well-educated man, I was less than happy with his use of the word *we.*

"Now..." he waved his spanner, "...you're going to tell me that these are enlightened times. You're going to say that such beliefs have faded, and that no sane or sensible fellow now believes in such things."

"You put my case for me."

"And, indeed, you are right. Especially in this last century. Forests have been felled. Farmsteads abandoned. Even in the matters of the land, science has replaced the old beliefs. And the power of those spirits which stemmed from those beliefs has also faded. But where have they all gone, eh? What do you think's happened to them?"

I laughed. I felt I had to. "If I didn't know you better, James, I think you were talking of fairies."

"It's not a term I use, for the reasons of which your expression speaks eloquently. I much prefer elementals." His face was entirely composed.

"Elementals..." I nodded. Part of me was wondering why I had allowed myself to be drawn even this far into the thoughts of someone who was clearly loosing touch with reason, although I was also consoling myself that, at the very least, I had an amusing story to be told tonight at the club. But I also had a genuine fondness for James, and he was always a persuasive talker, and perhaps a small part of me already believed.

"If you hear of superstitions now, they're much more likely to be some presence in some sooty workshop or alley in the East End, or a ghostly tram glimpsed at midnight, or a shop bell which sounds when the shop is closed. It makes perfect sense. After all, think of how many of us there are crammed so close together into this metropolis. Think of all the dreams and hopes and delusions and prayers...!

"I've wandered endless streets and back alleys, explored the far corners of factories. Long exposures of photographic plate will sometimes capture a movement, but merely as a faint blur. I've recorded drops in temperature, but only by a half of a degree. I've registered small changes in the potential of charged electric wires. I've tried dustings of flour or iron filings, on which the elementals leave vague disturbances, and of course all the more common methods by which one might trap a thing of more ordinary substance, all of which failed. But then I had a thought. After all, I'd already theorised that elementals arouse spontaneously out of the life and industry of the city—so why not simply create one myself...?"

He trailed off for a moment. He seemed to have achieved whatever it was he'd been trying to do with the leaking pipe, whilst I had so many objections to what he as saying that, when I opened my mouth, all that came out was a gasp.

"I can see," he said, "that you still need proof. And that's understandable—and commendable. Come this way, my friend..." He beckoned towards a low doorway, "...let me show you."

The space beyond led steeply down a dark set of stairs. The heat increased as we descended. I had almost forgotten that my stomach was queasy and my head ached in my amazement since entering the house. But the feeling rushed back to me now.

The space into which James had led me must once have been a large cellar, but this one seemed abnormally large even for so fine a house. Perhaps it had been extended. Or perhaps, the ridiculous thought struck me, his house had been built above some sort of natural grotto. Whatever its origins, it now resembled a cross between a workshop, a factory and a cave. All the buzzings, thumpings and gushings which filled the rooms above met their junction here, where they thudded to some final rhythm like some huge mechanical heart. Iron walkways had been built across some of the deeper spaces, I might almost say chasms, where the thicker pipes crossed and coiled. But there were pipes everywhere. And wires, and pumps, and coiled devices I vaguely associated with the gimmicks I'd seen performed on stage to demonstrate the effects of electricity, and clattering relays which made me think of telegraphs, and hissings mantels of gas flame. I banged my head on conduits, my vision swam, as James led me through and around into a somewhat clearer central space, in the centre of which stood a tall grey object. It was rectangular, about three time as high as it was wide, and constructed of wire mesh shaped around a bolted metal frame. If it reminded me of anything at all, it was of a crude birdcage or upright rabbit hutch.

"What on earth's that?" I thought to ask.

"A Faraday cage, named after the great man himself. They've been used for many decades to isolate a subject from exterior influences and fields."

"And what subject would that be?" I peered forward, still half-expecting some bird or animal to be scurrying within.

"Can't you see?" James gave another laugh. It was the sort of sound which you might hear some dying soprano give in the final act of an opera, it was so high and long and fluting. "Don't you *believe?*"

I looked more closely, as one might at a disappointing zoo exhibit. And as I looked, James Woolfendon ducked and prowled amid the hot and hissing interstices which surrounded us, still gleefully talking. And as he talked, I became less and less convinced that the space within the Faraday cage was totally empty. Churning within the centre of it was a *something.* My skin pricked. The hairs on my neck started to rise.

"Ah—you see it now, don't you? More clearly. That seems to be some part of the process of how elementals work. It was just a small thing to me at first. A mere churning ball of energies. Columbus must have felt much the same when he first sighted land."

The thing was so vague that it was hard to discern as a shape at all—more of an idea than a vision, a sooty smudge, a heat shimmer, a blur cast across the eyes in a glimpsed after-image, and I thought at first that it had a bluish tinge. I saw it as a slide of falling darkness defined by dancing sparks.

"You created this, James?"

"If created is the word. And I don't think it is."

The light was coiling more clearly now. But it was no longer blue— or if it was blue, it was the same bluish tinge which you often see close to sunset hovering above this city—a blue which is also edged with grey, and with flecks of sooty black, and with swirls of bilious green, and with edges of fiery yellow. It made you think, as well, of other things. The elemental was a murmur of telegraphs—a clatter of squiggly numbers and half-murmured letters. And it was the roar of furnaces, and the clamour of trams, and the cry of newspaper vendors, and the grind of railway points, and the odour, which caught now in the back of my throat, of a thousand gushing sewers, and a million pouring chimneys. And James, darting and prancing about me like an elemental himself, was still talking.

"Yes, yes! *There* it is. Almost as strong as I've ever seen it. You see now—you see what has happened? Trapped under the streets, crudely contained in wires and cables, within the mechanisms of factories, are endless elements, powers, energies. Imagine, the servant who turns on the gas, or the lover who waits for a telegram…Imagine each time we fill a cup, or pull a plug in a sink…These are rituals, endlessly repeated by millions. These are the presences we believe in so strongly that we generally take them entirely for granted. But we *depend* on them, we *believe* in them, as much as a forester once believed in the powers of the seasons. And with at least as good reason. The elementals are there. They are *here*. They exist. And they can become self-sustaining.

"Of course, the term elementals could in itself be seen as misleading. What I've created here is a vortex of *all* the energies of the city, not just one. I tried at first using gas light, or tap water, or pressurised steam, or surges of electricity alone. Not one of those experiments worked. In fact, I've come to believe that the ancients were wrong when they associated elementals with particular powers, be they fire, water or earth. For elementals are essentially emanations not of one power, but of all of them. See, how it pulses and changes, moment by moment? One minute, you think of a flame, the next of glinting water. But I do feel that the ancients had a method in their beliefs. For what good is untamed power alone? It must be channelled, contained. That, I feel, is why the elementals of old were associated with a particular spring, wood, or field. The reason was purely practical. That way, the water was persuaded to run pure, the fire to burn more strongly, the crops to grow without disease..."

James was in full flight now—whirring and laughing around me. Talking of elementals for trams and elementals for train timetables. Of shop window elementals, and elementals for money. The hot, confined space within the Faraday cage seemed to grow stranger and darker. Now, the shape was becoming clearer to me. So clear, in fact, that I wondered how my previous vision had been so vague. The elemental was a tall thing, roughly human in shape and size, although the sense of swirling movement remained. It was cloaked in light of flickering shades. It had arms, a gaze—a face. Eyes like an ever-changing flame. The thing now struck me as beautiful as it floated there, its falling hair a glitter of light. It smiled and reached forward to me. The hand was thin and pale—it was the most graceful thing I'd ever seen. And, as would as any man alive, I reached towards the cage to take hold of it. I would have given anything to touch, to see, to believe.

Then James was helping me up. "Almost fainted there, my friend. I've found it's best avoided, touching the cage. But what did you *see?*"

In my dazed weakness, I found the journey back through the cellar and up into the house even more difficult than the descent had been. Still, it was a relief to be back in the hallway, and an even greater one to lurch out through the front door and escape this pounding, gurgling, stinking place.

Then the good residents of that select square just off Grafton Street had another cause to feel offended as I hunched over in the gutters to be copiously sick.

●

THUS IT TURNED out that the story I'd hoped to tell to my friends at the club wasn't one that could sensibly be told. Was James mad? Had I really seen what I thought I'd seen? Had I, too, been infected by his madness? There were too many questions left unanswered, not least my own somewhat nervous thoughts every time I asked my butler to turn on a light for me, or to run a bath. This city, so populous and busy, seemed strangely changed to me throughout the rest of that summer. The trams rattled by like fairy carriages. The smoke above the chimneys formed angels.

Although I kept quiet, and made no further efforts to visit that square off Grafton Street, I felt an odd sense of pride, you might even say vindication, when it was announced that James Woolfendon would, at long last, being giving another of his famous lectures in that little theatre just off Drury Lane. No one else seemed to have any idea what it was about, but there was a consensus that it was of an import which would push Newton, Archimedes and Galileo to the sidelines of scientific thought. And it *was* science—that was what I found reassuring, even though it was nothing more than James had repeatedly said himself.

After several postponements, the lecture finally took place on a Wednesday afternoon in late October. I say afternoon, but the day had been so dark that the carriages swept by with their lamps blazing, but still were only vague presences in the fog. You could get lost on your own street. The city was a changed maze, filled with unrecognisable shapes and half-heard sounds. If there was ever a day for believing in elementals, this was it.

I arrived at the theatre early and stood at the side of the aisles to watch as the great and good of curious city society entered coughing and red-eyed. There were writers and professors, journalists and inventors, there were the highly knowledgeable and the merely curious. In those days, the distinctions were not so very great.

The theatre that day had absorbed much of the fog itself, along with breath and pipesmoke and all the mixed emanations of humanity. The apparatus which cluttered the stage was already the subject of much surprised comment as people settled into their seats. But it made a kind of sense to me. Theatres, after all, have always drawn considerable amounts of the city's resources, and these had now been formed into a cat's cradle of wires, pipes and pulleys around a tall, sheeted rectangular object at centre stage. The surrounding mechanism already thrummed and pulsed. It dripped and gave off odd smells, sharp judders, even small gouts of flame, which caused some members of the audience to gasp or express concerns about its safety.

Prompt as ever, although looking even more ragged and weary, James emerged to loud and expectant cheers.

Pacing the stage, occasionally stumbling over the obstacle course which he had created on it, he talked without script or lectern in that high, passionate voice. More than ever, I was reminded of some diva in an opera. All he needed was a cloak and a mask—and then an orchestra. There were shuffles, nudges and glances. After all, this was a theatre. Even when the subject was scientific, people came to such places to be amused. That sheeted shape, meanwhile, stood at centre stage like a mute sentinel. Let them doubt, I thought, as James talked in much that same way as he had to me that summer of powers and presences and the lost beliefs. Let them snigger. They will soon be amazed.

"I ask you to picture for one moment the household of the future, when the size of these Faraday cages—" he gestured behind "—can be reduced. Once elementals are stabilised, there will no longer be any need for all the external wiring and piping which so clogs up our city. Not only that, but I believe that elementals can be made to multiply and divide. What I bring you, gentlemen, is a new world of infinite energy!"

After that, and much turning of taps and knobs which caused the whole stage to rattle and throb even more loudly than it was already, and then a flourish which was only slightly reduced by the number of pipes which got in his way, James dragged the covering sheet off the Faraday cage. There were gasps. It was a moment which I, for one, had been waiting most of an hour for, not to mention all the time since I'd called in at James' house that summer. People might mutter and sneer—my own dreams might have become clotted with fevers— but here would be incontrovertible evidence that elementals were real, and that James Woolfendon was not insane.

The gasps continued. There were cheers and jeers..The harsh lights poured down a cheaply made metal box of chicken wire surrounded by a crippled snake's nest of pipes.

Apart from a few hanging specks of theatre dust, the Faraday cage was empty.

●

IN MANY SENSES, James' notoriety after that failed lecture was at least as great as it would have been if his revelation of elementals had turned out to be a success. People, after all, had come to be entertained, and that they had been royally. The initial confusion of that first moment, which was followed by James' own dumbfounded inspection of the Faraday cage, and a rising tide of laugher which seemed to sweep out from the theatre and then across all of the city on thick spumes of fog, gave him a far greater fame than his widely verified researches into other less spectacular areas had ever done. He was a feature of penny dreadfuls. He became a subject of an extra verse in popular songs. Anyone with a far-fetched idea was, for a brief time until some other figure to be pilloried came along, likely to be chided for being a James Woolfendon.

As for James himself, as far as I knew, he retreated back to his house, and to his studies, and the sort of obscurity which only comes after a certain kind of short-lived fame. I, meanwhile, listened to all the jokes with ashamed good-humour. I was, of course, quietly grateful that I had never seen fit to mention to my friends what I was still certain I had witnessed on that summer's afternoon. I had no desire to be tarred with the same contempt which had been aimed at James. But it sat oddly with me. Did elementals exist, or did they not? And when, as that particularly foul winter persisted, and fellows would stumble into the club flapping the odorous fog from their cloaks and loudly proclaiming that they been assaulted by several particularly mischievous elementals on their journey, I would join in with their laughter, but feel a twinge of guilt.

Although my life went on in its normal desultory fashion that winter, my thoughts often returned to James Woolfendon and his bizarre theory. I almost wrote to him. I nearly had one of my servants call with my card. Whilst out walking, my steps would sometimes tend towards Grafton Street, but they never quite got me there. Much though I might have thought of contacting James Woolfendon, a combination of fear and lassitude held me back.

It was an evening late into long winter when everyone else had forgotten about James Woolfendon when, of all things, he finally came to me. I was at my club. You can probably picture the scene. The seven courses of dinner had been predictably fine, and the claret with which we had washed it down with had been of a good vintage. I, meanwhile, might have been gazing at the new electric bulbs which had been affixed to the chandeliers, perhaps noticing with my sated gaze how each of the tiny filaments seemed to dance and flicker into tantalising shapes, and how, when a log shifted, the flames of the fire within the vast fireplace would almost form a face. How, indeed, the very air itself and the vapours which came from the dark well of my glass of port all seemed to move and entwine as if nearly alive. But then a card presented beside me on a silver tray, and I, sleepily half-bored, turned and inspected it. I imagined it to be nothing more than an invitation to some soirée. But the handwriting was far too jagged, the message too abrupt.

I must see you now. JW.

The porter indicated in whispers that the author of the note was waiting in one of the club's private suites.

I don't know quite how I expected to find James. When he presented himself as he often did in my dreams, it was as an undefined shape caught in a theatre's floodlights beneath a floating, mask-like face. So it was a relief to find him solid and living, for all that the details of his aspect were undoubtedly odd. In the opulent brightness of that private suite, surrounded by French china, Dutch paintings, Kidderminster carpets and Venetian glass, he looked not so much out of place as somehow *imposed* onto the opulent chair on which he was squirming like a ragged scrapbook cutting. His presence, for all that it was unmistakably vital, seemed to have been pushed through from some other place.

"My friend…" I held out my hand and he half-raised himself to take it. It was a shock to touch him. His skin was both hot and cold, and yet it was neither. The room itself, along with my own sense of being in it, gave a pulse and drew away. "…I'm glad to find you back amongst…" I stopped. It hardly seemed appropriate to say *the land of the living* when he plainly wasn't dead.

The sense of urgency and excitement which had always been part of him, and which had been so obvious last summer and at the theatre had, if anything, increased.

"I'm so sorry that things didn't go well for you that afternoon at the theatre," I muttered. "Still, these things happen, and Newton and Galileo…well, I'm sure they both had their problems. Ideas are slippery things, aren't they? They come and go like…" I was conscious that that I was babbling. "…well, like elementals."

He clapped his hands as he sat down to squirm in his chair. "You've hit the nail on the head."

"Have I?" I felt uneasy. For all that he was an old friend, I had no particular desire to hear someone like James Woolfendon telling me that I was right.

"I realised the truth almost as soon as the lecture had finished. You see, I was just standing on that bare stage and staring at that empty Faraday Cage, when the elemental began to reappear." He laughed. The sound was high as a gull's. "Soon, it was as strong as ever—and I realised the simple truth. It was the very thing I'd been telling you last summer! The power of the elemental's being is governed by the level of belief which surrounds it. Look…"

He burrowed in his pockets, then unfolded what I thought at first was an old handkerchief, but turned out to be a grubby sheet of paper.

"The equation for an elemental's existence is as simple as are all the great calculations—those which govern the turn of the planets and the geometries of this very room. It's purely a matter of putting the square of the level of belief over distance."

I—who had always avoided maths lessons at school in favour of extra time at the cricket nets—was hardly equipped to judge the calculation. It did strike me, though, that a supposed means of improving the supply of power and sanitation which relied so strongly on pure belief seemed dubious, even if mathematically expressed. I think I may even have voiced such a thought, but there again James was ahead of me, and telling me that that was exactly *the point*.

"What is required," he went on, "is a process of *solidification*—a means of re-framing the calculation so that b over s squared is always more than one. It's a simple matter of giving the elemental a physical being..."

And so it went. I believe I may have ordered a drink to settle myself. I was braced for some odd request, or even odder revelation, but never in a million years would I have anticipated what came next.

"I'd like you to take me out, my dear friend—out to one of those parts of the city, beyond, I believe, the markets, of which you and the other club fellows are always telling such uproarious tales."

"You're talking about finding *a girl?*" I could scarcely believe that I was having to ask James such a question, but I also quietly relieved. In my dazed state, I imagined that this request had come about from the sort of abrupt change of subject of which James was always capable. At least, I thought as I called for my coat, he's putting aside all this dangerous nonsense about elementals and is attempting to discover the traditional pursuits of a gentleman.

●

THE GUTTERS RIVERED. The overflowing river shone. It was pouring rain.

The cab which the porter had organised turned out to be one of the then new-fangled motorised things. It sat outside the club's entrance fussing and clattering and spewing smoke. It would hardly have been my transport of choice, but this was no night to argue. After I'd shouted my instructions to the cabbie through the slide window which admitted to the front, we moved off.

After the great establishments, the banks and the newspapers, the main offices of big businesses, the other clubs, the buildings lowered. Then the streets narrowed. The cab rocked and clattered. It was too late, or too early, for the markets to be open, and the theatres had long closed. The girls who went about their business here—the better, healthier ones, anyway—would have either found themselves a client, or gone home, or would never have come out on a night such as this. There was no illumination here beyond the needling lights of the cab, not gas or candleflame, and I was no longer entirely sure of where the cabbie had taken us, but it was the sort of place which would have seemed dank and dark, even in dry daylight.

"I really don't think," I shouted to James, "that we're going to have any luck this evening. Perhaps if we tried again some other night. Either that, or I believe Madame Suzie's—"

His hand grabbed mine. "There's someone! Look..."

I peered out of the streaming window, not sure at first if he was right, and then not particularly wanting him to be. A thing of rags even more sodden than the dreadful night itself was lying before us in the streaming street. I still wasn't sure whether it was alive, or that it was even human.

"I think she'll do," he said. "In fact, she's perfect."

Perfect for what? But I was certain, as James and I helped the girl—for the thing did seem to be female, and perhaps even young—up from the mud and into the vehicle, that my friend's intentions had never been the simple amatory ones I'd so stupidly imagined. The creature just slumped there as the cab moved off, and foul pools of water sloughed off her. She was scarcely there. Her face was a thing of hollows: the mouth, the eyes, the nose. The stink of illness was incredible. She was plainly dying—and a risk of contagion—and I contented myself (although contented is hardly the word) with covering my mouth with a handkerchief, and reasoning that, whatever it was that James had planned for this wretch, the city itself had plans far worse.

The night, our journey, must have proceeded. I certainly awoke next morning in my own bed in my own apartment with the not unfamiliar sensation of not being entirely sure how I had got there. My butler was little help. Neither did my usual restorative breakfast, or the irritation of several letters from tradesmen about unpaid bills. All I was left with was an impression of returning to the better streets of this city burdened with the grey, wet creature we had found. Then, we had surely arrived at James' house. But the stairway into the cellar down which we struggled seemed endless, and my confusion and weakness were great, but the cab driver was with us, and he was huffingly strong. Or perhaps there was some new mechanical device of James' own invention, for I thought I glimpsed a slide of steel and pistons within his cloaks and leggings, a sparking grit of oil where there should have been eyes and teeth. Then we were down once again amid a mass of pump engines and pipes which looked capable of powering, lighting and cleansing half of the city. And set in the middle was the Faraday cage, and within that cage, towards which we dragged and carried the girl, was a swirl of darkness.

And then we somehow had the girl propped in it, or rather she was standing now as if borne up by some impossible breeze. Her filthy hair flailed about her. Her drenched robes floated and tore. And James was leaping from pipe to pipe, switch to switch, valve to valve. He was opening every sluice and circuit. It seemed as if the whole cellar, the entire city, came flooding around us. And he was shouting, shrieking about how this could only have happened because of me—because his precious equations required someone who *believed*…

From there, everything faded into a tumbling roar. Somehow, I must have left James' house. Somehow, I must have got myself home. It would all have made so much better sense, I decided as I fiddled queasily with my breakfast and pushed aside the bills, if I had been seriously drunk.

●

I HEARD NOTHING from James Woolfendon after that strange night, although as spring progressed into summer I found to my surprise that the name of a cousin of his called Chloe Sivorgny—recently arrived from the country and making a name for herself amid the so-called new smart set—was being mentioned at our club.

But who *was* this Chloe Sivorgny? From the occasional glimpses I had of her face in the society photos as I flicked through the Times on my way towards the racing results, and one brief sighting as she emerged amid much hoo-ha and fawning from a carriage outside the Clavendon Hotel, I detected a resemblance to the creature we had rescued from the gutters on that rainy night several months before, for all that the two beings could scarcely have been set further apart in station and apparent wealth. How had James managed such a trick? Was this just a feat of clever dressing, training in deportment and style? A dying gutter-snipe turned into the talk of the season by the action of some strange machine…? Once again, I found that I had the makings of a story too impossible to tell.

I wish I could entertain you now with all the tales about Chloe Sivorgny which were circulating then. About her grace, her wit, her beauty, her deportment—but I was cross with these fawning nincompoops. And I was confused. And I had my own life to lead, or at least to continue drifting pleasantly through—or at least so I told myself. And I didn't want to believe, to be part of James Wolfendon's bizarre equation. And I was essentially incurious by nature, and I had other matters to deal with in my life, which soon became all-consuming.

My father telegrammed to call me back to the family estate. Travelling beyond the city had become an unfamiliar experience for me. I remembered the adventures of my Grand Tour, the lost sense of risk, excitement and discovery—that feeling that the whole world is yours, and simply waiting for you to perform the huge favour of discovering it. But, as I struggled to find the correct platform at Kings Cross, and then the right carriage, the whole experience seemed changed and alien. Even when I'd settled into my seat, I could scarcely believe from the accents, clothes and manners of the people who surrounded me that they, too, were travelling first class. Staring out of the window at the fading city as the train pulled out,

I caught the reflection of someone staring back at me through the glass. I started with a yelp, and the other people looked at me. But it was only my own, sadly aged, face.

What had James said about elementals fleeing the countryside for the city? The landscape certainly seemed under-inhabited, a scatter of empty farmhouses, abandoned mills and fallen stone walls. Our estate was in the same sad way. Once, it had been a monument to the South American trade—or at least the money which came from it. Fountains had fountained. Lawns were laid like cool summer sheets. Lakes had glittered like watery jewels. But much of it had been shut down or turned over to grazing and the rest looked as if it had given up the effort.

So did my father. He sat slumped wheezing in an armchair in his a dark study, surrounded by an oddly appalling stink. The fire in the grate which his few remaining servants attended was like him; half dead, and muttering and spitting. The desk in the corner, which I had once thought of as a fine thing, a hugely-prowed vessel veneered with walnut and ebony which he'd steered through the seas of commerce, was equally diminished. Drifts of papers, telegrams and share statements were piled upon it in sedimentary layers.

"Ah—it's you, " he spluttered, although I got no impression that he realised he had summoned me.

"It's a long journey," I told him, "from the city."

"The city?" he still looked puzzled. Then he nodded, his loose jowls quivering. But it wasn't a nod of assent. The tiny sparks of life which still remained in his blurred and rheumy eyes flared. "It's the city that's dragged us to this state. Don't tell *me* about your city…"

He went on like this for some time. What he said is scarcely worthy of recording. You've probably heard it expressed far more eloquently. I had, certainly. At the club, especially, as people disgustedly threw aside the share reports in their newspapers and complained of how the banks had let them down. Or the government. Or the French, or the Belgiums. Or your typical working man, who was fundamentally lazy. All I was thinking as I heard this diatribe was that I had delayed far too long in taking a proper interest in the family investments, and that I would see my solicitors as soon as I got back to this city which my father still wheezingly berated, and have the necessary powers of attorney drawn up to enable me to take control of the family affairs, or at least to appoint some competent underling to do so.

"Do you know what our family business really entails?" my father asked me.

I shrugged. "As I always tell people, our interests reside mainly in South America."

"But have you *seen?*"

"I study the share reports," I lied. "But no, I suppose I haven't seen in any literal sense. I mean, these dealings in the sales of materials and produce originate far from our shores And the Americas are a long way off—savage lands, so I imagine. What is there to see?"

"I think it's time you did..." My father nodded and blinked. I'd never seen someone look so exhausted, or so grey. But at the same time he still held some little power over me, at least until my solicitors made it otherwise, and I was suddenly struck by the terrible idea that he was proposing that I might actually visit South America. The dim room seemed to palpitate. I felt dizzy, and weak.

"It's here somewhere..." My father's hands flickered and his bare scalp shone as he rooted half-blindly amid the litter which surrounded him. Instead of producing the steam ticket for passage aboard some ghastly merchant vessel which I'd been dreading, he lifted up a small box. Even in this filthy room, the thing seemed cheaply made, but he offered it up to me in his trembling hands with all the reverence of a priest raising a chalice.

"Go on. Open it up."

I did so. Expecting—I don't know, some lost family treasure, deeds or jewels or letters of intent. But instead there was just this grey powder, and with it came a terrible stink. It was the smell, I realised now, which had been hanging at the edge of things since I'd entered the room. In fact, since I'd entered the house. It was the sort of smell that, once you've smelled it, never really goes away.

"Go on. Breathe it. Look at it. Touch it. *That's* where all your precious wealth comes from. All the life you've lived, the schools you've been to, the clothes you've worn, the food you've eaten—and all the women, I don't doubt, with whom you've laid. Or it did."

"I don't understand."

"It's guano. Comes from South America by the boatload and we've traded in it for generations. The world's best fertiliser. Things will grow in it to feed all the gaping hungry mouths in your beloved city in a way in which they will grow in nothing else. Dried bat shit—the shit of a particular bat which lives by the million in certain huge caves in Peru. I believe it's quite a sight to see them. The walls and roofs are crawlingly alive. They darken the sky when they come out to their prey each evening. The locals say they bring their own night. And they shit prodigiously, and they've shat for centuries, and the stuff lies across the floors of the caves in mountainous heaps. It's alive, as well, with billions of insects. Fall into it, and you dissolve, you die…"

Even without this unwanted description, the stuff was disgusting. Enough to put you off food, once you knew what it grew on. Enough to put you off business, as well.

"Perhaps you can see, my son, why we've chosen to distance ourselves from our trade. Yet, for all the talk of futures, options and indices, it all comes back to the same thing. Or it did."

I longed to close the box, but somehow couldn't. The guano breathed out at me.

"The guano trade is failing. Shit as they will, the bats cannot produce the stuff as quickly as we need it." My father coughed. The fire crackled.

"What are you telling me?"

"I'm telling you that it's all gone. That it's too late."

Dark things seemed to crawl across the ceiling as the room swayed biliously around me. I shook my head. "It's never too late."

●

MY FATHER DIED not long after that last interview. Long enough,
though, for me to find time to contact my solicitors, and for them to
reply that had received several summons and notices of possession
with which, seeing as the old man was clearly no longer competent, I
should also be served. Men in bowler hats and cheap cellulose-collared
shirts—the sorts of creatures who would once have been sent away
with a threat of the police—arrived at the steps of my club. Now, they
were meekly admitted. There followed scenes of a kind of which we
members were unfortunately starting to become familiar. Things were
thrown. Objects broken. Various deities—imaginary or real; I was no
longer sure that there was much of a distinction—were cursed.

Without the aid of my solicitors and accountants, and with the
resignation of my butler, along with the withdrawal of credit by several
shops and suppliers, I was forced to attempt to make arrangements
for the old man's funeral almost entirely on my own. Then I had to
arrange for his body to be disposed of, seeing as our family chapel had
collapsed beyond repair. Despite the early promises of economy which
I was given, the then-new process of cremation was costly. All to be
given a box of cheaply made wood, filled with a disgusting grey powdery stuff. I cannot say that my father's remains really smelled like the
sample of guano which he had shown me, for the smell—rich, ammo-
nic, inescapable as a rotting facecloth laid stuffed into your sleeping
mouth—seemed to have infused my life already. It was everywhere
long before what was left of my father blew over me and lodged itself
in every crevice of my flesh and ears and eyes when I attempted to toss
his remains into the river from a city bridge.

●

SUMMER FADED AMID the usual gouts of rain. My apartment wasn't
the place it had been; the place seemed dark and under-inhabited.
Even my neighbours complained that the rooms stank. My club was no
refuge. Like its members, it had gone down in the world. The gypsum
business had fallen on the rocks of some obscure new process for the

making of cement, the coal deposits beneath the old grand estates were almost exhausted, and the workings had caused the once spectacularly beautiful homes to fall towards ruin, whilst the railway companies had successfully challenged old deeds for various parcels of land. So I was confronted each evening with vistas of rotting velvet and damp stains where the club's roof had leaked in the autumn deluge, with servants confused to the borders of senility and with dusty spaces where once-valuable paintings had been sold for far less than they were worth. And all of it had happened so quickly—in fact, impossibly so. I studied my old friends in the dwindling gas light of torn mantles and the flames of cheap, sulphurous coal. Old suits leaked trails of gritty dust, crumbling limbs staggered on walking sticks, faces corroded by gout, too much good living or the clap stared glumly into other faces much like their own. My own skin had greyed even more, and had an odd powdery texture, and—I supposed from the way some people recoiled from me—an even odder smell.

Was I the only one who saw all of this? Was I the only one who understood? The power of this city was a swirling thing, bluely dark and sparklingly capricious. I saw it under railway bridges and in the shadows of the new electric lights which now lined the embankment. I heard its shimmer in the clatter of telegraph relays and the hum of transformers and the tingle of the new telephones. And it was there in people's eyes and in their clothes—the new sort, anyway, the sort who arrived in their new motor vehicles outside bars and clubs which seemed, like them, to have sprung up from nowhere, but to yet have been there forever. Wealth, even of the newest kind, has a sort of permanence. Poverty and ill fortune is temporary as frost.

I wandered the changed streets towards the bizarre new outroots of the city. I saw the fairy towers of the new pumping houses which bore fresh water from some remote man-made lake, the metal forests of the pylons, the spires of the new chemical factories, the steel castles of the gas silos, the ceramic dragons of the sewerage works. And all of it was strange to me, and yet all of it made a kind of sense. I cursed James for his talk of elementals, and I cursed myself all the more for believing in it.

I was no longer the man I was. I had become one of those types of creatures you see often enough in this city, muttering to themselves, bearing some other kind of stink and wearing ragged once-good clothing, although you make a wide berth as they pass you by. One day, you have a decent living, a fine enough place to live in, prospects so solid they sometimes almost seem a burden. The next, your debtors are foreclosing, your club has been closed to be redeveloped and your apartment has had its locks changed. And you find, when you stumble back out into the street, that Christmas has passed without you noticing, and it's snowing.

White stuff. Falling everywhere. Lying lace on the railings. Stinging like ash on your face. You stumble onwards, and the other people, if people is what they are, pass you by as vague presences, swirls of city dark. But then I glimpsed something—I cannot say it was more solid, but to me it seemed more real. Human in shape, or at least approximately human, and wild and ragged, but seemingly *pushed through* from some deeper space towards which I, too, felt myself falling. Even before I glimpsed the ruined mask of the face which had once belonged to James Woolfendon, I felt a sort of affinity with whatever he'd become. I called out after him or it. I ran. I followed.

So, in pursuit of shadows, I found my steps leading once more towards Grafton Street and then the square off it. Sleek new cars were drawn up in fussing lines outside the finest and whitest of many fine white houses. I had to blink and peer at the place through the wafting blizzard to convince myself that it really was James' old townhouse, and not some illusion of the falling snow. But it was, and some kind of party or gathering was proceeding there—the sort of thing which I would probably have avoided in the old times, but which now seemed filled with an almost unattainable pomp and glamour. I heard laughter and music as I moved closer to the steps like the surge of the greatest of all symphonies. I saw lights blazing at all the windows like those which call dying sailors to their rest. And I felt a near-impossible warmth. I limped towards it all, stumbling up the steps.

There was no sign of James, but there were footmen at the door. Their job was to collect hats and fur coats, shake off umbrellas, and offer the first of many warming cups of punch. No doubt, they were also supposed to keep out undesirables of the type I surely was. But their gaze—as I lunged past a German countess and her paramour who were exclaiming over the sheer *fuss* and *bother* of their journey—seemed to pass through me. And then I was inside.

The reception rooms of my friend's old house were filled with loud voices and even louder clothes. Everything, under the searing blaze of the electric chandeliers which hung like glass suns from the gilded ceiling, seemed newly made—and freshly cut, washed and dyed. Especially the people themselves. And it was so *hot*, as well, although the firegrates were filled with nothing but enormous flame-like arrangements of flowers. Newfangled radiators squatted like ornate iron sea monsters in every corner. I was dripping, I was sweating, I was breathing like some ragged animal, and I surely stank, but no one seemed to even notice my presence. People were talking in the usual clusters which form at these gatherings. The men were grinning widely and the women were tossing their heads back as they laughed. They were all taking drinks and canapés from the passing servants, who seemed oblivious to me as well. In many ways, the whole scene was recognisable, but I no longer fitted. I was the lost piece of some other jigsaw. I was no longer part of it. I wasn't really *there*.

I stumbled back out into the hallways. The door into the library—now, that did seem like a remnant of the old house. I pushed inside through the hotly glittering air. No books fluttered from the ceiling as they had when I had glimpsed the place on that hot summer's afternoon when I had called in on James. In fact, the whole scene was immensely orderly, and beautifully lit by many electric lanterns and the sheer whiteness of the day which washed in from the garden. There was still no sign of James, but a woman was sitting at the wide desk. She was writing, and surrounded by gifts, wrapping paper, cards.

She looked up, directly at me. She took me in her gaze. It was a pleasant surprise to be seen at last. Then she put down her pen and stood up to move with impeccable grace around the desk across the fine Persian carpet. I knew that this was the famous Chloe Sivorgny. She was so beautiful that I let out an unintended groan. The idea of any resemblance to that creature which James and I had rescued was instantly ridiculous. But I did recognise her nevertheless: she was the vision I'd first glimpsed within the Faraday cage on that first afternoon made flesh. Although flesh was scarcely the word.

"And who are you…? No." She paused. A smile played upon her lips. You could tell that she did everything in this same teasing manner. That life for her was all a dance, a play, a game. "You're one of James' old friends."

"What have you done to him—to this place? I'm sure I saw him outside. You know this is his house, don't you? You and your friends have no right to be here."

"I'm sure James is about somewhere. He generally is, although this kind of occasion has never been his metier, as you as a friend will surely realise. As to the house…" she smiled again. "Things change within families and life moves on as I'm sure you're aware. This house belongs to my side of the family now."

Even though my gaze was swimming and my head ached at the wrongness and strangeness of all that I had witnessed, I almost found myself smiling as well. It was almost impossible not to be drawn into this woman's sense that everything was a harmless game. "I know…" I managed to make myself mutter, "I *know* how you were made. You came from the gutters. You came out of the rain."

"You really think so?" She moved towards the tiers of books which rose on either side of the library in leather and gold. Unhesitatingly, she selected a particular volume. There was no doubt, when it fell open, that the page was the one she intended. As she bore it close to me, I found myself wanting to kneel, and holding my breath. "You will see here that the Sivorgnys go back as a landed family to a deed of grant for services in the crusades. And here…" Her finger travelled down the columns of spinning words. "…you will notice that an ancestor of mine married a certain lady Woolfendon soon after the

Reformation. And the association has continued since." She chuckled. The sound was like cool water over mossy rocks. "So you could argue, if you wished, that we Sivorgnys are in fact the senior, more elevated side of our esteemed family. As for our current status, and although I hardly feel comfortable in talking about something so crude as wealth, you see across the page…" The flickering pages made a soft breeze. "…that we owned a large amount of property in a certain village in a valley in Wales. That valley was flooded to provide the water which is needed to quench the ever rising thirst of this city. From that," with a delicious shrug, she closed the book, "I admit that we have done well."

I gazed at her. The clothes she was wearing were so finely chosen, so appropriate to what she was, that you hardly noticed them as clothes at all. She was all of a piece. It was the same with her face, her manner, her riverine scent, her flowing hair. I was reminded of the statues I'd seen in fountains in Italy, in the way the silk in which she was dressed in flowed across her body. But the effect was sheerer and far darker. It was shot through with flares of light.

"You're not human," I heard myself mutter, more in awe than in accusation. "You're an elemental—a thing made of the hopes and dreams of this city."

"Am I?" She had to laugh at that, and I found that I, too, had to suppress a smile. It would hardly be more ridiculous to accuse the finest Derby-winning filly of not being a horse. "Elemental…" Still, she turned the word over as she placed the book in its space on the shelf and ran her fingers along to another level, and took out a thinner, far dustier and meaner volume. It split open with a wizened cackle. "Is this what you mean?"

There were dark woodcuts and barely legible words on cheaply printed pages inky with damp and neglect. Images of goblin-like creatures squatting over wells, of lumpen things half earth and half flesh wrestling with the moon or the sun. Things of flame and things of scudding air. Sylphs, nymphs, salamanders, gnomes. It was plain to me as I looked down into it that the contents of this book didn't belong in the modern world.

"Do you really believe in such things?"

Looking at her, looking into those blue eyes, I knew that the idea was ridiculous. But still—but still part of me couldn't yet shed everything which James had once told me, and which I'd in felt my own heart, and witnessed with my own eyes.

"Yes," I muttered. "Yes, I do. But what I didn't realise before—the thing which James never explained to me—is that we're all elementals. Made not just from the stuff of flesh, but also from electricity, water, money, stocks, trading options, land grants, sheer and simple greed... I've seen it happen all my life. The way old friends and acquaintances fall on bad times—how you don't notice them at parties and gatherings any longer, even if they're there. How the chairs where they used to sit at the club lie vacant for a while, and then just seem to fade. And then come the new people, the fresh ones who've some made lucky marriage or inheritance—even those who've fallen into wealth and fame through their own genuine efforts. How they have that new gloss, that special glow...But it's down to what we believe. It's all down to the powers and energies which flow beneath and above us across this city."

Chloe Sivorgny gazed back at me, unblinking and proud. And for a moment, I thought I detected the smallest change about her. A surge of something, a weakening, a rush of chill air. For the pulse of one impossible moment, she almost seemed to fade. But then she shook her head, and I saw that she was taller than I was, an infinitely younger, and more beautiful—and infinitely stronger as well.

"You have," she said, with the smile still on that face of hers as if it had never faded, "the most extraordinary ideas."

Then I heard something crackle. Looking down, I saw that the tattered book which had once recorded those ancient scenes was collapsing in her hands. Not falling apart, but folding in on itself like some impossible parlour puzzle until there was nothing left. Not even a dark smudge. Not even dust.

The library seemed to flee from me, the spines of the books slipping by like the rails on a track until I was standing outside in some empty hallway, unnoticed by the milling crowds who seemed to lie in every other direction but the one in which I found myself. I might have left then. But the house seemed to have changed and grown so vastly that I stumbled along stairways and corridors, uselessly lost.

And then I saw something. It was a shape framed in a tall mirror at the end of a long space of crimson carpeted hall. No wonder, I thought, seeing myself reflected there, that I'd been ignored. I was scarcely there, and scarcely recognisable as human, if that was what I was still. I and my reflection aped each other's movements as we stumbled towards each other. Then, as I reached it, I saw that what I'd imagined to be the frame of a pane of polished glass was a doorway, and that the figure which was emerging from it, weakened though it was, was subtly different from my own.

"Is that you...?" I think James and both spoke at the same time, and that our fingers reached to touch each other at the same moment. Both met barely nothing, and we jumped back like startled animals. In some other time and place, it would have been enough to make you laugh.

"It *is*, isn't it?"

"My old friend."

We were too faint, too tired, to embrace.

"Everything you said was right," I told him.

"That's hardly a consolation, is it?"

"No..." if James had still had a proper head, he would probably have shaken it. As it was, he was just a shadowplay of smoke. "You were only person who ever believed."

"What happens to us now?"

"We continue to fade as we are already fading. Me with my discredited theories, your with your lost South American trade. With it fades what we were, what we did, what we owned. It's not such a bad way to go, is it? And it still fits entirely with my theory. If elementals arise from the energies of life and power which surrounds them, so must they also decay."

Decay was an uncomfortable word. Looking down at myself with what now passed for my sight, I could see the process all too clearly.

After all, what had my family been founded upon, of what were we made, if it wasn't for seething piles of bat shit? And that was me now, a centuries-long rain of shit and piss, a fog of odours and insects and dead things piled in the subterranean dark of some other continent. I would have screamed if I had the strength left in me. But instead, I had what might have been my last thought, my last idea.

"But this is still the house in which you did your experiments—it still has that cellar with the Faraday cage?"

●

IT WAS LESS of a doorway now than the entrance to an abandoned cupboard, and the sounds of the party were a million miles away as we squeezed what little was left of ourselves past lumps of old furniture and ruined scullery equipment. Even the steps down, which had never been grand, had deteriorated into a slide of rubble of the sort you might expect to find in some ancient pyramid.

The cellar, or cavern, was still there. But it was a dangerous place, filled with the stink of sewergas and rumblings of suppressed flame. The miles of pipe and wiring had turned in on themselves into a pulse of bared fists knotted around the central Faraday cage amid the damp and cobwebs. Inside it, although almost undiscernibly faint, was a swirl—a presence—the raw stuff of which all elementals are made.

I gestured towards James in a spill of darkening wings. It seemed only right that he should go first.

"No, it must be you," I heard something mutter. "You are the one who believes."

The cage was a dusty, rusty thing. It wheezed like an old gate as I squeezed my thinning being within it. And the elemental aura was feeble. I could barely feel it even though I knew it must be flickering somewhere within me. But beyond the cage, amid all these coiled presences of the city, something moved with a dervish purpose, leaping from spigot to transformer like a wind-blown flame, and the semi-slumbering mechanisms in the cellar shuddered and drew themselves up as new power surged into them—and into me.

I wish I could say that the process was extraordinary, but it wasn't. I felt like nothing more than awakening, like stretching yourself and getting up from your own bed. And it felt like quenching a mild thirst and warming your hands before a fire after a brisk walk. It felt like the most natural thing in the world. I was simply *there*. I was *me*. Now I understood now why Chloe Sivorgny had found me so amusing. I amused myself, to think that I could enter her fine library as a thing of stinks and shadows to berate her for not being humanly real. As I stepped from the Faraday cage, I laughed out loud.

"Look at you—it must be working…"

Seeing only shadows, I glanced around for the source of the voice. "It isn't working," I declared. "It's *worked*."

"But you understand what to do for me?"

I did. Of course I did. I nodded. I smiled. I looked down at myself. A mirror, perhaps, would have been helpful, but I already knew how fine I looked, and how well this whole city would take to me. I knew it with the kind of certainty which only comes with the utmost self-confidence, and of that fine certainty of knowing that things are exactly as they should be. The world no longer owed me anything, for whatever I took would already be mine.

Something scuttled towards the Faraday cage. The door wheezed open. Then it closed.

"…now…"

The presence, whatever James was or would become, was growing stronger within it already. Just as I had done, it was gaining substance and power. No longer a ragged mist, but the dawning of a man of the kind this new age would be certain to welcome. A man of exciting prospects. Of new ideas. And one of the ideas was this cellar itself—or at least the mechanism which was contained within it. I could see it strengthening as James Woolfendon himself became more of what he longed to be. No longer a leaky contraption of old pipes and lost workings, but a sleek device, an outpouring of new energies. It thrummed and sheened. And the Faraday cage itself was no longer some rusted bird cage, but a finely-shaped device, a beautiful sarcophagus which would house not death but endless life.

In one way, I realised, James had been wrong. He'd talked of some prosaic device to improve the supplies of gas and water in this city when what he'd really been creating was a means of making improved human beings. He was becoming one himself now. Or almost. I could see the fine figure he would soon cut. And I could hear his voice, calmer now, but still beguilingly fluting, and knew that not just I but everyone in this city would listen and believe. And from there, the whole concept of elementals would become the discovery which would re-shape everything, and I would soon be surrounded by people who moved as I moved, and felt as I felt. It would be heaven on earth, forever remade. An endless, endless, parade of elementals in their fine houses and gaudy clothes. Elementals who would vie for me for power and influence. Elementals who would compete, and would always succeed.

The way the machine worked was a matter of sheer simplicity to me. Turning it down, stemming the flow of its energies, was easy. But as I did so, there was at first a strange resistance. It wasn't that the wheels, handles and switches had stiffened in being opened, worn and old though they had previously been, but that they wanted, they willed, the creation of the elemental machine which James had formed from them—just as did the thing of shadows which flailed and screamed within the Faraday cage. But soon it was finished, as it had to be. It was as simple as turning off a tap.

The wires loosened. The pipes ceased their thrumming. I was surrounded by nothing more than the same remains of old endeavour and industry which you will happen upon if you dig up any city street. I wished again for that mirror, but decided I did not need it. I brushed a little dust and picked away a small cobweb from the nap of my fine suit. As I prepared to head back up the remains of the stairway to meet the happy throng who I was sure I would now welcome me, I already felt renewed, complete.

IAN R. MACLEOD

This, as well, completes my story of James Woolfendon and his theory of elementals—bizarre though I am sure it seems. As you can imagine, my own life has continued well enough. I am married now. I found an heiress to one of the patents of the new steel Bessemer process, and we are lucky enough to be happy in each other's company, as well as being a fine match in our connections and trades. We even have children, and they are bright and alive things as only children can be. As for the return of my own personal wealth and success after the brief period of doubt and decline which I have narrated, and although I find it crass to speak of such things directly, it began easily enough from among the first acquaintances I made at Chloe Sivorgny's winter party. There was a man there, a keen young man of the sort which you will often encounter if you keep the right kind of eye out for them, and he had an idea, a theory, an actual patented invention, which he was sure would bring nothing but wealth and success if only he could find the necessary backing. A backing which I, who understand better than anyone that money accrues around self-belief in the same way in which a pearl forms itself around a speck of grit in the depths of the ocean, was happy to supply. So now, I no longer say that I make my living in the South American trade. What I do instead, or at least employ others to employ others to do for me, is to finance the new chemical processes by which the nitrogen which the farmers still crave is now provided. The guano trade is so long gone that it is barely remembered at all, but I take some pride in the fact that I am still making my fortunes, just as my dear father did, out of helping crops to grow.

There are many people of new wealth now. People who have made new kinds of living in this new century. People such as my wife who base their fortunes from the processing of new kinds of metal which I believe are especially good for the machining of guns, and others who make barbed wire, or build battleships in endless competition with the Germans, or who experiment at government subsidy in the manufacture of new types of poison gas. Indeed, this is a fine time to live, and I am blessed to have such lovely children, three boys and a girl, and I rejoice that they may live amid the fruiting of so many new possibilities.

And as to the rest, as to James Woolfendon and his odd theory, that is so far gone, such ancient history, that I wonder how I ever believed. Or at least, I do most of the time. And if sometimes, when I wander the electrically lit embankment after a fine evening at the Palladian building of my new club, and see some odd shadow swirling in a place which the fall of light in this dazzling city does not seem to match, I shake my head and move on. If I believe in elementals at all now, it is the remnants of a belief which I hope the record of these pages will erase, and which I now pass on to you.

The CAMPING WAINWRIGHTS

IT'S A STRANGE smell. Part-familiar, yet feral and strange. Deep odours of trodden grass and wormcasty earth mingle with canvas and fresh air. Even folded fully dry and rolled up and brushed clean of that year's harvest of grass and beetles, then put away to slumber its winters in our attic, our family tent had a presence. I could imagine it, smell it, resting above the dark joists beyond my ceiling as I lay in bed—its lumpen shape reminiscent of some alien mummy surrounded by cobwebbed summer offerings of frying pan, peg, groundsheet, folding chair. On those other occasions when I went up into the attic, those seasonal visits to collect the Christmas decorations or put away my year's worth of school exercise books, its aura was far stronger than anything else. Stronger than that of my old toys, or my rusty pram. Stronger than Christmas itself, even in the times when I still believed in the promises made by tinkling strings of half-dead fairy lights.

We Wainwrights—Dad, Mum, my elder sister Helen and I—were a camping family. We camped. Even back then in the early eighties, the word *camp* had other meanings, but Dad could get away with such statements standing talking to the neighbours, or to the blokes he encountered down at the pub. He probably announced it to the kids he taught at his school as well, and most likely didn't get a single snigger. Camp. Camping. To camp. That was us: the tent, the sizzle of bacon, the great outdoors and the midnight walk to the shower block carrying a damply unravelling roll of toilet paper. We were all defined by the two weeks each summer, and the several weekends, which we routinely spent under canvas.

Camping, for Dad, was an endless adventure. There were the plans, the trickily unfolded maps, the plastic patchings of the ground-sheet and the trips to renew the gas canister which powered the cooker. There were his camping clothes—his shorts, of course, canvas as well—which he kept folded away in a special drawer. There were the winter's nights of slide shows. I can still hear him humming in the way he only did when he was involved in anything to do with that tent. The compressed atonal sound comes back to me now, along with the endless *tink tink tink* as, crouched out on the patio in freezing mid-November, he gleefully hammered pegs straight in preparation for next summer's trip.

We were all involved. There was no alternative. There were the family sessions, which he scheduled, proclaimed, for whole weeks in advance, during which he would spread out his latest collection of leaf-lets, brochures and Ordnance Surveys across the kitchen table before Mum, Helen and I, and explain at unstoppably great length exactly what we would be doing in the summer ahead. I remember how the tart and musty smell of the tent seemed to seep down from the attic on those evenings to pervade the house. Later in the night, when I wres-tled with sleep, Dad's voice still droned through the bedroom wall as, punctuated by Mum's monosyllabic replies, he talked about the drives we would take, the many historic sites and morally improving locations we would visit.

I wouldn't say that my sister Helen and I were particularly close—we had our separate interests, and were three years apart in age—but we'd occasionally discuss our schoolfriends' holidays, which involved package flights to some sunny part of southern Europe. The idea of those bright, white concrete apartments with their proper beds and sea views, a private toilet—shower, even—and chairs that didn't fold up when you tried to sit on them, seemed an impossible dream. We wondered over the idea of beaches so hot that the sand was impossible to walk barefoot, of lands where you didn't have to shelter in the damp-smelling "family room" of some out-of-the-way pub from the endless rain or, worse still, sit huddled playing endless rounds of Travel Scrabble in the dripping communal space of our tent. Once, I ducked into a travel agent's on the way back from school and grabbed up some package tour brochures on the mumbled pretext of a geography project. I smuggled them home with all the guilty excitement other lads might have experienced with a copy of *Penthouse*. It was all there in those glossy pages, even the sex: those beaches sprawled with bikinied bodies instead of deserted expanses dotted with a few hardy families huddled behind windbreaks and some locals exercising their dogs. I could almost feel the sun, and taste the absence of canvas. Then, one evening, I lifted the brochures out from their hidden space under my bedroom carpet and found their pages savagely creased and muddied. As if a dog, although we Wainwrights didn't own a dog, had dragged them across several wet gardens. But what could I have said? Even if I'd confronted Dad, he would have denied all knowledge, or come up with a semi-plausible explanation.

After all the months of preparation and talk, the day would loom when we were finally to set out again for our summer camping holiday. Mum, who was quiet at the best of times, became quieter, whilst Dad grew louder. His hummings broke into song, or simple ringing shouts of excited affirmation. The process of bringing the tent and all the other camping accoutrements down from the loft was protracted. Everything had to be cleaned, re-assessed, mulled over. There would be lightening trips to obscure shops to buy new aluminium pans or a peg hammer. And it all required an audience, and small delegations. Little tasks which Mum and Helen and I were all expected to perform, and which generally went wrong in strangely unpredictable ways.

Our tent was a reasonably modern affair; mid-green, with separate inner compartments, and a metal-poled frame which was high enough for even a man as tall as Dad to be able to move around freely within it. The mummy-like sack which it filled was too big to sit in the back of the Volvo, and was laid out in one of those awninged trailers which you still often see on summer roads. When the early morning start of our holiday eventually arrived, with the trailer and the car and all our bags and supplies packed and every possible detail itemised, re-checked and accounted for, we would crawl yawning into the car and set off through a world made strange by dawn mists and buzzing milk floats. The route was scheduled long in advance, as were the stops we were supposed to take on it. Dad disliked motorways, so Mum was constantly occupied in deciphering his complex handwritten directions as we veered along A and B roads. The accompaniment to these journeys was Dad's humming and occasional shouts, along with the cassette tapes which he banged into the slot mouth in the Volvo's dashboard with all his typical holiday relish. Being the age he was, a child of the fifties, Dad had an especial liking for the works of Mantovani, Syd Lawrence and Perry Como.

"Listen to *that!*" he'd shout over the saccharine racket whilst Mum struggled with all the spewing bits of paper. "So much better than today's rubbish!"

Inevitably, we ended up getting lost, although nothing could dent Dad's holiday mood as we repeatedly circled a roundabout or sat at a junction as holiday traffic growled up behind us. For him, one of the highlights of these long hours of travel was to slow down on the street of an obscure village, wind down the Volvo's window and beckon some wandering indigene towards him. *Absolutely lost,* he'd declare. *No use asking my navigator. Absolute waste of time. But perhaps you...?* Whether or not the randomly-chosen local had the faintest idea where we should be going, the one-sided conversation would continue. *We're campers, you see, us Wainwrights. Always have been. Can't beat the great outdoors, the British scenery...*One of Dad's favourite occupations was talking pointlessly with strangers.

After several such stops, and occasional pauses for Helen, who grew carsick, to hunch retching over a verge whilst Dad kept the motor revving and sang along to *What Did Della Wear Boy*, and after he'd taken the navigation over from Mum and cheerily pointed out to us all exactly where she'd gone wrong, we'd finally arrive at the site, and the proper process of camping began.

Everything had to be choreographed. We all had responsibilities. *Found the drinking water tap yet, our Terry?* he'd say to me, *think it must be over there*, after previously sending me off in the opposite direction. All the pegging and the hammering and my getting the guyropes *twang-tight*, as Dad liked to call it, and searching for this and that small but essential item, which one or other of us were supposed to have packed—and it was never Dad—and which had either gone missing or turned up strangely damaged. That pale, disappointed look on his face again, beneath the smile, now with the two bright red spots on his cheeks which the outdoors always brought out in him.

Cloudy skies, damp grass. Uneven fields scarred by the yellowed outlines of previous camping families. The smell of slurry from a nearby farmyard, the twittering of skylarks. Further off, the drone of some arterial road. Dad, already in his shorts, and humming, whistling, occasionally letting off those weird shouts, would soon be off to *test the lie of the land* or *reconnoitre the toilet block* or *check out what the site shop has to offer* whilst us other three Wainwrights were still struggling to perform our allotted tasks. Hands deep in his voluminous pockets, clayey white legs protruding, he'd strike up conversations with the families of nearby tents, and even some of the caravans, although he disapproved of the latter as *too easy* and *not quite the real camping experience*. Then he'd join in with the football match which many of the younger kids spent most of their holidays playing, calling vigorously for the ball.

"Ah, this is the life..." he'd pronounce as he eased himself back down into one of our folding chairs. "Isn't the tea up yet, darling? What on earth have you lot all been doing over here...?"

After the traditional camping meal of burnt yet undercooked sausages which Mum had struggled to prepare with some vital utensil missing, the evening, and the even longer night, drifted in. Summer nights are surprisingly dark in Britain, especially in the sort of low, deep, river-strewn valleys which are generally set aside for camping. Surprisingly cold, as well. By ten or ten thirty, as I braced myself for what I hoped would be, but probably wouldn't, my last trip to the reeking, slippery cavern of the shower block, I would already be shivering.

"Not going to bed already, our Terry?" said Dad, jiggling his knees in his shorts. "Warm, beautiful night like this! Call yourself a camper, eh?"

But I knew that the dew would have already have dampened my sleeping bag. And that, just I was unentangling my underpants from my feet before pulling on my pyjamas, my inner tent would unzip, and Dad's head would appear. *Everything alright in there, our Terry?* he'd enquire cheerily with those two red spots flaring on his cheeks as I hopped about, freezingly naked. Eventually, I worked out that Dad could see what I was doing from the shadows my torch threw against the tent's lining, and I got changed in darkness instead.

A chorus of goodnights. Hawks of sputum. Dad's humming. Canvas zipping and unzipping. That tent-smell, compounded now by the rank rubber of the lilo. Twisting about as you try to find comfort without loosing your precious core of bodily heat. The debate, which can fill whole excruciating hours, as to exactly when the moment will come when you'll have to get up and head for the toilets. Despite the tent's separate inner compartments, any sense of isolation was illusory. Along with the sounds of the night, you could hear every sigh, move, scratch, swallow, fart or breath anyone else made. Dad snored—snored with the same loud relish with which he did everything else when he was on holiday—but in the proximity of the tent, I was also party to the sounds of his and Mum's love-making. It would start with a lower-sounding version of Dad's usual humming. Then, after enough shuffling of sleeping bags and squealing of lilos to set the entire tent swaying, came a stutter of surprised sobs from Mum: the sort of noises you'd expect someone to make in the throes of grief rather than any sort of ecstasy. Followed by owl calls and the tick of the rain as the tent subsided and Dad's breathing slowed into the rhythm of his snoring, all of it overlaid with the aching sense of my bladder's imminent over-brimming.

For all that, there's something strangely *right* about camping. It's where we humans come from—the more northerly sort, anyway, who were never free to sleep under the stars. When I say *right*, I don't mean that camping ever felt good, and it certainly wasn't homely. There was just this mustily atavistic sense of doing something which already lies deep under your skin. I felt it when we visited a Neolithic tomb on one of our camping holidays. Stooping under the ancient lintel into the earthy space beneath, I realised instantly from the smell, and the whole dark, damp sense of confinement, what my ancestors had had in mind when they had raised this mound. They had wanted to create a long-lasting replica of the sort of space their dead chieftain would have spent his entire life living in: it was a stone tent.

Such visits were a common part of Dad's schedules for our holidays, and we'd be quizzed about them afterwards on the drive back to the site. *Now, tell me, Helen, according to the latest geological research, were those lintels brought here from Brittany, or from Cornwall?* We were never right, and Dad—who'd been studying the leaflets and guidebooks all winter—was never wrong, but those upturned bowls of earth, upright slabs and vaguely defined ditches spoke to me with a kind of sympathy. I almost felt awe, standing on low hills in the freezing rain, watching the wind-driven mist shimmer around teeth-like circles of stones. Gods were worshipped up here, I realised, and they were the gods of this muddy earth, of this rain, of lives lived barely sheltered in fluttering constructions of leaking animal hide. Something cold arose as I gazed down at the puddled grass and thought of the blood which had once been let here, the sacrifices which had long been made. Lying in our own tent that night after a meal of greasy chicken in another pub's family room, and listening to continuing rain, the presence of these demanding and capricious beings remained. They drew me closer than I had ever been to making some kind of sense of what it meant to be a camping Wainwright.

IAN R. MACLEOD

●

EVER SINCE I could remember, there had always been a feeling of
things being marginally askew, of a universe perpetually misbehav-
ing. Early incidents are hard to separate from childhood's general mess
and chaos. Like my favourite Corgi car vanishing, only to resurface
months later rusting in the flowerbeds, or the Action Man doll which
was left to writhe and melt on the cooker after I'd placed it somewhere
else. Such things happen to all kids, and perhaps sometimes I was
responsible for them, but I'm as sure now as I was then that, mostly, I
wasn't. Mum, when I came up to her hot-faced and uncomprehending
after some new incident, would patiently tidy things up with promises about putting them back together, or dispose of whatever it was
straight away if it was clearly ruined. Helen was little better. They had
something similar at the back of their eyes—a smudge of resignation
which asked *What else did you expect, our Terry?* This, I soon understood as balls of wool unravelled in Mum's occasional stabs at knitting
and Helen's dolls lost their eyes, was part of their lives as well. Dad,
though, was always solicitous, caring, fascinated as he turned over the
evidence of the latest disaster in his long-fingered hands. *Perhaps you
dropped it, eh, our Terry? We don't always remember exactly what we did
with things…Maybe a cat took it—they do come into the house sometimes. Perhaps it was blown off the table by the wind. Or perhaps you
forgot, eh lad? Perhaps it's that, our Terry. Perhaps you just simply forgot
about what you really did with it…*As I grew older and the incidents
and Dad's explanations grew more baroque, I learned to hide whatever
was especially precious to me, although, as with those package holiday brochures, that tactic sometimes failed. It was just another part
of our lives, of being a Wainwright—the existence of this capricious
poltergeist, which could remain dormant for months, then visit you
with some trivial destruction and kneel down afterward to inspect the
damage with a broad smile and two pale pinks spots on the cheeks of
its equine face. It wasn't something we other Wainwrights discussed.

138

After all, these things—the dead mouse which turned up in Helen's old doll's house, or the lines of Mum's washing which were repeatedly torn and muddied as they fell across the lawn—are part of the life of every family. As I grew older and Mum's mutterings became more clipped and monosyllabic, and Dad remained happy as ever to explain things in his own inimitable way, it seemed that there was little else we other Wainwrights could do, other than get on with the life that we were living.

Camping was always at the core of these odd happenings. Holidays of any kind are prime times to lose, damage or forget things, even if they don't involve laying out all your belongings in some windy field. So it was always especially hard when we were camping to tell exactly how much of what went wrong involved any external assistance. You didn't need Dad around to discover a frog in your sleeping bag, or dead beetles in the bottom of your plastic beaker of Fanta. Or perhaps you did. Where did it start? Where, beyond all the humming and Mum's sad groans and getting ridiculously lost on the way to the site and then finding that the holiday pack of cards had got themselves smeared with dogshit, did being a camping Wainwright end and ordinary life begin? In our tent the cold, mustily playful fingers of those vicious outdoor gods were always threatening, demanding some small new sacrifice or abasement. There was no escape.

●

THE JOURNEY TO Wales for the last holiday all four of us camping Wainwrights ever took together was just like every other journey. We got lost to Mum's directions along B roads as Dad hummed and banged the dashboard and sang along to Perry Como. *Hope you've got your passports*, he shouted as we crossed the border. *Can't you even try to repeat that Welsh phrase I told you, our Terry?* He was as happy as I'd ever seen him, and revved the Volvo's engine into cheery clouds of fumes as Helen crouched coughing and retching at the roadside. His only disappointment came when the old woman he pulled up beside didn't understand his version of Welsh. And it started raining. Of course it started raining; on Wainwright camping holidays, it always rained. When we finally reached our site, which was too wreathed in wet cloud for us to have any idea of its surroundings, Dad climbed out and stopped humming for long enough to sniff the air loudly and proclaim, *Good, fresh, Welsh precipitation!* just as he had praised the rain of the Lake District, Cornwall, the Scottish Highlands and other portions of Wales on previous holidays. We, the tent and all our belongings were soaked by the time everything had been transferred and erected.

Opening out my bag that evening in the wan light of the dripping tent, I discovered that several of the cassettes of current hits which I had carefully taped off the radio on my portable player had unravelled themselves into balls of shining brown ribbon. I didn't feel particularly shocked as my fingers slid through them. In fact, this was far too petty, too trivial...

"Problem there, our Terry?"

I looked up. Stupidly I'd left my inner tent hanging open and Dad's long face, smiling as ever, was looking in on me.

"Just this..." I remembered the hours I'd spent with my finger hovering over the record and stop buttons. But I wasn't going to let him see me cry.

"Those tapes, eh? Well, never mind. Must have got jolted loose in the car. I've told you before that every cassette really needs to be kept neatly in its case."

"That's impossible," I said. "You did it."

Dad's smile scarcely changed. "Like I say, Terry. These things happen—"

"No they don't!"

"But there's the evidence right in front of you." He gazed down at the balled up mess of ruined cassettes.

I drew back. I could tell that he longed to touch and inspect them.

"I suppose it's no great loss," he mock-sighed. "After all, there's nothing to beat the old crooners, the classics."

"Just leave me alone! It's like all the other stuff—everything in our lives that's ever been wrecked or ruined or broken!"

"Now, Terry…" For a moment, there was a change at the corners of Dad's smile, and those bright points of pink which always flushed his cheeks on holiday darkened. "…you really think *I* did all of those things?" There was something else in his gaze. Something which I had never seen. It could have been denial, or wonder, or a sort of anger, or a kind of sorrow, even. Then he retreated, leaving me shivering.

Despite the drum of rain, such conversations in a tent are never private, and its chilly echo lingered as we ate dinner off plastic plates. The food was semi-cold: Dad had delegated to Mum the task of replacing the gas canister this year, and the thing now turned out to be empty. *Maybe you just picked up the old one by accident…You are sure you actually went…? Of course, it could have leaked. This modern so-called workmanship…*We'd heard the same or similar explanations a million times and Mum, in particular, seemed frail and hollow-eyed at the start of this holiday—far older and wearier than her forty-something years. Iller, too, although almost everyone looks unwell in the greenish light of canvas. Apart from Dad, that is. I kept glancing at him as he ate, hating the pink spots which had returned to his cheeks, the open-mouthed way in which he chewed and how he rested his plate on his bald, bared knees and drummed his fingers on the arms of this folding chair to the beat of the rain. That night, I lay in bed listening to the continuing rain, re-acquainted with that feeling both of stifling confinement and empty exposure which you only ever experience in a tent. Dad's face loomed. I cowered, drowning in canvas. The drenching clouds swept by, and I dreamed of sacrifices to the gods of a windswept earth until I was awoken in the still dark by the absence of the rain and the soft, nearby sound of something mewling. A mouse, I thought at first, being slowly dismembered by a fox or a cat in a nearby hedgerow; the sound was that high, that hopeless. Then it was punctuated by a characteristic series of soft ohs and I realised that it was Mum. And I knew that this had nothing to do with anything resembling love. She was simply crying.

Something extraordinary happened next morning; we awakened to find the Welsh hills bathed in sunlight, and what looked like the whole blue Atlantic glinting beckoningly beyond a low fence. The breeze was warm and mild—barely enough to flutter the sides of the tent as Dad, hands stuffed deep into the pockets of his shorts, strode around it, muttering about the forecast being wildly wrong; how he'd been expecting, had *planned* for far harsher weather. The day, which had started deliciously warm, soon grew warmer. By noon, even the deep pools of mud outside the shower block had started to shrink.

For the first part of our holiday, everything basked in incredible heat, and everyone on the site bore a dazedly cheerful expression. This, after all, wasn't how camping holidays anywhere in Britain were supposed to be—especially in Wales. There was a small village nearby with a whitewashed pub, giddy cliff walks, and steps which led down to a vast, rock-strewn, beach. I remember the clean smell of the salt as I splashed in and out of the tepid shallows in the swimming costume I normally only wore on the afternoons when we escaped into some municipal swimming pool from the rain. Mum and Helen lounged on towels on and read doorstop novels. We all got mildly sunburnt. This was nothing like a usual Wainwright holiday. This, in fact, was almost like those brochures which I'd once smuggled home from the travel agent's. Dad, for whom camping was all about battling storm and tempest, did his best to hide his disappointment. He wandered resentfully in his holiday sandals, boring the neighbours with his endless stories, scowling at the blazing sky and joining in the kids' football match which had decamped itself to the beach near to a place where Mum and Helen sunbathing. Unsurprisingly, and although I don't think it was Dad who actually kicked it, the ball once hit Mum in the face.

At night, lying in the clean dryness of my inner tent and feeling the pinprick itch of my sunburn, I wondered at all these new sensations. Was this how other families lived their lives, had their holidays? Was this what it meant to be actually *happy*? But I knew it couldn't last. When I climbed out of our tent on Saturday morning the sun was still blazing, but already there was a different tang to the air. Dad was walking briskly up the grassy slope from his trip to the camp shop with a bag full of sausages and bacon and his copy of the *Daily Telegraph* rolled like a baton. His shorts flapped in the breeze. I'd never seen him grinning so broadly.

"Haven't you heard, our Terry? I'd make the best of today if I were you—your pretend-swims. And better tell that lazy sister and mother of yours to wake up and start getting things shipshape." Cheeks redly gleaming, he scanned the Welsh horizons, then let out a shout—a yelp—of sheer joy loud enough to set the seagulls screaming. "There's a big storm coming. Good job I managed to find a gas canister to replace the one your Mum forget to get fixed. We'll need something warm inside us this evening..."

Already, people were packing up. Tent poles tinked and car engines revved as cheery voices called farewell to holiday acquaintances they knew they would never see again. *Not going yet, then?* someone called. We shook our heads. After all, we were the camping Wainwrights, and Dad loved a big storm. Just like that Carpenters song which, despite its relative modernity, he was humming and singing in odd barks as he organised things, he was on top of the world.

By noon, the sky had clouded over and the site was already near-deserted. Those few other hardy beings who were planning on staying were taughtening canvas, knocking blocks under the wheels of their caravans, hammering in more tent pegs. Grass shivered, briars creaked, clumps of hawthorn waved their limbs, and there was a sense of siege as I hung my sodden trunks to flap from the guyropes after what I knew would be my last *pretend-swim*. All those recent happy days of warmth and sunlight already seemed like a dream. Even now, the tent was starting to give off its characteristic odour of soured canvas. The old, capricious gods of wet earth, of drumming rain, and of endless small destructions and sacrifices, were returning...

Then a loud gasp came from within the tent. I ducked inside, and saw Mum crouched beside Helen in her inner tent. They were both looking down into my sister's clothes bag, and what seemed for a moment like blood was smeared over their hands.

"This is everything I've got left to wear," Helen muttered, gazing at the inky mess where two or three of her girlish multi-coloured biros had seemingly leaked simultaneously across most of her clothes. "God knows how we're going to get them clean."

"Isn't there a washing machine in the block by the office?" I asked hopefully.

"For what good that will do." In this bilious light, Mum's eyes were black. Her face, as if lit like a Halloween lantern, had a waxy, greenish glare. She pulled out a tissue from her pocket and began to wipe her fingers. "I suppose I'd better get started before the storm kicks in. I mean..." She balled the tissue hard inside her fist so hard I heard it squeak. "I mean, it could be worse..." She trailed off. The sides of the tent bellied as the wind moaned. "I mean, it could be..." She trailed off again. I heard something in her throat click. "It's like that bloody gas canister. It's like—we can't go on like this, can we? We've got to—"

She stopped as the sound of Dad's humming and the tramp of his sandaled feet grew close across the grass outside. We heard the jingle of his keys as he shoved his hands into his shorts. He was standing right beside us now, a dark shape looming just beyond the canvas. He let out an abrupt shout.

"Talk of a bit of rain, and look what happens," he called. "Half the campsite disappears. But we'll show them, eh? Us Wainwrights'll have the time of our lives, eh? Eh?"

In the late afternoon, the site owners drove their beaten-up Landrover around the field, offering the shelter of a mouldy caravan which lay at the edge of the site. Dad, legs apart, stripped down to nothing but his shorts, fists planted on his bony hips as he stood in front of our tent, the absolute epitome of Wainwright resilience, smilingly shook his head. By now, huge, boiling banks of cloud, the far-flung arm of some tropic tempest which had reached all the way to us from across the Atlantic, were massing. There was a second leave-taking as most of the remaining campers decided against braving the elements on this exposed Welsh field. The sun gave a final bloody glare as it poked through the mountainous horizon, and I rechecked the guyropes and the pegs and the rubber hoops and the tent-ties and the metal poppers which held the frame together. I was looking for the flaw, the fault, the strain or rip or tear or twist or breakage, which I was sure lay hidden somewhere amid all Dad's cheery preparations. But I couldn't find any-thing—and that absence, as the tent's canvas began to throb whilst Mum set about boiling up a meal of Vesta curry beneath the dripping remains of Helen's stained clothing, was the wrongest thing of all.

Mum, Helen and I ate stoically. Dad, though, was taut as a guy-rope, and humming, smiling, jiggling. In its way, it *was* exciting to be here inside our the tent as it began to bow and creak when the first heavy drops of rain started to thud against it. Then the heavens opened, and we just sat there wishing the hours away, for this was far too much, despite the many wet nights us camping Wainwrights had experienced. Normally, we'd have played cards, but the hissing, flap-ping roar of the storm as it beat against the tent was all-absorbing. Shining runnels of water pooled. The frame leaned and creaked in each roaring hammerblow, dimming our dangling gas lantern. Even in raincoat and plastic trousers, I was instantly drenched on my last trip to the toilet. There was a moment of blind panic on the way back when I slipped in the mud and found my torch illuminating nothing but streaming rain. I was sure I'd lost our tent. But there it was: inner-lit, standing out against the pouring dark, it really did look almost safe; nearly welcoming.

"Bit of a breeze out there?" Dad shouted in his typically yo-ho-me-hearties way as I wrestled to zip the flap back up. "You lot can all just go to bed. I'll keep watch for all us Wainwrights, make sure everything stays absolutely shipshape..." Pulling off my wellingtons and plastic overthings, too tired to bother with anything else, I crawled into my sodden sleeping bag and curled up there. Sleep, I told myself in the moment before I tumbled headlong into it, was impossible.

And I dreamed. Although the sun was so bright I could barely see, I knew that all us Wainwrights were here, and I stumbled in search of Mum's and Dad's and Helen's holiday-happy voices. Slowly, I realised that the gleamingly painful light came from the gloss of the pages of the brochures into which I had fallen, with their bright poolside bars and plasticky palm trees. And, being mere pictures, the whole thing was flat; a disappointing wasteland. *Come on, our Terry!* Dad's voice remained typically hearty. *Could do with some help here...*But I was still faltering, trying to work out exactly where on earth *here* was. My feet skidded and my hands slid. My fingers tore at the paper in my anger and frustration, which clumped and grew damp. Everything was sodden and filthy now, wet and reeking of soil and canvas as it closed over me, weighing down my flailing arms, wrapping my face and blocking my mouth in a filthy, turfy, earthy, musty reek. I fought against it. I couldn't move, scream, breathe—

Could do with some help here, Terry, Dad was still saying as I rose out from my dream to find that I was still choking, wrestling with flapping sheets. His torch danced amid the storm, showing streaming turf, blurring rain, a glimpse of his bare white knees. Dad, who was still wearing only his canvas shorts, was battling to secure my corner of the tent before the wind lifted the whole thing away.

"Well done, our Terry! Are you awake in there, Mum? Helen—you as well! Could really do with a little more help out here..."

His voice came and went over the thwack of the tent and the wild roar of the wind. Half-buried in mud and canvas, batting away flailing bits of rope, I struggled against the wet grip of my sleeping bag until I finally managed to scramble my way out. The noise was tremendous. You feet slid. Your legs buckled. The air was sucked from your lungs. Dad's torch played across his face. He was smeared in grass and mud, and the rain streamed off him, but still he was grinning—and he was humming, singing, letting out those bizarre shouts.

"This is it, eh? Some wind! But could do with a bit of extra help here..." He grappled with a stretch of canvas. "Keep a hold of this for us, our Terry."

I did as he said, even though the whole nightmare force of the storm seemed to buck against me. Mum and Helen crawled out from their corners of the tent just as the frame started twisting. Lightning flickered. They looked like muddy zombies. I suppose I did as well.

"Ah! There you are! See that guyrope, Helen? Try to keep a hold and stop it from lifting—And you, darling..."

But it was too late. With a splintering screech, the frame broke, tearing as it did so a widening rent in the canvas. There was an odd glimpse of the fragile indoor normality of our camping life: the towels and the tins and the games and the cooking things and all the flip flops and the wellingtons and the hanging stuff we'd vainly hoped would dry, and then the night ripped through it, pulling everything apart. Packs of playing cards and Scrabble letters spewed. An empty water bottle took flight. Someone's lilo slalomed downhill. There was a wild anger about this storm, a sheer physical presence which, as the edge of the tent which I'd been struggling to keep hold of ripped finally itself from my fingers and slapped viciously against my face, I knew it was impossible to fight.

Dad, though, was having none of it. He was still laughing and barking out orders. For him, no matter how bad things got, this was just another story he could tell the neighbours and the kids at his school and those unwary strangers he stopped at the roadside, another camping adventure, a fresh wave of destruction which he'd brought to our lives and would grinningly inspect and discuss with us across the kitchen table through all the endless evenings afterwards. I realised, even as my legs buckled and I slipped back into the mud, there would be other nights, other tents, other holidays—that the lives of us camping Wainwrights would continue to go stupidly and unbelievably wrong.

Lightning flashed as I scrambled back to my feet, and I saw that Mum was gripping the famous blue gas canister, about which there had been such dispute this holiday, in her hands. The thing was heavy now that Dad had had it refilled, but she held it as if weighed nothing. Dad, who was crouching as he attempted to stop the tent frame's last straight leg from twisting, looked up as she stood over him. The rain had washed Mum's nightdress pale. Her hair streamed black around her white face. Lightning flared again, and Dad's grin broadened. Even though Mum looked strange and eerie and angry, he probably imagined she was going to use the canister to weigh down our rapidly collapsing tent.

"That's great, darling, if you could—"

With a strength I didn't imagine she possessed, Mum swung the canister down and around. Dad looked surprised when, with a wet, splitting sound, it struck the side of his head. "...careful...could really have hurt—" His grin loosened as Mum swung and struck him again. The side of his skull had become oddly shaped, and his voice was slurred. "Could *still* do with a bit of help here..." His mouth began to bubble with dark fluid. "If you could just—" The gas canister flashed for third time, and all expression dropped from Dad's face. He wavered for a moment, then toppled forward, landing in a splash of limbs amid what was left of our tent. Mum just stood watching, the dripping canister still in her hands, as his body gave a series of spasming jerks. So did Helen. Dad had dropped his torch as he fell. I stooped to pick it up from where it had slid across the mud.

"Turn it off!" Mum shouted.

The torch was darkly slippery. Its beam seem to brighten and fan out as my fingers struggled with the switch, lancing across the field.

"Here—give it..." Helen, nearly falling across Dad and the mess of the tent, wrenched it from me. But still the light wouldn't go out. Mum joined in, and our struggles with that stupid and unobeying object filled our attention for what could have been seconds, minutes. Then the wind gave a surging moan, a wall of wet darkness slammed into us, and we realised as the torch finally blinked out that something strange was happening to Dad and the tent. It was mainly a sound at first, a huge ripping and tearing. Then, as the clouds flared again, we saw that the whole thing was rearing itself up in the wind. Dad had become part of it. We saw the flail of his limbs tangled in ropes and canvas as poles twisted and parted, then the bony white mask of his face. He even seemed to be struggling grinningly against the strips of rope and bloody canvas which had wrapped themselves around his body, although more likely it was merely the storm which was animating him. The tent streamed up and out. Then, as some last restraint gave in a groaning tear, it took off and began a tumbling movement down across the campsite, lit by the lightning's stuttering flares, and bearing Dad with it. It was one of those things that you see and yet don't see; that your mind struggles to grasp even as you witness it. Amazed, we followed. The storm tore with wild hands, straining to lift us as well as we stumbled across the sodden field and the thing danced ahead like some weird black jellyfish. Shedding aluminium pans, wire hangers and plastic plates—the whole detritus of our lives as camping Wainwrights—in its wake, it finally snagged against fence which separated the land from the sea. There was a loud bang as one of the posts snapped. Then another was ripped from the earth and barbed wire unravelled in a series of bright screams until the whole edge of the land gave and Dad and our tent tumbled off into the night.

●

THE RESCUE SERVICES were incredibly busy that night, but there was still a rigorous search. As Mum, Helen and I sat huddled in blankets and waiting for news in the bland florescent glow of the campsite owner's kitchen, I still half-imagined that Dad would be found alive. After all, it was just like one of this stories, the whole way he explained the world. *Well, the tent caught certainly me up, but it acted as a sort of parachute, and then it floated...Sounds strange, near-impossible, I know...* CAMPING MIRACLE. MAN BORNE ALOFT IN GALE SAVED BY TENT. I could see the headlines, and the twin red spots on his cheeks above his smile. But Dad was dead. They found his body not long after dawn at the far edge of the same beach on which Mum and Helen had sunbathed, and I'd paddled. He'd died, we were told, from the injuries sustained from his fall off the cliff. Most probably, we were reassured by several doctors and policewomen, he hadn't suffered.

We returned home to find the house wrapped in its usual holiday post-drowse, and a note on the doormat from the local camping shop apologising for having accidentally given Mum an empty gas canister the week before. The place seemed quiet, empty, ridiculously dry and clean and spacious, but then, at the end of holidays, it always did. There was a spate of the things which happen after someone dies—visits from relatives, an inquest, many forms to fill in, more relatives, solicitors, a funeral—and then life returned to what us three remaining Wainwrights would eventually come to think of as normality, even if the evenings did seem longer and quieter as autumn set in. The pension and insurance policies which Dad had paid for through his school and his teaching union were quick to pay up, and Mum soon bought a new car—a much smaller, sportier, redder, prettier thing than Dad's old Volvo. It took the three of us out on expensive meals quite different to those you eat in the family rooms of pubs, or to the cinema to see the kind of stupidly comedic films of which we knew Dad would never have approved. We sat there in the dark gazing up at the screen, listening to the sound of other people laughing. And then we went home again.

Christmas, as anyone will tell you who's lost someone, is a hard season. The idea of going up into our loft and rummaging around for the lights and the tinsel close to the space where all our camping stuff had laid—*have you sorted out those new bulbs like I asked you to, our Terry. Pity about what happened to that plaster Santa Claus*—was never something about which any of us felt happy. Instead, Mum came home one evening with bright handfuls of brochures for holidays in parts of the world which are still warm at that time of year, and it was almost like the old times as we spread them out over the kitchen table and looked at the vistas of palm trees and swimming pools, and talked of times and dates and facilities. The odd thing was how often life continued to go wrong. The downstairs sink cracked, my schoolbooks got unstapled and Helen's favourite perfume evaporated—all seemingly spontaneously. The only thing that was missing was Dad's humming, those bright spots on his cheeks, his occasional cheery shouts, and his bizarrely pointless explanations as he stroked the ruined objects with his fingers.

Then the school term ended, and Christmas came, and all three of us were kept quietly busy wondering what to bring with us to this strange, hot land where people swam and sunbathed and ate fresh salads in December. The pots, the pans, the folding chairs, the games of cards and Travel Scrabble, were all gone anyway, although it felt odd to be getting ready to go somewhere without them, and without the pervasive smell of our lost tent. But the flight itself was early in the morning, and the business of going to bed early knowing you wouldn't sleep was familiar. But I slept anyway, and dreamed that Dad was crouching in front of me in his canvas holiday shorts, and that he was turning over and over in his long fingers something which looked like his own ruined head. *You really imagine I do all those things, our Terry?* he was asking with a strange, sad and wounded look on his face. Then the alarm went off, and I dragged myself up from darkness to get dressed.

I paused outside my sister Helen's door as I hauled my suitcase towards the stairs. We didn't normally enter each other's rooms, but something about the way she was standing by her window made me go in. She had one of her favourite new multi-coloured biros in her hand, and it was covered with streaks of blue and black and red.

"I left it last night on the radiator," she explained. "And see what's happened—it's leaked. Just from the heat. It was probably the same with those ones I had in my bag last summer. I mean, you remember how hot it got inside our tent."

I looked down at her hands, which were stained and twisting. "I suppose some things do just happen by pure accident," I acknowledged. "But not all of them. I mean, my cassettes—

Helen barked a laugh. "Those ridiculous tinny recordings you make! Your taste is even worse than Dad's—you really thought any of us could bear listening to those terrible, stupid songs of yours all the time cooped in our tent?" Taking her ruined biro more firmly in her right hand, she mimed holding something with her left, and then stabbing it, twisting it through the heart and turning and turning with the biro's tip. I realised that she was miming unravelling one of my cassettes.

"You never said."

The HOB CARPET

I'M A MONSTER, an aberration. I've never really known what it means to be human. You could try to trace what I am back to the life which supposedly formed me. Try, and most probably fail. In that, at least, reader, and even though you may try to deny it, I'm much like you.

I was raised in a family of moderate influence and reasonable wealth. My father's line were successful merchants—men who had once plied the Great North Water, but calculated long before I was born that there was more money to be earned trading along its banks. My mother's side were paler-skinned than is common, and perhaps more savage and unpredictable in their moods as a result. That was her, certainly; a waxing, waning Moon to orbit my father's calmer earth. Her lineage was of the temple guards, and her father was proud of the spear-wound which a skirmish in his youth had inflicted. I remember him baring his shoulder as we sat in the lazy aftermath of a processional feast, inviting me to place my finger in the cratered dimple in his shoulder. It was like touching a second navel; another part of my birth. In those peaceful times, the wound had most probably been inflicted during training. The man drank to excess, and grew bitter performing duties which were entirely ceremonial. I still believe that there was intent in the riding accident which brought about his early death.

I imagine it was this very unlikeness which first attracted my parents to each other, and which eventually drove them apart. That probably also explains why I was the only fruit of their union although, as I of all people should understand, it is dangerous to peer too deeply into truths of love—if any such truths exist. But, for whatever reasons, I grew up largely alone, and somewhat pampered, and perhaps had more freedom to roam my own thoughts and obsessions than was good for me. That, at least, has often been said.

●

OUR HOMESTEAD AND its grounds covered many acres. It rose— still rises, for all I know—above the banks of the same river which had brought my family its wealth, beyond Eight Span Bridge and upstream from Dhiol. It was a pretty place, if anywhere so large can be called simply pretty, emerging from the cliffs like the prow of some unimaginable vessel on thick, golden-stone ramparts which had become bedecked with mosses and flowering ivies since they had lost their military function, and were a roost and feeding ground for many varieties of bat and bird. The battlements, viewing towers and high perimeter walkways along which I wandered were decorated with flags and ceramics, fruiting arbours and fishpools. The arrowslits which had once been constructed for purposes of defence were set with filigree metals and stained glass. There were spectacular views of the Great North Water and all its barges and sails passing far below, and the towers of Dhiol hazed the middle distance and the vast forests of Severland reared beyond to meet the peaks of the Roof of the World, which still shone white with snow at the height of summer even in those more beneficent times. Turning to the inward side of the battlements revealed all the gameboard neatness of a typical middle class homestead, with its ditches and canals filled with all the patterns of the sky and the trees which shaded them. At some point as the eye proceeded inwards along this dazzling patchwork of the produce fields towards the main house which rose at its centre, those fields became gardens, although the moment of transition was hard to discern.

My family homestead now seems like a kind of heaven. Of course, I then took it entirely for granted, but if there was one thing which I ignored more than any other, it was the presence of the hobs. Walk along the avenues that spanned the manicured distances towards our house, and their stooped backs would be as common as the swallows which then wheeled in the summer twilights. They were the first thing I saw each morning as their hands parted the vast curtains of my bedroom. Pinching out the candles and lanterns as the shadows deepened until they became shadow themselves, they were the last thing I glimpsed at night. But imagine for a moment, reader, that all of this is new to you, then think of a part of your existence which is always there, something which you would notice if the effort seemed worth such foolishness but which you never do. Imagine the smell of your own flesh, or the taste of your own tongue, or the blink of your eyelids, or the feel of your own toes. Then think of the hobs.

●

LIKE YOU, I was raised in their presence. I was never close enough to my mother to ask her whether one suckled me, but I imagine that that statement in itself provides an answer; most likely, I grew plump affixed to the nipple of some nameless surrogate hob. Certainly, the hands of numerous hobs would have dealt with all the messier tasks which the rearing of a baby requires. Then as tradition demands on the brightening of my thirtieth Moon, and in a ceremony which I cannot even remember, I was presented with the beginnings of what my parents no doubt fondly imagined would be the beginnings of a large retinue in the shape of two young hobs.

I imagine you expect me to record how I developed an especially strong and sentimental bond with these creatures, but I honestly did not. I called them Goo and Gog. Babyish sounds which, to an imperious three year old, seemed to fit to their mute and trusting natures. In retrospect, I can see how cleverly they learned to understand my moods—to sense whatever I wanted long before I had made the appropriate hobbish gesture; often, in fact, before I had even fully decided what I wanted myself. But they were typical of their sort. Blue-eyed. Pale. Slope-headed. Guiltily deferential. Stooped. Tonguelessly mute, of course, and entirely lacking in any sense of gender, although I was too young to understand the meaning of the shiny scarring I sometimes glimpsed within their slack mouths and beneath their crude kilts. I was like, as the saying goes, like any other child with a new hob. In the few occasions when I didn't take Goo and Gog entirely for granted, I passed the time by signing them to perform pointless and undignified tasks. *Get. Put down. Bring back. Take away. Roll over. Wave feet. Eat shit. Pant like dog. Bring back.* When I think now of my two silent and mostly ignored companions, I cannot summon the misty-eyed nostalgia which I know many humans seem to feel for their first attendants, be they called Pip and Pop, or Boo and Baa. All I feel is a sense of emptiness, and a vague guilt, which strengthens to something resembling disgust when I remember the many times when either Goo or Gog—have I mentioned that I never troubled to tell them apart?—was bound and flogged as punishment for my own misdemeanours until their backs streamed with blood.

●

HOBS ARE EVERYWHERE in our world, but those which do not belong to our retinues are generally shy as fauns. They slink back along corridors or hide in the vegetation as soon they sense our approach. So quickly and efficiently do they vanish that it barely ever occurs to us humans that they are there. If we were to consider this trick at all—which I then never did—it seems almost magical. But the fact is that hobs hear and scent us long before we are seen. To put it bluntly, we smell as strongly to them as they do to us, and they have trained themselves to notice our presence just as rigorously as we have trained ourselves not to notice theirs. Hob, or Human. Ignored, or noticed. That, it sometimes seems to me now, is where the true distinction ultimately lies.

Even if I was unconcerned by such questions, I was a busy and inquisitive child, and my parents saw to it that I was provided with academics and priests to keep me occupied and out of their sight. A restless learner, I much preferred to stride around the grounds and hallways of our homestead than to be confined to the single high room in which I was supposed to study. My tutors, being in the main sensible, intelligent men and women—and, for academics, quick on their legs—were generally happy to walk with me.

Once I had mastered the basics of calligraphy and numerology, I became a child of endlessly changing enthusiasms and fascinations. Why do the petals of a flower only come in certain numbers? Why is the sky is blue, and why are the Stars are only visible at night? And what, exactly, is the mechanism by which the seasons come and go? Later, I came to ask even more imponderable questions, such as how it is, if the Gods are endlessly wise, that people receive different answers when they pray to them. And why do hobs look so nearly like us, and yet remain so different...? Perhaps I asked that last question as well as I strode along the florid avenues and golden-paved battlements with some flustered tutor. And, as always, the garden hobs retreated as they sensed our approach, and the domestic ones who followed with their fans and awnings waited until they were summoned by a gesture, and our debate continued as we took our ease on cushions laid across their bent backs and were silently served with refreshments by their unnoticed hands.

In winter, Dhiol became a less favoured place. Although trade continued and the river never iced itself over in those days, it was customary for families of our class to travel downstream through the mountains and lowlands to escape the worst of the cold. Sometimes we crossed the Bounded Sea to sample the delights of the cities of Ulan Dor or Thris. Long before my age reached a century of Moons, I had stood on the Glass Pinnacle and counted—or tried to count— the sacred flamingos. I rode an elephant along the Parade of the Gods and blew the sacred horn to celebrate the flooding of the God River. I witnessed priests, crimsonly enrobed with the skins of their sacrifices, moving down the steps of the great temple of Thlug. But it was always the journey rather than the arrival which most appealed to me; the procession of landscapes as we headed down the Great North Water, then the glimpsed islands and broad horizons and all the changing moods of the sea. Being merchants, my family had the pick of the best vessels. No matter how rough the weather, they always felt like places of safety to me. Ships were places of exploration as well. After the endless avenues of our homestead, it was liberating to live aboard spaces so confined, yet within which—along gangways and inside storage spaces and beneath endless levels of deck—there was always some new surprise.

Afloat, the proximity of the hobs was unavoidable. Look up at the sails, and you would see dozens of them climbing like apes in a jungle. Look towards the waters, and there was the endless plash of the oars; a ship's heartbeat is the beating of its engineroom drum. On the decks themselves, ropes were always being fed through pulleys, as woods and irons and brasses were polished. I stepped around these activities much as you might step around a lamp-pillar in the street, but I also studied their processes in the abstract sort of way which seems to typify my intellect. I came to enjoy analysing the configuration of the sails, and quizzed the mariners about their differing functions. Occasionally, one of the figures which moved with such acrobatic abandon along the spars and ropes would mis-judge a leap and tumble into the sea. They never made a sound as they fell. The vessel pushed on without pause. I was reminded, I remember, of apples dropping from a tree. I even considered producing a poem on the subject, although, if I had ever written it, it would have been more about orchards than about hobs.

The masters, navigators and gangsmen were enormously proud of their vessels, and were as keen to show me their enginerooms, for all their stink and noise, as they were to demonstrate their understanding of the Stars. Down at the waterline, the sustained beat of the motive drum, and the movement which came with it—the slide and creak of wood, the tensing of hob muscle, the huge combined intakes and outtakes of hob breath—became a solid presence which thrummed within your chest. Striding down the gangways, the captain or master would explain in great detail the length of the oars and the mechanisms of the rowlocks and the number of *arms*—they never talked of whole hob bodies—which serviced them. The squeamish might find such scenes hellish, but as I was told about stroke speeds and sweeps of arc and shift times, I saw the hobs as these mariners saw them; as one combined mass of muscle. The stink and effluent, the shortage of good air, the bodies—*components*—which failed during shifts and had to be swiftly hoisted out, disposed of and replaced without loss of the rhythm, were all mere technicalities; the equivalents of how a drainage engineer might discuss rates of inundation and flow.

The first time I came consciously into closer contact with a hob beyond my thoughtless encounters with our domestic retinue was on one of these ocean journeys. It was a pale morning, and our vessel was surrounded by nothing but sea. I had risen early to discover everything misted, shining and slippery, and greyly dark. I was still in the phase of inwardly composing poems which I never actually wrote, and I recollect as I stood at the rail and looked out into the fading nothingness that I was thinking how the ship itself, in its stealth and greyness, seemed itself to be made of little more than mist. Doubtless, the engineroom drum was still beating and the oars were thrashing as they drove us on—the entire vessel would have thrummed and creaked as all such vessels do—but we had been at our journey for a few days, and all I felt was silence, all I breathed was stillness and fog.

The next thing I remember is a spinning whooshing, and being knocked sideways across the deck. When I recovered my senses, I discovered the weight of some other living thing lying on top of me, and a face briefly peering down into my own. What I saw, before it clambered off and loped into the mist, was nothing but the generalised features of a typical hob—beetle browed, chinless, broad-nosed, pale-skinned and set with a wild spew of reddish hair. Several mariners were already running over to me as I got up. Even as I attempted to explain what

had happened, it seemed impossible that I could have been touched—
assaulted—by such a beast. Then one of the men grinned and pointed
to the spew of rope and metal which had gouged itself across the
deck. A pulley must have broken somewhere high up in the masts and
come swinging towards me out of the mist. If it hadn't been for the
intervention of that hob, I would have been killed.

●

ANOTHER WINTER FADED, and my family returned with the birds
towards the mountains and forests of the cooler north, to find our gardens emerging from their winter swaddlings, and the house perfectly
clean, and our beds warmed and aired, and fresh fruits and sweetmeats
laid in bowls on the tables, and fires crackling in every hearth. The
gardens, in particular, were a delight in this coming season of growth.
In response to my endless questions about the purposes of insects and
the mechanisms of fruiting and growth, my parents placed me in the
company or Karik, the most senior garden gangmaster.

Everything that's ever said about hob gangmasters is true. Karik
was tall and unstooped. His face was broadly handsome. His skin
was aristocratically dark. All in all, he was about as far from the
near-hobbish caricature of his type as you could possibly get. But in
every other way he fitted the bill. As he promenaded the fields and
gardens, he would pause in his explanations of when the soil should
be turned, or a tree pruned, and call over some creature which I,
in my absorption, had not even noticed, and strike them hard and
efficiently with the cane he always carried. No explanation was ever
given. Glancing back as he and I strode on, I noticed how other nearby
hobs ceased their tasks and scurried over to see to the needs of their—
what *was* the term, comrade, fellow, friend, colleague? Perhaps it's a
sign of the beginnings of my obsession that I was starting to wonder
about such things. Karik was as skilled with his cane as he was with
the other aspects of his craft, and I'm sure that some of the hobs had
their limbs broken, although others remained capable of getting up

and continuing working. I suspect a few were actually killed. Karik knew what he was doing, and I suppose the hobs understood as well.

As well as a cane, Karik carried several gardening implements slung around his hips on a belt. An eccentricity of his was that he would sometimes stoop down towards the earth and actually snip a shoot, or even dig out a weed, with his own bare hands. In that busy season for new planting, he would sometimes take the pointed wooden object he called his dibber, and work it into the soil, and physically plant a tuber or seed. I watched this activity with amazement. It seemed as unlikely a thing as a human cook peeling a vegetable, a sweep personally climbing up a chimney, or dressmaker physically sewing the fabric of a dress. But when Karik encouraged me to try, I discovered that I actually liked the grainy feel of the earth and the dark scent it left upon my hands. I like it still.

As a student of horticulture, I also became a student of the work of the hobs. I felt by now that I knew our entire homestead. But, wandering with Karik and then on my own, I discovered new landscapes hilled with piles of mulching vegetation, and low arches which I'd long passed without noticing within the house itself, which led down narrow stairways into smoky caverns. The hob were endlessly busy. They were always carrying things away, or bearing them in, or wading ditches, or carrying laundry, or scooping out sludge. Pushing my way around unlikely corners, I would emerge into laundries and potting sheds. There were cavernous kitchens and huge glasshouses and busy workshops and subterranean acreages of dusty furniture waiting for their fashion's return.

Once when I was exploring the gardens, I re-found a turn along which Karik had shown me several Moons earlier. The potting sheds, I reckoned with my newly acquired knowledge, would be already busy with the planting for the following spring, but, contrary to my expectations, they seemed to be deserted. I hunched along the dark passages, curious as ever, and enjoying the feel and the taste—it was too intense to be called merely a smell—of the rich, loamy earth. Here and there were set rooflights, emblazoning the blackness with gilded veins of Sun. The roots and shoots exposed by my exploring fingers could have been formed of the finest coral. When I sensed something ahead of me, I moved softly on. I had learned that, if I kept downwind of them and moved quietly enough, I could sometimes catch working hobs unawares.

Ribboned in a dazzling fall of light, Karik and a hob were engaged in some strange mutual contortion. The scene was oddly beautiful. They were both making sounds and their voices, hob grunt and human cry, intermingled in a way which could have been a sacred chant. Their gleaming bodies rose and fell. The hob, who was bending, shook her mane of hair in a spray of gold. Karik was bucking and baring his teeth. He was rivered with sweat. And his penis, which was at least as long as his dibber, thrust and emerged from the hob's nether regions, and she thrust and bucked back. Then, with a rising bellow which began in the depths of Karik's lungs and which the higher scream of the hob's voice almost extinguished at its peak, the business which they were engaged in reached some kind of conclusion.

The two creatures, human and hob, fell back from each other towards the soft earth. Karik muttered something, and the hob replied in a growl as she climbed from her knees. Her gaze shifted along the tunnel to where I was standing as she swiped the dirt from her breasts, and she stepped back into the blackness, and was instantly gone. Karik turned to look in the same direction, his still erect penis trailing a glistening blob. When he saw me hunched there in the shadows, he tossed back his head and laughed like a God.

●

HOBS ARE BORN male or female. They do not lay eggs or have beaks or scales. They do not dwell in eyries or the depths of the ocean. Neither do they produce flowers or send out roots. They may have oddly pale skins and those masses of russet hair, and be broader and shorter than we humans are, but they are the only species I know of which chooses to walk on two legs just as we do. Their faces may be somewhat flatter than ours, but their eyes and mouths and ears and noses are arranged much like our own. In fact, their bodies are like ours in almost every significant detail. And they possess penises and vaginas—unless, that is, they have been physically removed.

As outdoor hobs routinely work naked, even a child far younger and less curious than I should long have been acquainted with these facts. Even you, patient reader, will be aware of the similarities of fleshy geometries which humans and hobs share. We are alike in ways that horses and dogs and sheep and cattle and all the other creatures which serve us are not. That, I believe now, is why we keep ourselves so far apart.

What I saw happening between Karik and that hob left me puzzled, and it was a quieter and less exploratory child who inhabited our homestead for the rest of that summer. One who, much to the relief of his parents and tutors, was happy to sit up in his room in the high tower and seek knowledge within ancient scrolls.

After its uncertain start, the weather that year turned hotter than anyone could remember this far north. People walked beneath fans and awnings when they walked at all, and received their guests seated in cool, lily-adorned baths. Carpets were taken up. Beds were placed on balconies. Gangs of hobs were diverted from their usual tasks to fan air along complex systems of vents. The gardens beyond my windows shimmered and blazed. Then, just a few days before my family were planning to flee this furnace for the cooler Winds of the coast, the skies above Dhiol finally darkened. I looked up from my work to silently urge the Gods to break their thunder overhead. And, like the opening of a sluicegate, they did. For all my newfound seriousness, I couldn't help but rush down the stairways and out into the lightning-split torrent like the excited child I still almost was. I spread my arms and tilted back my head. Jumping from the lip of an overflowing fishpond, I felt my right leg slip out, and twist and buckle with a grating snap.

●

IAN R. MACLEOD

IT WAS A bad break. I was delirious for several days with medicines and pain. When I finally awoke, I found myself immobile in a vast, strange bed. Looking up at the ornate drapes, painted wooden arches and door-sized cushions of which the boat-like structure was composed, I felt an odd flash of recognition. An echo of my fever came back over me, and I cried out. I feared for a moment that I had actually died, and was lying in my own tomb. Or, worse still, that I had been interred whilst still living. Pale and quick as a ghost, a hob face came and went amid the turbulent decorations. Intense pain shot through me. I cried out again, and struggled to fight my way out of this gilded tomb.

Footsteps came, followed by a flutter of hunting scenes and forests amid the fabrics. I cringed, expecting some ebony guardian of the Afterworld to emerge. But it was only my mother. I say *only*, but she was surrounded as always by a large retinue of personal hobs dressed in silks which complemented and blended with her own attire. They were bearing the golden poles of the great crimson canopy which evolved into a hat as it neared her head, and wafting the dyed and silvered ostrich feathers and incense burners which fanned her air, and laying down the rose petals upon which she habitually walked, and sweeping them up in her wake, and carrying her enormous silk train like some great living fishtail, and plucking the small instruments from which emerged the aura of sound which she always bore with her. Smiling down at me, actually taking my bare hand in her own gloved one for a few moments, she asked if I was feeling better. Despite the obvious stupidity of my accident, she was in a forgiving mood. She told me how she had briefly feared for the worst, and had had the family tombs re-surveyed and this ancestral bed restored in case the journey of my fever should take me further than this earth. I nodded and smiled as pain and surprise receded. Looking up at the tumbling, fruited carvings, I realised why I had dimly recognised this structure; I had come across it in on my wanderings through the vast storerooms which formed part of the hidden landscape of this house.

"The arrangements for our journey south," she told me, "are too far advanced to be postponed. Contracts have been set. Visits have been

164

promised. Sacrifices have been made. Feasts and entertainments have been agreed. Money, above all, has been paid. Your father and I will be travelling downriver as usual, but we have discussed the matter and decided that it would be impossible for you to come with us in your current state. You will remain here through the winter in our homestead, and you body will heal. Everything has been arranged."

A glorious vision, a jewel set within the perfumed glitter of her chiming, wafting attendants, she turned from me and the curtains fell back.

●

MY PARENTS SAW to it that I was provided with tutors to teach me things I was no longer interested in learning, and priests to remind me of the doings of Gods in whom I was certain that I no longer believed. Visits were also arranged from acquaintances and relatives, and reports required of them and me. I was given a pet parrot to keep me entertained—which soon flew out of a window to reappear a few days later as a sprawl of rainbow feathers in the frost. But, more than ever, there was no human company I was prepared to tolerate beyond my own.

It did occasionally strike me that the scene which my progress made through the house and grounds was rather extraordinary, even if it is something which you, reader, will regularly see passing beneath your window if you live in a city. But, with little else to occupy my thoughts, I was intrigued by the complexity and variety of the process by which the hob retinues bore my newly disabled self along. As our house was as rich in mirrors as our garden was in ponds, I was even able to study the strange manner of my progress as if I was watching someone else. There was the *simple half-crouch*, wherein two or three hobs would position themselves almost as if they were sitting as we humans do. I would recline on the silks and cushions which they had arranged upon their bodies, whilst four or six other hobs beneath that top layer would contort their backs in a variety of postures to provide the necessary motive power and support. For stairs and slopes, there was the position which I called the *rolling back*, during which a dozen or so hobs, more if necessary, would lay themselves face-upwards across the ascent, and push the rolling knot of upper hobs which still actually supported me up or down. Then there was *hands over arms* for the steeper ascents as the hobs formed something like a stairway of limbs, and, most strange of all, what I thought of as *the hob carpet* in which, once I had signed that I was weary of being seated and wanted to stretch my still-functioning limbs, my tumbling, ever-changing retinue would briefly contrive to convey me upright as though I was walking, yet still supporting my splinted leg as if it was not broken at all.

Here I was, riding about every day on my writhing throne of hob flesh, and also submitting to the sort of attentions which are otherwise usually reserved for infants, the elderly, the lazy, or the infirm. There is, it has to be admitted, a smoothly addictive quality to reaching towards something which lies beyond the span of your arms, only to find a moment later that you are actually holding it. It does not take much further effort, I can well imagine, to enjoy having your food chewed and every other conceivable outward process of your body performed on your behalf.

My bathroom lay along a corridor adjoining my suite of rooms. Each morning, I was lifted from my bed by the gentle touch of dozens of hands. Still supine and still half-asleep, I had leisure to see aspects of my surroundings which I had never previously noticed. Gazing up, I saw now how the long, high ceiling was marvellously arched, and spangled with fragments of polished stone. The bathroom itself was a larger room, its great heights dripping with candelabra which, in the dark of those winter mornings, glowed with thousands of candles freshly lit by an invisible army of hobs. This light played on tiles and marbles and filigree embrasures; it shone across the dreams of some long-dead architect rendered material by the labours of hobs even longer gone. It's a scene, reader, which I imagine you can probably picture from your own abode. In fact, you may well scoff at the plainness of my description, for if there is one thing we humans are good at creating, it's structures which involve the near-endless labour of hands other than our own. My bath itself was a simple affair, consisting of nothing more than a deep, steaming lake brimmed with white marble. The same hands and arms which had borne me from me bed now subtly divested me of my nightclothes and laid me afloat amid islands of rosepetals and scented candles. They somehow even managed to support and keep dry my splinted left leg.

All in all, it was an untroublesome way to start the day. Often enough as I drifted back towards easy sleep and the continuation of my dreams, it was barely a start at all. Inevitably, being male and of the age I was, these half-sleeps had a certain effect upon my anatomy. When I fully awoke, I would find that my member was rigid. That solitary winter, cradled by hands and steam, I discovered the means of dealing with this state.

I felt no particular shame as the signs of my morning's activities were washed away by the subtle hands which supported me. But I did feel an odd sense of curiosity. Sexual activity, even of this simplest sort, is peculiar in that way; I found myself wondering if this one thing could be done, why not others. Not, I have to say, that I was particularly experimental, but I soon discovered that I enjoyed the way the hands which supported me touched other aspects of my body as I reached the height of my satisfaction. Soon, I was commanding the hands to do this or that. In truth, once a small moment of initial resistance had passed, they required little encouragement.

The snows came rolling down from the mountains on dense banks of cloud which seemed far too dark to be capable of containing anything so miraculously white. Slowly, my leg healed. My cast was removed at the physician's directions and replaced by a light splint. I was encouraged to bathe. And, in each of those many baths, the contortions which I demanded of my retinue of hob flesh became more elaborate. Soon, the use of my own hand to pleasure myself became redundant, and I made use of a twisting, ever-changing array of hob vaginas, hob breasts, hob mouths and hob anuses. Then the water itself became an annoyance. By now, I was capable of walking, but I often chose instead to transport myself naked amid a writhing orgy.

I tumbled though the echoing corridors and state rooms of my homestead amid a many-limbed, backed and buttocked fist of mingled hob and human flesh.

●

THE SNOWS ABATED, the canals brimmed and the Great North Water roared with meltwater beneath the battlements. I was able to walk unaided and without a stick by the time my family retinue returned, but, looking down at the flotilla of craft as it moved and flashed upstream in the bright spring Sun, I saw the flutter of black flags and heard the trumpets of mourning.

My mother greeted me a day or so later in the chapel she had established within her quarters at the house. A dark grotto had been created within one of the great halls, set about with huge stones and ferns and moss to signify the entrance to the underworld. A waterfall hissed, and many diamonds were scattered across the flower-bedecked turf which had been laid across the usual tiles, in echo of tears she was supposed to have shed.

"Well," she said, looking me up and down as I entered this odd place to greet her. Dappled light played. She looked magnificent in black. "I am pleased to note that at least some of our prayers and sacrifices have been answered in this time of great loss." She gave a small sigh. Her retinue of hobs wailed and beat their bloodied torsos with flails. "Although I believe that the Gods were right to call your father when they did. In fact, I almost wish they'd done so sooner. He'd become weak and lazy long before the fever which struck him. It's up to you now, my darling, to be the man he once was."

●

MY FATHER'S BODY processed upriver in the great boat of his funerary bed through Dhiol and beyond the forests of Severland toward our family tombs in the Roof of the World once the embalmers had finished their work. We disembarked onto a carved obsidian platform which traversed the polished face of a great glacier on a complex system of ropes. The great mountains were all around us now, and I longed for quiet to contemplate the frailty of life and the vastness of eternity—but I still couldn't help but notice odd and irrelevant things. How, for example, the teams of hobs who worked all these pulleys wore scarcely any more clothing in this frozen land than their compatriots did in the lowlands whilst we humans hid ourselves in furs.

Our passage into the final chamber which my father had spent many years constructing was lit by clever arrangements of ice and mirror. Carved here were scenes from his life reproduced with a scale and a grandeur which already placed him amid the Gods. My mother and I stepped back from in his gold sarcophagus. The priests were retreating, and the final doors were already closing off the light. We were not just leaving my father behind, but enough supplies to ensure that he did not go lacking in the afterlife. In fact, a worrying amount of our family possessions lay strewn around us. Great trees under whose shade I had once studied had been uprooted and placed within huge pots. There were whole libraries of scrolls, and paintings and statues and chairs and rugs, not to mention a veritable farmyard of animals, whose soundings and smellings the priests did their best to combat with their clamour and incense. Inevitably, amid all the wealth which my father would bring to the underworld, there were also dozens of hobs. They, though, sat in a quiet huddle. The panic, I supposed, would come later as they began to realise that the labours of others of their kind had not only sealed off all light from this tomb, but also air.

"Well," my mother sighed as we stood outside again once all the doors had slammed shut and the splendid white of the mountains gleamed around us, "that's half a fortune gone."

●

ALTHOUGH I WORKED hard as a merchant, I realise now that my heart was always elsewhere, although exactly *where* still remains in doubt. I certainly enjoyed the sights and the journeyings. I liked meeting people from other lands, and finding out about how they lived their lives. But the stuff of actually doing business with them, of starting at one price and working around to another after many hours or days of mock outrage and subterfuge, left me bored. These were also seasons of unexpected rains, bad harvests and broken bridges, when the rich became cautious, and merely well off decided they weren't so well off at all.

It came as no surprise when my mother broached the subject of marriage. In every way, it was sensible for us to make alliance with another family of similar means to our own. By any standards, though, Kinbel was a great catch. A daughter of the priesthood, she was so exquisitely educated as to make my own knowledge seem half-made. Her eyes were amber. Her skin was like polished jet. She moved with the grace of a statue come to life. Above all, though, she bought fresh money and influence. In retrospect, I realise that, beneath all her layers of accomplishment, Kinbel was something of an innocent, but, in the few words and glances that she and I were allowed to exchange before the ceremonies of our wedding began, I found it hard to see beyond her outer perfection.

Being a union in which the priests were more than ever involved, the gutters which had been laid for that special purpose in the gardens of our homestead ran red with blood for days. It's a rarely observed truth that, with the possible exception of whores, priests are alone amongst us humans in doing anything resembling real physical work. There's certainly no doubt that the removal of an entire hob skin in one untorn piece, leaving only the hands and feet remaining on the shuddering carcass like shoes and gloves, is a feat of manual skill so great that one might almost call it hobbish. Granted, though, that the labour of many other hobs was then required to smooth out and stitch this gathering mass, whilst still warm and dripping, into one vast sheet, which was then folded over and tented in such a way as to create a roof and floor—indeed a carpet—of hob flesh.

The Hob Carpet

The drumming and the ululations reached new heights as Kinbel and I finally descended the offal-strewn steps from our separate thrones so that we might complete our tryst inside the weird structure which had been created for us below. A flap, which seemed to be made entirely of eyelessly peering hob faces, was pulled back. Kinbel and I then found ourselves standing together—but, inevitably, not alone—inside a rank cave.

I remember thinking, as Kinbel was finally divested of all her raiments, that, with her upturned breasts and sculpted thighs, she really was too beautiful to be real. I even remember staring at her perfect feet in the bloodied, pinkish light, and admiring the pearly sheen of her toenails. I was naked by now myself, but I had, as so often happens, become over-absorbed in odd abstractions. When I finally tried to meet her gaze, I saw that she was looking down towards my flaccid penis. I imagine that she had been told that such small obstacles were to be expected on a day of such magnitude, and a murmur of anticipation and delight went up amid the watching priests as she stepped forward, twined her arms around me, and pressed her mouth against my own.

What was suddenly the most important part of my body still remained ignorantly unresponsive. Sex had ceased to interest me in the years since my early solitary experiments, and I found it still left me disinterested now. But Kinbel was persistent. She drew me back and down until more and more of my body was in contact with the carpet of flayed flesh, which was inlaid as if by jewels with bits of hob ear, hob nipple and hob nose. Now, as Kinbel reached out to me and the priests cried out and clattered their bells, my member finally responded, and the necessary work was soon done.

●

IT WAS THUS in a spirit of genuine optimism that I entered married life. Kinbel was, I kept telling myself, all and more than I could have hoped for. We took informal solitary walks with no more than a few dozen hobs as our retinue. We even ate in the same room. People commented on how she and I made a fine couple in the statues which were being carved as a prelude to the commencement of work on our tombs. It was hard not to enjoy her presence; how she moved, the dark, sweet sound of her voice. Although my mother was avoiding these colder climes and spending more and more of her time in the warmer south, Kinbel even charmed her.

If Kinbel and I had differences, they manifested themselves at first in the way that she would protest about statements I made against things being merely the work of the Gods. I could scarcely credit that someone so obviously intelligent could imagine that the Sun had to be persuaded to rise through a thousand daily sacrifices on the steps of the great temple at Ulan Dor, or that there was meaning to be drawn from a random spill of intestines, or the shapes of the clouds.

But in the background lay a different problem. One which struck me at first as vanishingly small. As small, in fact, as my penis which, since its efforts during our marriage ceremony, had shrunk back into flaccid reticence and stubbornly refused to perform. Our marriage bed was a vast thing, cushioned and canopied on a scale more than large enough to allow both of us to lose each other and a hundred others in untroubled sleep, but Kinbel returned to me night after night across its soft landscapes with small entreaties, then more and more extravagant seductions, all of which, although I was able to appreciate their invention and aesthetic merit, left a crucial part of me cold.

"Why is it..." she asked finally, kneeing before me in the lamplit smog of incense and chimes which she had created on that particular night, her ebony body emblazoned with curlicues of gold, "...why is it that you could do this thing so easily on the evening of our marriage, and yet never since? Would it help, for example, if I summoned your mother to watch again?"

"My mother would scarcely thank you for such an invitation, Kinbel," I muttered, still feigning sleep underneath a landslide of pillows.

"Then perhaps the prayers of the priests of my father's sphere do not reach us as easily here as they might. We could arrange for some acolytes to place themselves in the higher reaches of this bed."

That was too much. I sat up. "Does it matter so very much? Is this a question of offspring, or pure inheritance—"

"Inheritance!" She barked a laugh so ferocious that I drew back. "Is *that* what you think this is about? Can't a man and a woman do that for which the Gods made them in their own marriage bed out of nothing more than sheer affection and joy?"

Affection. Joy. Even spoken in her delicious voice, the human words sounded odd. "If it's the mere act you want, Kinbel," I suggested, "couldn't you visit one of the houses which I believe have discreet doorways in the west of Dhiol?"

Now she was silent. Her eyes were shining. For the first time in my life, it struck me that human females are perhaps more different from the male than the small variations of our anatomy imply.

"Wouldn't that deal with the problem, and perhaps even furnish the heir which you appear to desire?" I continued. "Believe me, Kinbel, no one would rejoice more than I if—"

"You don't understand. All I want to know from you is, is...What is that I have to do to persuade you to make love?" A tear joined with the gilded swirls on Kinbel's left breast. "I've tried dressing and undressing," she muttered. "I've tried dancing and not dancing. Do you want me here? Or in this place instead? Even that, I really would not mind. Nor this. Whatever you want of me I would enjoy. Nothing would bother me as much as...this nothing at all. Or would you like me to summon some other priestesses to join in our couplings as well? Or priests? Perhaps a pack of the sacred dogs? You even mentioned, I recall, a parrot which you were briefly fond of. I'm not sure how such congress might be arranged, and I've certainly put on and taken off enough feathers, but if you really think—"

"Enough! Enough!" By now I was covering my ears. I was shuddering like a flayed hob.

Instead of turning away from me and shifting across to her own encampment in this land of cushion and silks, Kinbel drew closer. And she did a strange thing. She placed her naked hand across my own. "There must be something of this world that you desire beyond mere ideas. There *must* be something, and I'd like to help find it, no matter what it is. We could pray. We could call for sacrifices. We could sport ourselves naked in the purest snow. For all I care—and happily I would do this—we could frolic with the rats in the sewers. After all, there was that one time at the ceremonies of our betrothal, when seemingly the task was most difficult. And yet you managed." She gave a softer laugh. "I'm starting to talk like you, as if this were a terrible task, some difficult matter of enormous work…"

Her voice was trailing off now, and the pressure of her hand was loosening against my own. I knew that if I did not speak now, I never would. "There *is* something," I croaked. "Or there was. Once…"

Speaking in a low voice, as the candles guttered and the chimes stilled and the last of the smoke of the incense settled like mist into the hollows of mattress and coverlet, I told Kinbel about my winter alone, and my shameful, as it seemed to me now, congress with that retinue of hobs. And all the time I spoke, the pressure of Kinbel's hand against my own remained unchanged. Only when I had finished, and I feared that my own eyes were shining as much as hers, did she lean forward. I felt the strange press of her lips against my face.

"Have you not heard," her voice murmured into my ear, "that no human congress is considered worthy of the name without the assistance of a few hobs in fashionable circles in Yoha and Halu? In Jasih Noish, apparently, many use them as beds. And everyone knows the stories of gangmasters, and no one ever thinks less of them for it, or even cares. It's not, I confess, a variety of love for which…" I heard a click in her throat. "Something which I previously felt any strong desire. But now that you have told me I would be happy and proud to summon as many hobs as you desire. Indeed, they could be trained in such arts. I would submit—"

Something broke within me. Flapping angrily at pillows and fabrics, I pulled away from Kinbel's hold. "I don't want you to submit to *anything*! I don't want you to drag some army of hobs into this dreary cage of silks. I don't *love* hobs. I don't even desire them—or at least not now. It was just some childhood fancy which lingered for too long in some lost part of my brain. A taste which I briefly acquired and then discarded. All I care about now is knowledge. All I want to find are ways of understanding the world. Why can't *you* understand that Kinbel—and then, by all those ridiculous Gods which you seem to hold so dear, just leave me alone!"

●

THE NEXT MORNING, and after a night undisturbed by further entreaties, I woke up to find that I had slept alone. Kinbel had left word at my breakfast table that she would reside for the time being in her father's temple-house in Dhiol. I felt a twinge of guilty delight as I read the papyrus. Without Kinbel, and with my father dead, and my mother gone to the warmer south, and but for the presence of a few gangmasters, I finally had my homestead entirely to myself. Walking the battlements in the breezy Sunshine, I decided that seeing to the maintenance of this place would be the task to which I would apply myself from now on.

It's not that I ceased being a merchant, but there was something about the needs of my homestead which inspired me in a way which the mere business of buying and selling had never done on its own. I found bargaining was far more to my liking if, instead of taking money and promises of goods, I asked for labour and skills, or even plain advice. Other businessmen were surprisingly happy to lend me their roofing or drainage hobs once they had overcome their incredulity that this was something I was genuinely prepared to accept. It didn't take long for me to enhance my already growing reputation for eccentricity as I drew deals based on recovered slates and sacks of mortar. Let people stare, I thought. Let them say that I have lost all sense. Let them call me a fool and—yes, even then—a lover of hobs.

I believe that particular phrase came from several sources. It probably began with my endless questioning of gangmasters. Word may also have seeped out from my bedtime confession to Kinbel. Not, I remain certain, that Kinbel herself would have deliberately spread such a slur, but she was probably innocent enough to imagine that the confessional with a priest was sacrosanct, even if that priest happened to be her father. In any case, *hob lover* is a common enough term of abuse in some lands. I didn't care—or at least not so very much.

My gangmasters were required to have a daily meeting. There, we discussed not just the quickest and easiest way of getting their individual duties performed, but how we all might benefit from the smooth running of the homestead. When the owners of other homesteads were complaining about the poor summers and the vicious winters, I was doing better than ever. I had no time now for the fripperies of planting and ornamentation which my mother had encouraged. Even within the house itself, I was more than happy to see some of the staterooms being used for storage or as hob workshops rather than being left waiting for the grand dances and ceremonies which I had no desire to hold. I think I convinced a few doubters, although those who came to visit generally returned to Dhiol with stories of the increasing roughness of my dwelling, and the Godless way in which I went about my work. That, and my apparent kindness to all creatures of my homestead, which of course included hobs. It seemed self-evident to me that persuasion and reward worked better than punishment, and that it was better to keep and cherish something rather than to let it die of neglect or sacrifice. But stories began to circulate as a result, although most of them false. Threats were made. The priests of Dhiol grew restless. But I was content. Now that I had my homestead in a state of productivity and order which exceeded all of my neighbours, I was free to investigate all the many things which continued to puzzle me about this world.

I discovered that domestic pigs and the wild boars of the forest can be mated, and that they produce an offspring which had good, strongly-flavoured meat, and can be left to forage out of doors. I learned that milk, if turned over in a machine of my own design, separates into different, and entirely useful, parts. I also found out that most of my hob gangmasters, my old educator Karik included, had a poor knowledge of the more detailed aspects of hob signing, and used the stick or the whip too easily when they failed to get things properly done.

The Hob Carpet

I set out to learn more about communicating directly with the hobs. There was a quietness and a sense of withdrawing as, crouched inside the low walls of their crude and stinking dwellings, and often without even the company of a gangmaster, I watched and prodded and questioned and cajoled. Hobs are generally uncomfortable in human presence, and they grew all the more so when they realised I had grown capable of telling individuals apart merely from their facial features, and then that I had worked out the grunts and gestures of some of their names. Disputes arose. I believe deaths occurred. The world of hobs is, in many ways, as savage as our own. They perform upon themselves the common mutilations which we require, choose nominations for sacrifice, and are fierce in securing what we humans would consider to be laughably small distinctions in status, although I was unable to find any proof of the common slur that hob mothers routinely eat their own young.

But I was pleased by what I learned. Knowing hobbish to the extent which now made my gangmasters redundant, I came to understand hobs' tribal rivalries and separations, and set about issuing my own instructions to the lead hob of each freshly-organised gang. I was certain that the drains were being cut more efficiently, and fields better hoed, as result. I developed ever greater plans. Even as the forests of Severland died and produce shrank in the markets of Dhiol, I was convinced that every homestead in this northerly land could remain fertile and productive if only it were better run.

I was stripped to the waist in a ditch with some hobs one morning and demonstrating how they should install some new ceramic pipework when I looked up and saw a figure outlined against the grey sky above. So unused was I to any other kind of company that I'd grunted and signed in hobbish before I realised that the figure was human, and female, and then that it was my wife.

●

KINBEL SMILED AWAY my apologies as I climbed out. After all, she was plainly dressed, and had come alone without warning, or retinue.

"I've been hearing so many tales. I thought it was time that I found out." She looked around her. The fields which we had once thought might belong to both of us shone with new growth. "And I can see that you're doing well."

"I think I am." Signalling for a towel from the gang of hobs, I wiped myself down. "I believe that this place will one day be seen as a way forward."

Kinbel chuckled. The sound had lost none of its beauty. Neither had she, plainly dressed, unadorned and alone though she was. "All I hear in Dhiol is that you live with the hobs, and that you treat the Gods as if they do not exist."

I shrugged. We were standing on a muddy pathway. The whole aspect of the landscape which surrounded us had lost the posturing grandeur which it had once possessed, but it seemed to me to be yet more beautiful in its simplicity and efficiency. All the more so now that Kinbel was here.

"This place." She turned around, and I saw the sky and the fields mirrored in her eyes. "It's nothing like I imagined. Yet I think that you are wrong to tell yourself this not the work of the Gods. The Gods work through people as well, you know. I imagine that they even work through simple hobs. But tell me, that structure over there...?"

I was delighted by her interest. No longer the innocent, she had grown and changed. She was particularly amused when I described how merchants squabbled over a single crumb of gold, then yielded at the suggestion that they gave me a drainage screw which, with a few repairs, was worth far more.

"You must see us as wasteful," she said as I showed her the beasts of the stable, and the stinking lake of effluent which would feed next year's fields.

"Us?"

"I mean people. Humans."

A silence fell between us as we walked on.

"Your mother sends her regards," she told me as she stood at the homestead gates. It was starting to rain. "She wants you to be reassured that many sacrifices have been made in the most holy of sites on your behalf."

"You don't still think that your Gods are so stupid and angry as to be appeased by hob blood, do you, Kinbel?"

Kinbel looked at me in that dauntingly composed way she had. "What you believe does not alter the punishment the Gods are inflicting upon our world."

There was no doubt, by now, that our summers were shortening and our winters were growing more harsh. The white blaze of the Roof of the World had spread, and the growth of its glaciers threatened to destroy many family tombs. Even in the sacred homelands in the south to which my mother had retreated, the nights were apparently showing teeth of frost, and the inundations of the God River threatened the temples of Ulan Dhor. The processes of my agricultural research were long-winded and often frustrating, but I was certain that my discoveries would soon be crucial. I tried to tell her more, but she held up a hand to make me stop.

"What you've done here, and what you are doing is—well, it's everything you say. But there are things you don't understand. People in Dhiol are saying bad things about you—"

"They've been doing so for years." I gave a dismissive wave even as I felt a flush come into my cheeks.

"That may be so, but it has gone far above mere personal abuse. You probably know better than anyone that times are hard. But when times are hard, people look around for something to blame. Or, better still, someone."

"No-one can be so stupid as to hold me responsible for the weather!"

I still expected her to laugh and shake her head, but she looked at me gravely, and nodded. "Exactly so. It is even spoken of amongst us priests."

"Can't you do anything about it?"

"Can't *you?*"

"What?"

"If you acknowledged the Gods a little, and talked less to you hobs, that might be a start. But you must do so quickly. Otherwise, I fear that it will be too late."

"And so?"

"Then, if you do not listen, all that you have done and stand for will go to waste."

I blustered in reply, shouting that she was being ridiculous, that it was the fault of her kind—her and all the others—but already she was turning, walking off through the rain.

●

THEY CAME ON a winter's night. By then, I had long been expecting them. I had even considered reinstating my homestead into the fortress it had once been, but its walls were enfeebled despite the fine cliff face it presented to the river, and the waste of such an enterprise appalled me even more than the prospect of what was to come.

It was an impressive sight which I looked down on from the battlements along which I had once debated the number of petals in a flower and the shining of the Stars. This was certainly no random mob. It was a river of light, and of chanting, and of bells. Some of the priests rode on elephants. Others were transported by oxen on glinting wagons of sapphire and gold. The landowners came with their gangmasters, and the merchants with their suppliers and storeholders, and all around them dripped flaming sconces, and everywhere there was a humming and a clashing of gongs. The crowd was huge, and it was organised in a way which was reminiscent of the great southern ceremonies which are said to sustain the workings of the Sun, the God River and the Moon. And, like any other human crowd, it consisted mostly of hobs. They steered and goaded the elephants and oxen, and scooped up the ordure left behind. They carried huge glowing braziers, which glowed like giant coals, to keep the procession warm. They bore the tall poles and vast banners which would provide shade or shelter should there be rain or snow or Sun. They carried many of the lazier and fatter members of the general population in sedan chairs, or rolled and writhed to support their bodies in muscled engines of livery and tattoo. And it seemed to me, as the chants and the voices rose up to me, that even the accusations of my being a godless renegade, a devil-worshiper, a non-human, a lover of hobs, came mostly in the distinctive rhythm and grunt of the voices of hobs themselves.

I looked at the small gang of hobs which stood behind me in the flickering light which was thrown up through the chill darkness. They stood at the same distance from me which they always stood, as if still awaiting orders. They still behaved, the thought struck me, like any other retinue, even my mother's, although they were somewhat more roughly clothed. But I could tell them apart well enough to understand that they felt emotions almost as a human might, and that they were far more afraid than I was. I had already relinquished the rest of my establishment of hobs, either through selling them in markets distant from my tainted reputation in Dhiol, or by simply releasing them, and signing them to ford the river and head north, where I believed they stood a better chance of surviving than us humans did in this increasingly hostile world.

What do you want of us now? The lead hob, who, in a fit of nostalgia, I had chosen to call Gog Two, signed to me, and I looked back at him, and for the first time in my recollection, he met my gaze without turning away. He was a sturdy creature, beetle-browed and heavy-set, with particularly large and agile hands. How he disciplined his colleagues was in many ways harsher than any gangmaster, but it was always directed towards getting the job done. I thought of him as fair-minded, and I liked to imagine he thought of me in a similar way.

Nothing. I made the simple signal of reply which any human might make when they have no immediate need of their hobs. But instead of simply remaining where they were and waiting for their next command, he and the rest turned from me and began to walk away, moving with that characteristic gait which hobs have. Then, without any obvious exchange of grunt or signal, they broke into a run.

I watched them vanish along the battlements, and down the steps, scurrying out of sight across the darkness of the homestead's muddied fields which had once been a delicate chequerboard of gardens, heading towards the gates I had left open on the far side. Then I turned back towards the procession, which now lapped in a glittering tide beneath my homestead's walls. I clambered up onto the lip of the battlements. I raised my arms, and felt and stillness shiver out beneath me as the chanting ceased, and with it the rhythm of bells, as light trembled on ten thousand upturned faces. I almost threw myself down at that moment into the fine, living carpet of both human and hob which lay spread beneath me; perhaps that was even what was expected. But I drew back, even though I often wish that I had leapt.

●

AFTER THE INITIAL beatings and cursings when I was blindfolded and chained and taken into Dhiol, I was treated well enough. I was imprisoned in rooms in a high tower of the Temples of the Moon, which looked down on the many courtyards, balconied gardens, ziggurats and raised terraces where the priests regularly performed their exalted work. Beyond that, glowering through clouds or blazing white in the light of the Sun or the Moon, lay the ever-mightier peaks of the Roof of the World. In many ways, my lodgings reminded me of the tower where I had dwelt as a child. If anything, the furnishings and decorations were more sumptuous, although, by priestly standards, they probably seemed rough.

For many Moons, I was left to fend for myself. My only visitors were a daily attendance of hobs, who were not only mute and castrated, but rendered deaf and sightless as well. These strange, sad creatures moved by touch alone, although they seemed able to sense my presence by what I eventually decided was body heat, and skirted around me with the slow caution of a chameleon stalking its prey along a branch. When I tried touching their scarred and naked bodies, they scuttled back with alarming speed across the walls and floors. They left me food and water, and a few buckets and crude implements which, once I had finished using them, they took away again. After my initial nightmares about the ingenuity of the tortures which the priests, of all people, were capable of devising, I decided that this was to be my punishment: to have to do the things which no self-respecting human would ever expect to have to do unaided and alone.

If that was the punishment which had been intended, it was a failure. I remained fascinated by life's processes, even those which ended up in a bucket. I soon realised, for example, that a huge source of extra fertility went to waste by our peevish refusal to feed the land with human manure. And I found comfort in the simple preparation of food. Peeling an apple or a raw carrot can be an eminently enjoyable task, and the dissection of a slab of meat or some new kind of fruit always carried the promise that I might find out something new about the structure of animal musculature. And I enjoyed shaving as well, the careful craft of steering a soaped blade across my jaw, which was something I had never thought to do myself in all the years since hair grew on my chin.

Outside the window, and despite the glories of the architecture, the scene was less elevating. These priests of the Moon seemed to have little else to do with their time other than to sacrifice hobs. As the silver sphere which they worshipped processed and re-processed across the sky in its changing quadrants, I heard the cries and screams of many of my own hobs. They soon even reduced the resourceful and resilient Gog Two to a whimpering mess of bared flesh and bone. I supposed it was inevitable that the hobs which I had released into the wild would soon be caught. After all, the only life they had ever known was one of servitude and captivity. But it struck me as perverse that the priests should also track down, and then presumably re-purchase, the many other hundreds of hobs which I had legitimately sold. No doubt, they thought it was a fine spectacle, to kill the beasts which I had supposedly loved on specially raised platforms within my earshot and sight, and by methods that were even more ingenious than I had feared, and which were often almost impossibly slow.

Maybe they hoped to drive me to madness, although the chants I heard from beyond the temple's outer walls credited me with being mad already, and more evil than the foulest enemies of the Gods. But if there was one thing which my life, like the life of any other well-placed human, had prepared me for, it was the spectacle of hob sacrifice. Even though I understood the pleading gestures and moans in ways which few other humans are capable, and was left disgusted by the agony and the waste, I remained somehow unmoved.

If there truly was a pain which I was put though during my captivity, it was the perverse one of not caring and hurting enough. In my darkest times, I even began to wonder if people were right, and that I really was different—some kind of monster who lacked some crucial spark or spirit, or even soul.

●

THE SEASONS CAME and went with or without the aid of the priests, and grew increasingly cold. I took special delight in the return of a flock of swallows which I knew journeyed far downriver each winter to seek the better climes of the lands beyond Ulan Dor. They came to nest above my windows, and I watched the superb flight of the parents as they brought beakfuls of insects to feed their squeaking young.

It was on such a morning as I was staring from my window—for once, no sacrifices were going on, for which blessing I truly praised the Gods—and pleasantly lost in thought as I considered the play of the seasons and the way in which all life seemed to respond, when I heard an unusual noise; the turn of a key in my outer door. Not that my mute lizard hobs didn't still visit to me, but their pattern was strict, and they only came at night. Even more extraordinary, then, was the unmistakable sound of human footsteps, and of a human voice.

"Are you in here? Are you alive?"

I found myself frozen despite the relatively warm light in which I sat. It wasn't just that it was Kinbel's voice; it was that it was anyone's at all.

She ducked beneath the low stone arch. She was wearing a plain, hooded cape. "I'd imagined somewhere far worse than this…"

It had been such a long time since I had spoken to anyone that I was opening and closing my mouth like a frog.

"See, I've brought you gifts." She put down a bag and pulled back her hood and gave a laugh, which sounded almost like the Kinbel of old. But not quite; she wasn't any less beautiful, but she had changed. Her face was shaper, and so was her gaze. She still moved with grace, but it was a grace which reminded me of the swallows, or even of my mute hobs. It had that edge of wariness, and of caution, which all creatures which are preyed upon possess. "I wondered if you could use a mirror, although I thought twice about bringing one. But you look well enough. I should have brought scissors, though." She smiled. "Your hair isn't quite the current fashion."

"Here, here..." My own voice sounded even odder than hers as, courteous as a hob, I brushed down my only chair and turned it around. "There must be a lot of stairs to reach this place."

"Indeed there are." She sat down. Her hair had streaks in it, silver amid the dark. Fine lines drew around her eyes as she squinted against the window's light. "What's that sound?"

"That? Those are my birds." I felt my mouth shape a smile. "Not that I own them, of course. Or anything now. They come and go with the seasons, and return to exactly the same spot. They help keep me occupied."

"Birds—the whole way you look at things. You haven't changed so very much."

"I'm sorry."

"No, no." She shook her head. "I meant that as a compliment."

It was strange to talk to a human again. I felt my face flush.

Kinbel told me about the outer world. Things were as bad as I imagined, but life went on. My homestead had been possessed by the priests of her father's own sphere, and then sold on at what, I was pleased to note, was a considerable price, even if the priests had kept it all. The new owners imagined that they would be able to maintain the place as profitably as I had done, and I was even more pleased to learn that they had failed. My homestead was deserted now, apparently. So were many others. People were heading south, but, unlike my birds, they weren't returning.

"Your mother does well, or so the occasional communications which cross the storms in the Bounded Ocean assure me. She had remarried, of course. You didn't know? Stupid of me—how could you... The way she put it, some of kind of new alliance was essential because you have dragged the family name so low. She believes that she performs an important task in parading in pomp along the golden avenues of Thris. The way I hear it from my other contacts, she seems to be in so many places at once that people speculate that she employs two or three fake retinues, who process with all the usual scents and bells and awnings and rose petals by which she characterises herself. But without her at the centre, of course."

"That hardly seems to matter."

"No. For her. Perhaps it does not."

"You and I, Kinbel—are we still married? I mean, if we are, and if it causes you embarrassment—I mean, more than embarrassment..."

Kinbel looked at me. She still had that way of doing so. "Yes, we are married. Or at least as married as we ever were. Which isn't saying so very much. I still even get enquiries from the stonemasons who are storing those statues of ourselves we once had made. They ask if there isn't more work we should be doing if we are to gain the afterlife we deserve."

"Perhaps we'll get that anyway."

"Yes. Perhaps."

"And it doesn't bother you?"

"What? Being married but having no husband? Or not possessing a tomb? Or lacking a name I can safely proclaim—or a homestead I can call my own?"

I'd forgotten about those flares of anger; I'd forgotten how strange and unpredictable people can be. But the glare in her eyes subsided almost as quickly as it had come. In that, at least, she hadn't changed.

"No. We remain married. No one else would have me now even if I were not. In fact, I think it suits my priesthood to have me thus. Not that I've been asked to disown you. But I know that I will."

I felt a chill pass over me. "What do you mean?"

"Oh. I see. You imagined that this was the end of things—that you would be kept up here until you expired? I'm sorry, but that's never been the plan. There will be...I think the word they use is trial. A special hall is being built for the purpose. I believe you can probably see it from that window. Unlike the rest of us humans, you will be called to judgement in this life rather than the next."

"And punished?"

Her look melted. She rose from her chair. I believe she would have moved towards me, perhaps even embraced me, had I not shrunk back. "I should never have said..."

"No, no. It's important that I understand. And I had wondered what that huge new building that all those thousands of hobs are clambering to construct was, although I'd never have been arrogant enough to imagine it had anything to do with me."

"Oh, you're famous." She sat back down again. All the old distance between us had returned. "The priests wish to make you so."

Kinbel went soon after, having left the contents of her bag. There was a mirror, as she had promised—although it was removed that evening by the creeping hobs, and the knives which I was given thereafter to prepare my food and shave myself were so bunt as to be useless; it had never occurred to me before that I was being watched. Kinbel also gave me spices for cooking, which I was happy to experiment with. She had even obtained some scrolls which, although they were couched in the ridiculous language of the priests, recorded several useful aspects of natural science. But what pleased me most were the blank scraps of papyrus and a small cake of ink; both that she should think of bringing such a gift, and that I was free to write.

●

NOW, AT LAST, I could put my ideas down.

Above all, I kept thinking of those arrow-tailed birds. The priests, I discovered in one of the scrolls Kinbel had left me, took their coming to these northerly lands as an augury, and had recorded their precise numbers and the Moon of their arrival for thousands of years. There were far less now, and I wondered as I watched the swallows swoop among the spires at the many which must die during each long journey.

Here my heart started racing. Those creatures which flew and thrived the best, the thought rushed over me, would survive and produce offspring, whilst those which didn't would not. I'd be lying if I said that the rest came easily. But, looking back, I can see that it was but a small leap to consider that not only a change in habit might produce better chances in survival, but also the types of alterations which I had deliberately been engendering in my homestead's crops and livestock, but which, I reasoned, would surely occur naturally as well.

After her first visit, Kinbel came regularly to see me with every Moon. She brought news of the outside world, although she often seemed almost as distant from such goings-on as I felt myself. Far more importantly, she brought fresh writing materials. Soon, as well, she arrived with bundles of scrolls on the specific subjects I'd started to request. It would never have occurred to me to look for information about the natural world within sacred texts, but here was everything I could ever need recorded over aeons in pedantic priestly detail. I even tried to tell Kinbel about my vision, in which every type of beast and tree and plant and insect had changed and developed over aeons in response to the demands of its surroundings. And she appeared to listen, and sometimes even to understand.

"And if the pig and the boar are related," she once said, "if a tree and a bush are sisters, if the fish which inhabit the oceans are remote cousins of those in our rivers, what does that make us?"

"Of course, of course. That is why I need to find out more! That taxation scroll on the categorisation of different crops from the first dynasty you found for me was excellent, but perhaps there's something similar about livestock, or even fruit…?"

Outside, through the freezing mists, the great hall of my trial gathered its many roofs and domes, but it seemed vague, insubstantial compared to my theories and thoughts. I found it hard to believe that

Kinbel's world, with all the gossip and ceremonies and money of which she talked, was real.

Her nose was red. She sniffed. She looked weary and drawn. "I'm sorry. I have some small malaise which our priests cannot cure. Everyone seems to be possessed by it. Perhaps it's this cold summer. I do sometimes wonder if we humans were ever meant to live under such grey skies, and this far north. Apparently, the hobs get it as well, and have long done so, yet they thrive well enough. And now they seem to have given it to us. Shortly, many will be sacrificed as a result."

"Why? I thought everything was supposed to be my fault?"

She looked at me in that bitter way she sometimes had. "You mustn't let the grandeur of that building outside fool you."

"I'm sorry. I don't think I can imagine how difficult life is for you."

"No." She was still staring at me. "You probably cannot. But I've almost grown used to that. It's the way you are, and I don't think that's your fault. You see things, but you don't feel them. With you, that's almost an asset. But...those early difficulties we had in our marriage— I've learned since that they're not so unusual. And I have a theory of my own. A small one compared to yours, admittedly, but still...If we humans were brought up by our parents in the way that most other living creatures are—if we were suckled by them and touched by them, and perhaps cooed over and tickled as well. If we were allowed to laugh and cry and squirm and perhaps even feel love in the arms of another human instead of the arms of some trained anonymous hob...Well..." Suddenly, she appeared awkward. Her gaze travelled the floor. "I wonder if we might not all be better at being closer. I did tell you it was a small theory..."

I was flustered. I guessed that she was right, but I didn't know how to respond.

"Look at you now," she said, although still without looking at me. "Lost for words as soon as I mention human closeness. I suppose you'd call that evidence, wouldn't you?"

With a sweep of her cloak, and a sneeze, she left.

IAN R. MACLEOD

●

BY SOME PROCESS I longed to understand but didn't, Kinbel passed her malaise on to me. I coughed and sneezed for a while and thought it was nothing. Then I started to shiver. I crawled to my bed. The light of unnumbered days came and went at my window as I sweated and ached.

I had some new kind of fever, and that fever brought visions. I believed that I was no longer in my cell. I believed that I was flying even higher and faster than my beloved fork-tailed birds. I saw everything. I saw the human cities as they really were—not just the great buildings and squares, but also the desolate sprawls of hob dwellings that surrounded them. I saw the endless ranges of white plains and mountains which seemed to march in every direction from what I now realised was the tiny enclave of our human world. I saw the spreading glaciers, and the plains and savannahs, and the pull and flow of the great God River, and all the teeming life of the great tropic forests, and the storm-flecked grey and blue oceans which stretched even further than the wildest mariner's tale. I saw that our earth is vast, and I saw that time is even vaster, and that change is irrepressible and endless under the blaze of the ever-turning Moon and Sun. I saw, and understood, everything as I tossed and turned in my fevered shroud.

I awoke ringingly clear-headed to the sound of movement. I imagined at first that another quick day was passing and that it was the noise of the shadows dragging themselves about. Then I thought that it was merely my lizard hobs creeping about their usual duties. But the sound didn't fit that pattern, either. These were unmistakably human footsteps, and I felt a small flush of joy to know that Kinbel had returned. But the footsteps were many, and the air and light in my room seemed to be muffled by a presence which I realised could not be hers alone.

I opened my eyes.

The Hob Carpet

Gorgeous in their raiments and retinues, wreathed in incense, fluttering with fans and bells, a horde of priests stood around me, and I knew that the time of my trial had at last come.

●

THE NEW HALLS loomed even grander than I'd imagined as I stumbled across the frosted paving beneath the odd sensation of open skies. The rustle and murmur of a huge auditorium quietened as I was drawn inside. Thousands of faces from all the lands of humanity stared in my direction as I was led up and up a winding stairway to the high podium where I was seated on a kind of caged throne.

The first Moon of the proceedings were taken up in the initial bidding prayers and sacrifices. So was most of the next. Fires had been set in many places to keep the halls warm, and the whinnies of the suffering hobs and the stench of their offal mingled with wafts of undrawn smoke. Meanwhile, I had more than enough opportunity to consider the vast labour and invention which had been poured into the construction of this edifice, and to study the nature and reactions of the many humans who had gathered here: all the priests and the guards and merchants and mariners and other representatives who hoped to be persuaded that I was single-handedly responsible for every woe of the world, and, more importantly, be entertained. Even I shared something like their sense of anticipation; the idea that justice might be meted out in this world instead of some subsequent one appealed, although I was already certain that the justice would be false.

Kinbel was there, of course. She had a special podium far opposite across the great bowl of the main auditorium from my own. She was not alone there, but sat at the pinnacle of a whole swarm of other priestesses who, according to the current stage of the proceedings, sang or danced or silently mimed their shock or concern. Many eyes other than mine were drawn to her, and the light and the fires and even the smoke conspired to make her presence glow. She seemed less like the woman I remembered than some Goddess made flesh.

Inevitably, for she was never one to miss out on a big social occasion, my mother attended as well. I soon recognised the characteristic pomp of her retinue down amid some of the more expensive balconies, where for every one human there was a swarmingly decorative mass of perhaps a hundred liveried hobs. I sometimes thought I even caught glimpses of something small and withered and possibly human inside all that glory, although I was never sure.

I awaited the words of accusation with interest, yet was amazed at their length and invention when they finally came. I had supposedly done so many things that I felt almost flattered. All those foul desecrations, the terrible deeds, when I'd imagined that the worst that could be thrown at me an unnecessary love of nature, and of hobs. It went on and on. Despite the glory of the occasion, I began to feel bored, and cold. I started to wish the hours away, and to miss my happy days alone in my cell, and the company of my fork-tailed birds, who had fled again to escape a winter so savage that I wondered if, this time, they would ever return. Even though I studied her endlessly day after day from across the distance of this smoggy, dripping, gilded hall, I missed Kinbel's visits, as well.

Moon by slow Moon, the proceedings continued. The crowds shuffled and whispered, then became noisy with sneezes and coughs as they were possessed by the same malaise which had afflicted Kinbel and I. People came and went. Some didn't return. This winter city, set beside a frozen river within a great, ice-bound bowl, was cut off from the world, and struggled to cope with the inundation of representatives which my trial had caused. Looking down at all the faces, I studied humans as I had never studied them before. I saw the distinctions in attire and matters of custom which people from different regions affected. And I noticed, as well, the surprising variations in the colour of their skin. Although Kinbel's ebony beauty might be rightly prized, I was stuck by how many had a far lighter tint—even paler than my own, and my mother's. I was also struck by how, although the paleness of hobs' skin is cherished because of the fine contrast it makes with the red of blood, many, even in this high gathering, were surprisingly dark.

My eyes travelled. My mind wandered. High up though I was in my throne of imprisonment, there was a mechanism which seemed capable of raising it higher still. It ascended beyond the dome of the main hall, and long left me puzzled until one evening when I had returned to my cell. Winter was waning, and the Sun lingered over the rim of the mountains long enough for me to be able gaze across the snowbound city of Dhiol. I saw that on the outside of the main dome of the halls of my trial had been constructed some ultimate spire which rose high above every other spire and tower in the entire city, and that on top of that spire was a platform, and on that platform glinted an extraordinary machine. I'd seen such devices used to punish hobs, but this was far more extravagant. Poised and exquisite as some huge golden insect, the machine of my planned excruciation flashed its many pincers and blades in the last of the evening Sun.

●

SPRING ATTEMPTED TO arrive in Dhiol. Some of the snow and ice melted, and much did not. The priests who traversed with me to and from my cell now chatted freely amongst themselves, and I learned of the frozen bodies of deceased representatives which had been stored in the catacombs. I even heard it said that the great glaciers of the Roof of the World were expanding so mightily that the great tombs and their wrecked contents would soon be pushed into the streets of Dhiol.

Although I'd learned the language of the priests through the scrolls Kinbel had brought me, I'd long reached the point where all the prayer and debate of my trial passed me by. So it came as a surprise when it was suddenly announced that the vote on my verdict would commence the following day, and that I would be given a chance to speak beforehand. My heart gave a small kick. That night, I barely slept.

●

IAN R. MACLEOD

THE PRIESTS CAME with the dawn. I was led through the morning mud to my usual spot high above the vast hall. But today, I was released from my shackles to stand within the cage of my throne, and the crowd I looked down on seemed almost as big and expectant as it had been at the start of my trial. I thanked the Gods for this extraordinary chance.

I'm not sure how clearly I explained things, and there were times when many of my audience seemed lost or confused. After all, they'd come today expecting either a denial or a confession. What they received instead was a different way of understanding the world.

Living creatures, I began, amid gasps which subsided into incredulous silence, are not the work of the Gods. They come about through natural laws. Everything which lives, lives to survive long enough to reproduce, and those which thrive will have more offspring than those which do not. And each living thing is different. Each plant is as different in its own small way as one human is from another; it's just that, as we are not plants, we are not so good at telling them apart. (At that moment, there was laughter, and I knew that my audience was not yet lost.) But these small differences can be crucial—a fleeter foot, a broader wing, a stronger scent from a blossom—and they can combine and multiply over many generations to form a creature which is no longer the same as its ancestors. As different, indeed, as one type of flower is from another, or all the varied species of fish or bat. (There were murmuring nods at this suggestion; I think I had already taken people further than they realised).

This process of change and development, I told them, is slow but extraordinarily powerful. It explains not only the different plumages of different birds, but why there are birds at all. (A few of the murmurs here sounded hostile, but they were shushed by others who remained interested to hear what else I had to say). For the earth is almost as old as the Gods themselves (I hadn't intended to put that sop in, but it seemed to help) and it has been changed through frost and fire and inundation and flood. If living things were not able to adapt, nothing would have survived at all.

The Hob Carpet

I paused for a moment there. I felt light-headed and breathless. I'd said much of what I'd wanted to say, yet people were still nodding, and looking up at me as if half-persuaded by what I'd said. Even many of the priests seemed content. Perhaps they'd feared I'd accuse them of all the venery and corruption of which they were most probably guilty, but instead I'd produced this odd lecture. But I could see as I took my breath that some representatives had already lost track of the concept I'd set before them, whilst others, perhaps the quicker ones, were growing puzzled or restless. A few were even starting to look angry. The noise below me increased. But the designers of these halls had paid great attention to how well an individual voice might carry, and my position in my caged throne was unassailable. Even as people began to scream and block their ears, my words still carried.

It follows, I explained, all living things must stem from one primitive organism, and life in all its specialisation and variety has developed in simple response to the demands of competition and survival through the mechanism of selection and random change. Thus the pig and the boar are related (I glanced over at Kinbel; I even think that she nodded, for I was using her words) and the tree is cousin to the bush. The evidence is written everywhere in the way in which different animals share similar but differently-used organisms. You can see it in the bones of a leg, the arrangements of a flower...

I think I could have stopped there. In many ways, there was little more to be said. The few in my audience who were be able to grasp my theory had already grasped it. As for the rest—they had come to these halls for spectacle and superstition, and still cared for nothing else. So perhaps it was a kind of malice which made me then go on, or it might even have been Kinbel herself. As I looked across at her once more through all the light and fume, I remembered how quickly and elegantly she had grasped my meaning, and seen that it applied not only to trees and fishes and birds.

We humans, I told the gathering, are as much a product of chance and survival as any other species on this earth. Indeed (and now I did have to shout, for the gasps were growing to a roar) the evidence of our origins abounds in the natural world. Look at the monkeys and the great apes of the jungle. Look, above all, at our closest of relatives—the hob. So closely are we related, in fact, that we can mate and interbreed, just as the horse can with the donkey, and the lion with the tiger, and (and here the uproar grew even wilder) one or another kind of dog. Look at the colour of the skin of your own skin, and the features of your face, and then at the flesh of your retinue…

For some time, I had been aware of activity below me. Now, the last of my proclamation was muffled by an ungainly scuffle as my guardian priests scurried up the last of steps and heavy bodies fell across my own.

●

IT WAS ALMOST nightfall by the time I was returned to my cell. The Sun glittered on the arms and spindles of the terrible machine on Dhiol's topmost spire, then sank. I, too, slumped down in the gloom of my cell. All sense of elation was gone. Then I heard a sound just outside my window; a sound that was at once so strange and yet familiar that I felt an odd displacement of time. I was back in the days before my trial; free to explore my thoughts and the evidence of the scrolls which Kinbel bought me—without, it now seemed, a care in the world. But the sound was unmistakable. A few swallows had made their habitual journey to this unwelcoming northern clime. I smiled, although I knew that their chances of raising another batch of chicks in this savage land were probably as doomed as my life was.

I was still sitting and wondering what I had accomplished when the lizard-hobs began to come and go about their nightly tasks. This would be their last night. It was hard to imagine that the process of my excruciation would be delayed. As always, I ignored the grey hobs as they shifted and stirred. Then one of their number came closer than I was accustomed, and removed the hood which had covered its head, and straightened up. I was telling myself that I had never seen a hob so tall, or so fine-looking, or with skin so dark, before I realised who it was.

"They told me I couldn't see you," Kinbel said.

I was so happily astonished that I almost laughed, but her face remained stern.

"You know what will happen tomorrow?" she asked.

"Some kind of judgement will be announced. And then I suppose I will be slowly killed on that machine..." All sense of happiness and surprise drained from me. "I just hope it isn't as awful as I imagine."

"There's something else first. Why else do you think they've made me sit in those halls for all these interminable Moons? You've seen the way the delegates stare at me, and how my fellow priests chant and respond. I'm your wife, and they still want to hear about all the terrible things you did to me...Things..." She made a gesture. "Even worse than they can imagine, although I can't believe that that amounts to very much."

"If you're called to denounce me and make up stories, Kinbel, then you should do so."

"Even if that means I have to lie?"

"Things are so bad for me now, there's little you can do to make them worse."

"But it wouldn't be true. And I'm standing witness before our— or at least *my*—Gods."

"You don't still accept all that nonsense?"

"If you mean that the Sun will stop in his movement across the skies if the ziggurats of Thris do not run red each day with fresh hob blood—no, I do not. I think the Gods are far less eager for hob slaughter than most of the priestly spheres imagine. I'm tired of its stench. Even as a child, I used to hate the way my father would come home each evening with his vestments stained—like, I would say, a butcher's apron, although no self-respecting human butcher ever gets that close to the work his hobs do for him. I'm sick of slaughter. But, yes, I do still believe that there is more to this world than what we experience with our senses. That life's not just the product of struggle and vicious chance—"

"That's never what I meant."

"Perhaps it isn't. But this is hardly the time to debate niceties. I've watched you over these long Moons. I've listened to you. I sometimes almost think I could say I've known you, and that I've seen you for what you are, which is a good man. I'm a priestess and I know what that machine out there will do to you, and I don't believe you've done anything to deserve such agonies, nor that it's what the Gods would want of us—if, that is, the Gods want anything at all. Perhaps this world will be ruined by a coming age of ice, and perhaps we all are being punished, but if there has to be a sacrifice, let it not be you. Let it be someone else. Now…"

Kinbel unbundled something from around her waist. It was a grey livery much like the hobs were wearing, and her own.

"…put this on."

"How did you manage all of this? How did you persuade—"

She gave a laugh; the sound was half-happy, half-sad. "Even now, you have nothing but questions! You can't accept anything without trying to have it explained…I think, may the Gods help me, that's what I most hate and admire about you, you wilful, stupid man. But, since you ask, do you seriously imagine that you're the only human who has ever taken an interest in the welfare of hobs? And, in all your schemes and thoughts, did it never occur to you to find a way of communicating with these creatures who have cared for you for so long and so kindly in this cell?"

Kinbel was surrounded by them now. The mute grey creatures shifted about her in the dim light like shadows thrown from the edges of her robe. Their movement reminded me of the priestesses who had surrounded Kinbel during my trail, but the sense of true reverence and worship was much more strong.

"If you'd only taken the time," she said, "to learn to communicate with your hobs about something other than ditches and crops, you might have learned far more. Every living creature has its own story, and my friends here have been through such times and sufferings as you would not believe, even were you to ascend into that terrible machine tomorrow. All you ever had to do was to reach out with an open heart…"

I watched as her fine dark fingers traced shapes in the pale flowers of the hob's open palms, and then how the fingers of the hobs dipped into hers. It was a dance of touch and shade, a mingling of different lives, and the strange thought came upon that perhaps Kinbel was right—perhaps there was more to this world than could ever be proved by clever minds like my own. Then, at some signal from her which I did not see or understand, the hobs drew back.

"We all must go," she muttered.

"What about the watchers? What about the human guards?"

"You forget how used they are to having everything done for them. The people who guard this tower are as lazy as..." She paused. The phrase was as *lazy as a hob*. "As lazy as humans. Quick." Her hand moved to her neck. A key dangled on a piece of string. "We have to leave."

●

THROUGH CORRIDORS AND beneath arches. The hobs led. Kinbel and I followed. I stooped and scurried. I was a hob myself, a shadow, but I weaker than them, and clumsier, and lost. It was night, and pitch dark, yet I sensed that we passed through places with which I had once been familiar, back in the days of my youth—those far corners of my lost homestead, where every new turn and experience had been a lesson and a surprise. Great subterranean halls filled with the lost lumber of other ages and styles. Vast, vaulted kitchens echoing to footsteps amid the dangling metal of thousands of hooked pans. White ghosts of laundry rooms. Reeking lakes of wine and beer. Potting sheds, even, filled with the extra dark of waiting earth. We seemed to pass through all of these places, but now they were all chill and empty and distant as they waited for a summer which would never come.

The journey seemed even more endless than the darkness. I was bruised and tired and exhausted, but part of me was elated. It was as if the prayers which I'd never offered had been answered in the shape of these quiet and subtle creatures, and of Kinbel. We were, I reasoned, moving through these halls and passages not only beyond the chapels of the priesthood which had imprisoned me, but the entire city of Dhiol. Sometimes, I thought I caught voices, or glimmers of light shed along the cold, wet passageways. I was certain that I smelled human effluent, and worse. But we pushed on without pause. After all, what human would ever think to notice the passage of a few anaemic hobs?

Then we reached a final opening in which the darkness changed texture, and the breath of a cold night came rushing to touch my face. The archway was set in a hillside beyond the confines of the city, and my exploring hands as I levered myself out to stand on the cold earth told me that, like almost everything which is hob-made in our world, it was cleverly and finely wrought.

The hobs gathered around me, touching hands with Kinbel, yet avoiding my own. Some kind of message seemed to be passed between them as we stood beneath a thin Moon and a few cloud-chased Stars. I sensed a change in their posture. They even seemed to glance towards me with their ravaged eye sockets for a moment before they turned back towards Kinbel.

"From here," she said, "you and they have a chance of being free."

My teeth were starting to chatter. Iron air was pressing down from the dark shoulders of the Roof of the World. It took me a moment to understand.

"What do you mean? You and they?"

"I have to go back to Dhiol. Look, the Sun will soon be rising. If I beat on those gates down there for long enough, I'm sure I'll manage to wake someone, be it human or hob."

"Kinbel, you can't!" My head was rushing. I felt as the priests claim to feel when they feel the spirit of the Moon within them, or the turn of the Stars.

"If I go back, I'll be able to answer for myself in those halls. I'll have my chance to speak what I see as the truth just as you did yesterday. I'm a priestess. I still owe that much to the Gods."

"Don't you realise what they'll—"

She stopped me by taking my hand. "*You* realised, and yet you did what seemed right. You've got to give me that same chance."

"I just said what I thought. I could even be wrong. Especially what I said about humans and hobs—our mixed offspring and characteristics, the idea that we interbreed. That's just supposition. I have no proper evidence. What it needs is more study. What I have to do is—"

Kinbel stopped me by leaning forward and pressing her fingers to my lips. "There. Human touch. That's the only way I've ever found of shutting you up. But look, the Sun is rising. I have to go."

"You can't…"

"You've said that already. I must."

She stepped back, and briefly touched the ravaged faces of each of the hobs, which shone with edges of fire in the first flush of the rising son. Dhiol stretched below us, ashy shadow in a valley lit as yet only by the glittering ember of its highest tower. She turned and walked down the slope towards the city walls. And as I watched her go and did nothing to stop her, I knew that everything which had been said about me in the long days of my trial was true.

I'm a monster.

An aberration.

I'm less than human, and far less than hob.

●

OF ALL THE things which I've described to you, reader, it seems strangest of all to have written of the old seasons: of hot summers, migrating birds, budding flowers and misty autumns. Not that the weather doesn't change up here in these mountains, but we treasure the cold hard darkness of winter, and see spring as the harshest of times, fraught with avalanches, rockslides and dangerous torrents of meltwater, instead of as the most blessed. I say *Blessed*—as if blessings really existed! But, more and more, I find my myself thinking in these ridiculous priestly terms. I smile up at the cold white Sun, ask questions of the Wind or the Moon.

My mind must be weakening, or I'm getting old. Otherwise, why am wasting my precious supply of papyrus and ink on writing this tale?

I would once have filled these same scrolls with notes, descriptions, questions, calculations, theories. But the truth is that the part of my mind which once worked in that way—as hard as a well-whipped hob, as the saying used to go—feels worn out. And time is no longer precious to me. I have plenty of it. My colleagues or captors have little use for me. I sometimes feel that I have little use for myself. But it's pleasant to recall those old times—or many of them. And I enjoy the process of writing, even if, in doing so, I feel that very little has been explained, even to myself.

I still think of Kinbel's actions. And I still have no idea whether things happened as she intended. For, although she showed every evidence of knowledge, I cannot believe that she would have submitted to events had she really known what was to come. But even *I* knew, and I did nothing—I watched her walk down that hillside towards her city, and her fate. Around this point my suffering mind still revolves.

The climb away from Dhiol on that cold spring morning was hard: for me, who had been too long been at leisure in my cell—and for my mute and blind companions, who found themselves suddenly evicted into a place of wild, high air and jagged drops. But I could see, and they could feel and climb, and between us we made our way higher and higher across a maze of icy rock. We were all soon exhausted, and bleeding, but, hand over hand, and arm over arm, flesh against flesh, we still hauled ourselves up.

It was a bright, clear day. By noon, with no bay of hounds, shout of humans or grunt of hobs to signal pursuit, we took time to breathe. I looked down. Dome upon dome, tower upon tower, Dhiol was a perfect jewel wound about by the river's ice-flecked rush like a curl of shining hair. I had never been a lover of cities, but the place seemed beautiful to me now that I knew I could never return to it.

Perhaps I had allowed myself to briefly forget about Kinbel—monster, aberration, that I am. But even as I gazed down at it, the city breathed out a great and glittering clamour, a rush of trumpet and voices, a seethe of processions and flags. Then the noonday Sun blazed in an incredible beam through parting strands of clouds as if the Gods really were at work, and that beam found focus on Hilo's dreadful topmost spire which rose above the halls of my trial. The air which I gazed across seemed to shudder, and my blind companions gathered and trembled and touched hands. I felt as if I could see everything—as if I, too, were a God—and that which I could not see, I could feel, and that which I could not feel, I heard. It was, above all, the sounds of Kinbel's screams which filled that great space though all the long and terrible afternoon. I hear them still. After all the labour and expense which had gone into constructing it, I imagine that the priests had decided that their machine must be used. And if not on me, what better choice than my consort—the one who had engineered my escape and who, even in the terror of her excruciation, still refused to denounce me? Sometimes in my musings, I can briefly make it seem as if Kinbel's return to Dhiol and her prolonged death was inevitable. But I still like to pride myself on the rigour of my intellect, and I know that I could have taken Kinbel's fate from her, and that agonised death was something that I was certainly worthy of, just as certainly as she was not.

But I still cannot leave those events alone. They gnash their blades as if some machine of excruciation has formed itself inside my head. I wonder, for example, at the ease of my escape. After such time and investment, and on that of all nights, were the priests really so neglectful? Perhaps they saw the truth as clearly as I did, and knew that I bore no more responsibility for the worsening seasons than did the swallows, and that my death would cause nothing to change. Yet rash promises had been made about the many miracles the Gods would grant upon my death. The ice would retreat, the warm days return, the crops grow, the God River herself would flow with beneficent calm again. And, as they began to consider the consequence of all those unfulfilled promises, perhaps it occurred to them that it might be better and easier to let me escape, and uselessly sacrifice a scapegoat instead?

●

IAN R. MACLEOD

IDEAS, THEORIES—YOU SEE how I still cannot let them go. But life continues, and I, to my shame and disappointment, find small satisfactions—even hints of something resembling happiness—in observing the habits of the increasing numbers of hobs who have come to reside here in the Roof of the World. The ice tombs, ravaged though they are, provide a ready source of materials—even of food, for the frozen produce of lost offerings can, if properly heated and cooked, provide useful nourishment. Then there are all the stones, and the tools, and the furnishings. Hobs, despite all the sayings, are industrious, and they know how things work in a way which way no human has ever done. But rarely is anything put to the use for which it was originally intended. A funeral bed makes shelter for an entire tribe. A sarcophagus becomes a trough to feed the animals they so cleverly manage to raise here—once its previous occupant has been evicted, I might add. These changed ruins seem like some dream of the human world in which everything is twisted and transformed.

As well a being industrious, the hobs are intelligent. They understand that these funerary supplies will only last for a few years. And after that, I believe they will survive just as well. Already, parties go out to hunt for bear, goat and deer, and to collect the berries which still grow in what passes for summer. Sometimes, they even risk venturing into the lower lands around Dhiol, which are now mostly empty of civilised life, either human or hob. Hobs are used to hard times, and to difficult work. Above all, though, I believe that they will prosper because this cold land belongs far more to them than it ever did to us humans.

In the times when I permit myself to think in terms of my old theories, I feel an understanding of how humans and hobs came to live as we have done. Just as in the priestly myths, we humans, with our dark flesh, thinner limbs and intolerance of cold, came from the warm south. We spread slowly north in the time when the ice sheets were in retreat as the world grew warm; moving across and around the Bounded Ocean, towards the lands where my family eventually prospered on the trade of the Great North Water. There, we encountered our near relatives who, with their thicker-framed bodies and lighter skins, coped more easily with a colder Sun. We called these strange, half-familiar creatures— with their red hair, thick jaws and beetle brows, who signed and grunted instead of speaking, and wore half-rotted furs for clothing—hobs.

Perhaps there were times of co-operation and understanding. More likely, there was fear and distrust. Almost certainly, there would have been conflict as our numbers increased and resources grew more precious. But we humans won, and the hobs were subjugated, and we began to use and exploit them as they are used and exploited still. As to why it was that way around, and not some other, I cannot tell. Life, as I still see it, is ruled as much by chance as any other process. Perhaps there is some other version of our world where the hobs triumphed, and we humans worked for aeons to build hob cities. There may even be a world where, in a spate of even greater vindictiveness, we humans destroyed the hobs entirely, and their existence passed into records in the rocks in the way of many other lost creatures. But if that had happened, if the hobs vanished and we humans came to thrive alone, I struggle to imagine a better world than the one which I have known. Hard work would still have to be done, and I doubt if its burdens would have been shared equally. I shudder, indeed, to think of the means we would have used to divide humanity between the rulers and the ruled, the watchers and the workers, the fat and the poor, were it not for the convenient presence of hobs. It may have been something as ridiculous as skin colour, or the simple accidents of geography and birth.

●

THE HOBS IN this high place treat me mostly with distance, and a kind of respect. Sometimes, admittedly, there are small abuses and bullyings—they are as aware as the humans in my trial of the accusation of my being a hob lover, and seem to regard the idea with almost equal disgust. But they find me food, and supplies such as this papyrus. They even let me forage on my own, secure in the knowledge that I would die if I wandered off too far in this jagged place of bitter cold. Mostly, though, I keep to my cave, which was once the anteroom of a large tomb. In many ways, it isn't so different to my cell in Dhiol.

It suits them, I think, to have me as their willing captive almost as well as it once suited the priests of the Moon. Word sometimes reaches us from the hobs who flee here of human doings in the lowlands, and it seems my name has become an even bigger curse. I'm responsible now not just for the changing climate, but for the wars which have set human against human as the shortages increase. Of course, when I say human against human, I still mostly mean hob against hob, but the numbers of hobs who will unquestioningly do human bidding is decreasing, even if they are still in their millions. Our world is changing in more ways than simply by growing cold.

The other name of which I still hear, as if it didn't torment me enough already, is Kinbel's. The hobs revere her for reasons which I find too complex to fully understand. They say, for example, that, through her suffering no further sacrifice will ever be necessary, although I'm certain that plenty of hob sacrifice still goes on. Odder still, it's even signed in whispers that there are some humans who revere her as well. Could it be that Kinbel's death really wasn't in vain? Is it possible that what she did might somehow signal through history that hob and human can live together, not as slave and master, but as equals?

Again, my mind rambles, but I'm almost sure that humanity would have prospered better if we'd had to do things for ourselves. Maybe our temples wouldn't have been quite so huge or our gardens so elaborate, but we might have been pushed instead towards inventions which allowed more to be done with less effort. I remember the times when I was alone in my homestead with that broken leg, and how the hobs bore me about with the contortion known as the hob carpet, when it seemed as if I was walking unaided even though I was supported almost entirely by their work. That, it seems to me now, is how all of humanity has lived for far too many centuries. We imagine that we do it all ourselves, when fact we do nothing.

My hands are turning numb. Soon, I will find a place in the ice to consign these scrolls in the vain hope that they will be found and read.

The Hob Carpet

Are you there, reader? Are you human, or hob? Are you even from this particular world? Or perhaps you're from some other place, where humans worked so hard and alone that they made the very air so hot that they stopped the glaciers from their terrible return. Nothing but fantasies. This real world fades. My teeth chatter. My bones hurt. I sense the coming of another fever. Perhaps my final excruciation does not lie so very far off.

But the seasons still change, and life will go on. And sometimes things will be good, and sometimes they will be terrible, and most often they will be both at once with much that is neither intermingled. The hobs who come to our redoubt all bear their scars and stories of the horrors of the lowlands. Sometimes they arrive with other burdens as well. There was a young hob who reached here two dozen Moons ago. She was female and pretty (there, I've said it) if exhausted by her long flight. And she was noticeably pregnant.

I watched her with the same distant curiosity with which I watch most things as her belly grew and her term approached. One night, and not so very far my cave, I heard the unmistakable commotion of a birth. The hobs were too preoccupied to notice my presence as I watched. A baby was held up, mewling and screaming, still dripping from its caul. Then came a second, which is as unusual with hobs as it is with humans. I thought at first that the even greater uproar which ensued was simply down to that. But the two babies were very different. The first one was pale-skinned, and already had a fetching crest of red hair. The second was thinner, and longer. Its skin was dark.

The debate which followed was too quick for me to follow, but the result was plain. Even as the new mother nursed the child with the crest of red hair, the darker, more human-seeming baby was taken out along the smokily lamplit tunnels towards the snow-teeming night. Hobs, as I've long since discovered, may not practise ritual sacrifice or eat their young, but they not afraid of bringing death. I ran after them. I signed. I yelled.

Maybe I've saved or helped other creatures during my human existence, but I cannot honestly recall when, or how. Abstract theories and good husbandry are fine enough things in their way, but I've long grown sick of finery along with all other kinds of pomp. Through what I'm still convinced was my intervention, the dark-skinned child was allowed to survive. She's in her thirteenth Moon now, and is learning to sign, and to walk. Perhaps because of my special interest, she's less afraid of me than most of the other young hobs are. Her mother sometimes even lets her squat in my cave, and I try talking to her using human words, and she gargles some of them back in return. She's a sweet thing, precious beyond jewels, and has a hob name which I cannot record with these written symbols, but I call her Kinbel, and I've noticed that a few of the hobs have started signing to her by their own version of that name, as well.

On the SIGHTING of OTHER ISLANDS

●————————————————————→

THE ISLAND WHICH floated above mother ocean was composed of many things. Part metal, part forest, part city, part mountain, part orchard and meadow, it cast a shadow across the waters beneath and generated tides, currents, storms; it cast out nets of emerald lightning. Down in the barnacle dark of its turbulent underside, nameless sea-behemoths, flocks of blind seabirds and silvered shoals fought over its many kinds of spoor. Roots, chutes and fallings of metal sluiced, fed, or were torn apart by the endless clashings of waves. From some angles and sufficient distance, it seemed as if the island was somehow supporting itself on shimmering legs, or had just emerged from the sea, or was falling endlessly towards it, but from most, even as the eye strained to take in the scale of what it was seeing, the island appeared to be what it truly was: a bulkingly beautiful, yet seemingly impossible, vision made real.

Those who lived on the island never saw it from such a distance. To them, it was land and it was their home, and beneath there was only mother ocean, and the drop which separated the two was too vast and terrible to contemplate. For mother ocean, it was commonly believed, was endless, and the only qualifications to this watery infinity were those rare events known as sightings. In the island's topmost towers, the question of when and where the next sighting would occur, and then what it might mean, occupied the minds of the greatest of the dreamers. Some who lived and worked in the more mundane lowerlands claimed that the dreamers actually possessed maps of mother ocean, although such documents would surely have consisted almost entirely of ever-changing greys and greens and blues, and were thus hard to envisage. Others speculated that the dreamers steered the island in some direction or another in active search of new sightings, although it was mostly accepted that the island steered itself—if, indeed, it was consciously steered by anything at all. Strangely, the more common assumption was that sightings only occurred because the dreamers called them into existence out of a conjunction of their various slumbers, and that, once they had drifted beyond the horizon's haze, these other islands vanished back into the watery, sleepy stuff from which they had entirely been made.

After each sighting, the dreamers in their towers would put away their sacred telescopes and set about long and stringent debate as to what this particular conjunction of stone, roof, precarious field and hazy mountain signified. From there, decisions on such crucial matters as the planning of the harvest, levels of hemline and the financing of new sea-drains were then made. Over the innumerable lives and sightings through which the island measured its history, there had been many different visions with which the dreamers had had to contend. There had been islands glimpsed at dawn, and islands which appeared to drop from the nowhere heat of cloudless midday. There had been islands which looked to be transparent, or perhaps were made entirely of smoke, or possibly ice or glass. There had been islands of iron, and islands seemingly banded with precious stone. Sometimes, and yet more memorably, there had been several islands at once, which, even in the brief period in which they could be studied, had doubled and rejoined. Most spectacularly of all within the memory of recent generations, there had been the strange, far lights of an island glimpsed at midnight, and the horror of an island hanging upside upon a blood red sea. But most sightings, rare though they were, were far more commonplace, causing the island's more daring thinkers to posit that the beings who surely dwelt on these edifices lived lives which were perhaps not entirely dissimilar to their own. Sometimes, it was said, the dreamers with the best sight and access to the strongest and most sacred telescopes had glimpsed high towers formed in shapes of a near-recognisable architecture, or caught the sunflash of lenses trained back on them. But this, too, was merely another part of the pattern of sightings, and was soon re-woven into the fabric of the dreamer's dreams as the island drifted on, floating vastly on shimmers of storm above mother ocean's endless haze.

SECOND JOURNEY of the MAGUS

HE TRAVELLED THE same way, but there was heat this time instead of the dark of winter, and nothing of lands which he had passed through more than thirty years before was the same. Gone were the quiet houses, the patchwork fields, the lowland shepherds offering to share their skins of wine. Instead, there were goats unmilked, bodies bloating in ditches, fruit left to rot on the branch. And people were fleeing, armies were marching. Fear and dust hazed the roads.

He followed hidden tracks. He camped quietly and alone. He lit no fire. He ate raisins and dry bread. He spoke no prayers. Although an old man, weak and unarmed, he felt resignation rather than fear. His camel was of far greater value than he was, and he knew he could never return to Persia. At least, alive. The Emperor, if he ever knew of his journey, would regard it as treason, and the Zoroastrian priests would scourge his body for honouring a false God.

He came at last to the Euphrates. There were palms and green hills rising from the marshes, but the villages all around were empty. He sat down by the broad blue river as his camel drank long and loud, and quietly mourned for his two old friends. Melchior, who had first read of that coming birth in the scriptures of a primitive tribe. Gaspar, who had found the right quadrant in the stars to pilot their way. And, he, Balthasar, who had accompanied them because he had ceased to believe in anything, and wished to see the emptiness of all the world and the entire heavens proven with his own eyes. That, he supposed, was why he had chosen to bring an unguent for embalming corpses as his gift for this king he never expected to find.

A boat was moored, nudging anxiously into the current as if feared to be left alone in this greenly desolate place. It was evening by the time Balthasar had refound his resolve and persuaded his half-hobbled camel to board the vessel with murmured spells, then made small obsience to the gods of the river, and poled into the inky currents beyond the reeds. The sky in the west darkened as sprites of wind played around him, but, even as the moon rose and stars strung the heavens, even as he re-moored the boat on the far side and set off across a land which soon withered to desert, the western horizon ahead remained aflame.

He knew enough about war to understand the dark eddies and stillnesses which he had already witnessed on his journey, but it seemed to him that the battleground he encountered as the dawn sun rose at his back and brightness glared ahead was the stillest, darkest place on earth. All Persians should be grateful, he supposed, that this resurgent Hebrew kingdom had turned its wrath against the Empire of Rome. A strategist would even say that war between powerful neighbours can only bring good to your own lands—he had heard that very thing said in the bars of Kuchan—but that presupposed some balance in the powers which fought each other. There was no balance here. There was only death.

Blackened skulls. Blackened chariots. Heaps of bone, terribly disordered. The way the Roman swords and shields were melted as if put to the furnace. The way the helmets were caved in as if crushed between giant fists. Worst still, somehow, was the sheer *value* of what had been left here, ignored, discarded, when every battlefield Balthasar had ever witnessed or heard of in song was a place ripe for looting. This great Roman army, with its engines and horses, with the linked plate metal walls of irresistibly fearless men and raining arrows, had been obliterated as if by some fiery hurricane. And then everything simply left. It was hard to find a way across this devastation. He had to blindfold his camel and soothe the moaning creature with quiet visions of oases to keep it calm. He wished that he could blindfold himself, but, strangely, there was nothing here to offend his mouth and nose. There were no flies even as his feet sunk through puddled offal as he climbed mountains of bones. The only smell was a faint one of some odd kind of perfume, such as the waft you might catch from the beyond the curtains of the temple of some unknowable god.

The noon sun was hot, but the blaze in the west had grown brighter still. He remembered that star, the one which Gaspar had been so certain would somehow detach itself from the heavens to lead them. Had it now reignited and settled here on earth? Was *that* what lay ahead? He swathed his face against the burning light and drifting ash. It seemed to him now that he'd always been destined to re-take this journey at the end of his life. If nothing else, it was due as penance.

The three men who had taken this journey before had thought themselves wise, and were acknowledged in their own lands as priests, kings, magi. Then, unmistakably even to Balthasar's dubious gaze, a single star had hovered before them, and did not move as the rest of the heavens revolved. It went beyond all reason. It destroyed everything he understood, but the people they asked as they passed through this primitive outpost of the Roman Empire could speak of nothing in their ragged tongue but vague myths of an ancient king called David, and of a great uprising to come. They did not understand the stars, or the ancient scripts. They only understood the gold which the three magi laid upon their palms.

Finally, though, they reached the city called Jerusalem. It was the administrative capital of this little province, and truly, from its fallen walls and the pomp with which the priests of the local god bore themselves, it did seem to be the remnant of a somewhere which had once been far greater. The local tetrarch was called Herod, and even to the cultured eyes of the three magi, his palace was suitably grand. It

was constructed on a sheer stone platform with high walls looking out
across the city, and surrounded by groves of fine trees, bronze fountains, glittering canals. Thus, the three magi thought, as they were led
through mosaic-studded halls, does Rome honour and sustain those
who submit to its power.

They were put at their ease. They were given fine quarters, soft
clean beds and hot baths. Silken girls brought them sherbet. Dancing
girls danced barefoot. Here, at last, they felt that they were being
treated as the great emissaries that they truly were. Herod, bloated
on his throne, struck Balthasar as a little man made large. But he
could converse in the Greek, and the three magi could think of no
reason why they should not ask for his advice as to the furtherance
of their quest. And that advice was given—generously, and without
pause. Astrologers were summoned. Holy books were unfurled, and the
bearded priests of this region who clustered around them agreed that,
yes, such was the prophecy of which these ancient scriptures spoke—
of a new king, of the lineage of a king called David who had once
made this city great in the times of long ago. The three magi were sent
on their way from Jerusalem with fresh camels, full bellies and happy
hearts. Herod, they agreed, as they rode toward the star which now
seemed even brighter in the firmament, might be a slippery oaf, but at
least he was a hospitable one.

The roads were clogged. It was the calling, apparently, of a census,
despite it being the worst time of the year. Not an auspicious moment,
either, Balthasar couldn't help thinking, for a woman to travel if she
was heavy with child. He discussed again with Melchior as they pushed
with the crowds and the sleeting rain past the camps of centurions and
lines of crucified criminals. Remind me again—is this child supposed
to be a man, or a god? But the answer he got from his friend remained
meaningless. For how can the answer be both yes, and yes? How can
something be both? Difficulties, then, with finding somewhere to
reside, for all the documents of passage Herod had so kindly given
them, and Gaspar's navigation was no longer so sure. For all that this
star glowed out at them like a jewel set the firmaments both day and

night, no one could offer guidance on their quest, and none bar a few wandering shepherds seemed to notice that the star was even there.

Then they came at last to a small town by the name of Bethlehem, and it was already night, and it was clear that whatever this strange light in the heavens signalled had happened here. They enquired at the inns. They spoke once again to the so-called local wise men, although this time, more warily. They made no mention of gods or kings. At the start of this journey, Balthasar had imagined himself—although he had never believed it would truly happen—being led to some glowing presence which would rip down the puny veils of this world. But he realised now that whatever it was that they sought would be painfully humble, and all three magi had begun to fear for the fate of the family involved.

It was a stable, at the back of the cheapest and most overcrowded of all the inns. They would have been sent away entirely had not Melchior known to ask as the door was being slammed in their faces about a family from a town called Nazareth. So they had reached the place toward which the star and the prophecies had long been leading them, on the darkest and most hopeless of nights, and in the coldest time of the year. There was mud, of course, and there was the ordure. There was little shelter. Precious little warmth, as well, apart from that which came from the fartings and breathings of the animals. The woman was still exhausted from birth, and she had laid the baby amid the straw in a feeding trough, and the man seemed…not, it struck Balthasar, the way any proud husband should. He was dumbstruck, and in awe.

They should, by rights, have simply turned and left. Offered their apologies for the disturbance, perhaps, and maybe a little money to help see this impoverished family toward their next meal. Balthasar thought at first that that was all Melchior planned to do when he stepped forward with a small bag of gold,. But then he had fallen to his knees on this filthy floor before the child in that crude cot. And Gaspar, bearing a bowl of incense, did the same. These were the gifts, Balthasar now remembered, that his two friends had always talked of bearing. Now, he felt he had no choice but to prostrate himself as well, and offer the gift which he had never imagined he would be called to present. Gold, for a king, and frankincense, for a man of God—yes, those gifts were understandable, if the prophecies were remotely true. But myrrh symbolised death, if it symbolised anything at all. Then the baby had stirred, and for a moment, Balthasar had felt he was part of *something*. And that something had lingered in his mind and his dreams through all the years since.

He had spoken about that moment with Melchior as he lay on his deathbed back in Persia. Yes, his old friend agreed in a dry whisper, perhaps a god really had chosen to manifest itself in that strange way, and in that strange place. Perhaps he had even moved the heavens so that they could make that long journey bearing those particular gifts. But Melchior was fading rapidly by then, falling into pain and stinking incontinence which the castings of spells and prayers could not longer assuage. As his friend spasmed in rank gasps, Balthasar couldn't bring himself to frame the other question which had robbed him of so many nights of sleep. For if that baby really was the manifestation of an all-powerful god, why had that god chosen to make them the instruments of the terror which happened next?

The three magi had left the stable at morning under a sky doused with rain, and they knew without speaking that they must return quietly and secretly to Persia, and should spread no further word. But, through their vain discussions in Herod's opulent palace, it was already too late. Rumours of a boy king was the last thing this restless province needed, and the remedy which Herod enacted was swift and efficient in the Roman way. Word came like a sour wind after the three supposedly wise men that every male child recently born in Bethlehem had been slaughtered, and they returned to their palaces in Persia half-convinced that they had seen the manifestation of a great god, but certain that that god was dead.

So it had remained in all the years since, through Balthasar's increasing decrepitude, and the loss of his wives, and deaths of his oldest friends. But then had come rumour from that same territory in the west of a man said to have been born in the very place and manner which they had witnessed, who was now performing great miracles, and proclaimed himself King of the race the Romans called the Jews. It had been four years, as Balthasar calculated, since this man had emerged as if from the same prophesies which Melchior had once shown him on those ancient scrolls. And it seemed to Balthasar now that this last journey had always been predestined, and that the only thing which he had been waiting for was the imminence of his own death.

He was entering a green land now. It was fertile and busy. The creeks bubbled with water so pure and sweet that he feared both he and his camel would never stop drinking. The roadside bloomed with flowers more abundant than those tended in his own place grounds. Fat lambs baaed. The air grew finer and clearer with every breath. All the dust and pain and disappointment of his journey was soon clensed away.

The first angel Balthasar witnessed was standing at a crossroads, and he took it to be a tall golden statute until he realised that it wasn't standing at all. The creature hovered two or three spans in the air above the fine-set paving on four conjoined wings flashing with many glittering eyes, and it had four faces pointing in each of the roadway's four directions, which were the faces of a man, a lion, an ox and an eagle. Its feet were also those of an ox. Somehow Balthasar knew that this creature belonged to the first angelic order known as Cherubim. There was a singing in his ears as he gazed up at the thing, which was too beautiful to be horrible. He didn't know whether to bow down in tears, or laugh out loud for joy.

"Old man, you have come as a pilgrim." It was merely a statement, sung by a roaring choir. "You may pass."

This land of Israel truly was a paradise. He had never seen villages so well tended, or lands so fecund. Trees bowed down with fruit even though it was too early in the season. Lambs leapt everywhere. The cattle were amiable and fat. He felt, amongst many other feelings, ridiculously hungry, but withheld from plucking from the boughs of the fig trees until he saw the many other travellers and pilgrims feasting on whatever took their fancy, and farmers freely offering their produce—plump olives, fine pomegranates, warm breads, cool wines, glistening haunches of meat—to all.

He knew that night was coming from the darkening of the eastern sky behind him, by the west glowed far too bright for any visible sunset to occur. A happy kind of tiredness swept over him. Here, he would merrily have cast himself down here in these hedgerows, which would surely be soft as a feather bed. But a farmer came running to him from out of the sleek blue twilight, and insisted on the hospitality of his home. It was a square building, freshly whitened, freshly roofed. Olive lamps glittered, and the floor inside was dry and newly swept. He had never encountered somewhere so simple, yet so beautifully kept. The man himself was beautiful as well, and yet more beautiful were his wife and children, who sang as they prepared their meal, and listened gravely to Balthasar's tale of his journey and the terrible things he had witnessed, yet laughed when he had finished, and hugged him, and broke into prayer.

All he was seeing, they assured him, were the sad remnants of a world which would soon be extinguished as the Kingdom of their Saviour spread. Their eldest son was fighting in the armies of Jesus the Christos, which they knew would be victorious, and they did not fear for his death. Even in a house as joyous as this, that last statement struck Balthasar as odd, but he kept his council as they sat down to eat on beautifully woven rugs, and the meal was the best he had ever tasted. Then, there was more song, and more prayer. When the man of the house finally beckoned Balthasar, he imagined it to show him the place where he would bed. Through a small doorway, and beyond a curtain there was, indeed, a raised cot, but a figure already occupied it; that of an elderly woman who lay smiling with hands clasped and eyes wide open as if gripped in eager prayer.

"Go on, my friend" Balthasar was urged. "This is my grandmother. You must touch her."

Balthasar did. Her skin was cold and waxy. Her eyes, for all their shine, were unblinking. She was plainly dead.

"Now, you must tell me how long you think she's been thus."

Troubled, but using his not inconsiderable knowledge of physic, Balthasar muttered something about three to four hours, perhaps less, to judge by the absence of odour, or the onset of rigor in the limbs.

The man clapped his hands and laughed. "Almost two years! Yet look at her. She is happy, she is perfect. All she awaits is the Lord's touch to bring about her final return in the eternal kingdom which will soon be established. *That* is why we Christians merrily do battle against all who oppose us, for we know that we will never have to fear death..."

That night, Balthasar laid uneasily in the softness of the rugs the family had prepared for him, and was slow to find sleep. This clear air, the happy lowing of the cattle, the endless brightness in the west... And now the family were singing again, as if out of their dreams, and joined with their voices came the softer croak of the older woman, happily calling with emptied lungs for her resurrection from undecayed death. In the morning, Balthasar felt refreshed for all his restlessness, and the beast the family led from their stables was barely recognisable as the surly creature which had borne him all the way from Persia. The camel's pelt was sleek as feathers. Its eyes were wise and brown and compassionate in the way of no beast of burden Balthasar had ever known. He almost expected the creature to speak to him, or join with this family when they broke into song as they waved him on his way.

Thus, laden with sweetmeats and baked breads, astride a smooth, uncomplaining mount on a newly softened saddle, Balthasar completed the last leg of his strange second journey to Jerusalem. The brightness before him had now grown so intense that he would have feared for his sight, had that light come from the sun. But he could see clearly and without pain—see far more clearly than he had ever seen, even in the happiest memories of his youth.

The encampment of a vast army lay outside the great city's gleaming jasper walls. Angels of other kinds to the creature he had first witnessed—some were six-winged and flickered like lampflames and were known as the Seraphim; others known as the Principalities wore crowns and bore sceptres; stranger still were those called the

Ophanim, which were shaped like spinning wheels set with thousands of eyes—supervised the mustering and training with the voices of lions. The soldiers themselves, Balthasar saw as he rode down among them, were like no soldiers he had ever seen. There were bowed and elderly men. There were limping cripples. There were scampering children. There were women heavy with child. Yet even the seemingly lowliest and most helpless possessed a flaming sword which could cut as cleanly through rock as it did though air, and a breastplate seemingly composed the same glowing substance which haloed the city itself. Seeing all these happy, savage faces, hearing their raucous song and laughter as they went about their everyday work, Balthasar knew that these Christian armies wouldn't cease advancing once they had driven their old overlords back to Rome. They would turn east, and Syria would fall. So would Egypt, and what was left of Babylon. Persia would come next, and Bactrai and India beyond. They would not cease until they had conquered the furthest edges of the world.

He entered the city through one of its twelve great, angel-guarded gates. The paving here was composed of some oddly slippery, brassy metal. Dismounting from his camel, Balthasar stooped to stroke its surface just as many other new arrivals were doing. Like all the rest, he cried out, for the streets of this new Jerusalem truly were paved with gold. The light was intense, and there were temples everywhere, as you might find market stalls, whorehouses or watchman's booths in any other town. He doubted if it rained here, but the golden guttering ran red with steaming gouts of blood. The fat lambs, cattle and fowls seemed not to fear death as they were led by cheering, chanting crowds toward altars of amethyst, turquoise and gold. Balthasar, who had dropped his camel's rein in awed surprise, looked back in sudden panic. But it was too late. The crowds were already bearing the happily moaning creature away.

Most of the people here in Jerusalem wore fine but anonymous white raiments, some splattered with blood, but Balthasar recognised the faces and languages of Rome, Greece and Egypt amid the local Aramaics. Yet even when strange pilgrims of darker and paler races encountered spoke to him, he discovered that he understood every word.

Second Journey of the Magus

The story which he heard from all of them was essentially the same. Of how two figures had appeared atop the main tower of what had then been the largest temple in this city on the morning of the Sabbath four years earlier. Of how one of the figures had been dressed in glowing raiments, and the other in flames of dark. And how the glowing figure had cast himself as if to certain death before the gathering crowds, only for the sky to rent from horizon to horizon as many varieties of angels flew down to bear him up. Even the most conservative of the local priests could not deny the supernatural authority of what they had witnessed. When the same figure had arrived the following day at the closed and guarded city on a white horse in blazing raiments and demanded entry, Pilate the Roman prefect, who was subsequently crucified for his treachery, ordered that the gates be flung open before they were broken down.

Everything had changed in the four years since. Jerusalem was now easily the most powerful city in the eastern Mediterranean, and Jesus the Christ or Christos was the most powerful man. If, that was, he could conceivably be regarded as a man at all. Balthasar heard much debate on this subject amid the happy babble as work toward celebrating his glory went on. Man, or god, but surely not both? It was, he realised, the same question he had asked Melchior many times on that earlier journey. He'd never received what he felt was a satisfactory answer then, and the concept still puzzled him now.

The city walls were still being reconstructed in places from more huge blocks of jaspar which angels of some more muscular kind bore roped to glowing clouds. For all the imposing depth and breadth of the finished portions, Balthasar could not imagine that this city would ever be required to defend itself. Many of the buildings, for all their spectacular size and ornamentation, were also works in progress, raised from the support of what looked like ridiculously frail scaffoldings, or perhaps merely faith alone, as new gildings and bejewellings were encrusted over surfaces already bright with gems. The Great Temple, which rose from the site of the far lesser building from which Christ had thrown himself down, was the vastest and most impressive building of all. Great blocks of crystal so sheer you could almost walk into them formed turrets which seemed mostly composed and fire and air.

Controlled and supervised by angels, crowds flooded the wide marble steps beneath arches of sardine and jasper. Most of those who came to worship were whole and healthy, but some, Balthasar noticed, had terrible injuries, or were leprous. Others, perhaps impatient for the promised resurrection, bore the dead with them on crude stretchers, variously rotted or well-preserved. As was the case throughout the entire city, there were none of the expected smells. Instead, that fragrance which he had first encountered at the site of that battlefield was much stronger still. It was part spiced wine and part the smoke of incense, and part something which your reeling mind told you wasn't any kind of scent at all. The interior of the temple was, of course, extraordinary, but by now Balthasar was drunk and dizzy on wonders. All he yearned like the rest of the crowd was to witness was the presence of Jesus himself.

There he was, beyond all the sacred gates and hallways, enthroned at very furthest of the vast final court of the Holy of Holies, which Balthasar had no doubt was the largest interior space in the entire known world. Angels swooped amid the ceilings, and huge, strange beasts, part lion and part bird, guarded a stairway of rainbows, but the eye was drawn to the small-seeming man seated at the pinnacle on a coral, emerald and lapis throne.

In one way, Jesus the Christos seemed frail and small, dwarfed by these spectacular surroundings. You noticed that he wore his hair longer than might seem entirely manly, and that his raiments were no whiter than those worn by many in the crowd. Noticed, as well, his plain leather sandals and how, for all that he was past thirty, he still possessed a young man's thin beard. But at the same time, you knew without thinking he was the source of all the radiance and power which flooded from this city. At first he sat simply gazing down with a kind of sorrowful compassion at the wild cries, prostrations and offerings of the crowd. Then he stood up from his throne and walked down the steps into the masses, and absolute silence fell.

A sense of eternity, moved amongst them, and everyone in that great space felt humbled, and judged. It really did seem that some of the dead were resurrected with the touch of a hand, a few quiet words, and that the leprous regained their limbs, but equally a few of those who had imagined they had come here in good spirits collapsed as if dead. Then, without the Christos having come close to Balthasar, a clamour of trumpets sounded, and his presence vanished, and the audience was at an end.

Balthasar had come all this way, lived all these years, in search, he now realised, of just one undeniable glimpse of the absolute. Just to know that there was something more than the everyday magic—the dirt and demons—of this world. Some blessed certainty. That was all he'd ever wanted. Or so he'd believed. And now, the presence of a supreme being had been demonstrated to him and ten thousand other witnesses in this city of crystal and gold. So why, he wondered as he left the Great Temple with the rest of the milling crowds, did he feel so let down?

There was no way of telling in Jerusalem whether it was day or night. What stars he could see were probably the auras of angels, or glittered amid the impossible architecture which rose all around. But he noticed that a patch of deeper dark had settled at a corner of the Great Temple's wide outer steps. People were making a wide berth around it, and as curiosity somehow drew him closer he caught a jarringly unpleasant smell. Swarms of flies lifted and encompassed the shape of what he now saw was a man. Here, he thought, was someone so hopelessly sin-ridden as to be beyond even Jesus's help.

Balthasar felt in his pockets and pouch for what scraps of food and money he had left and tossed them in the poor creature's direction. Not that he imagined that such material things would be of much use in this city, but what else could he do? He was turning and pondering if he was likely to find a place to sleep when a preternaturally long arm extended to grab the edge of his robe.

He allowed himself to be pulled back. The man had large brown eyes. He might once have been beautiful, if you ignored the flies and the sores and the rank and terrible smell which emanated from him. He licked his scabbed lips and looked up at Balthasar.

"You know who I am?" he asked in a voice which was a faint whisper, yet echoed in Balthasar's mind.

Just as in the temple, Balthasar knew and understood. "You are the Christos, the Christ—the same Christ, and yet a different one—as the Christ I have just witnessed perform many wonders in this temple."

"There is only one Christ," the man muttered, glancing at the crowds which were already gathering around them, then up at the various angels which had started to circle overhead. "I am always here."

"Of course, my Lord, you are all-powerful," the theologian in Balthasar answered. "You can thus be in many places at once. And in many forms."

"I can be everywhere, and everything," Jesus agreed with a slow smile, bearing what teeth he possessed within his blackened mouth. "What I cannot be is nowhere. Or nothing at all."

Balthasar nodded. The crowd around them was still growing. "Do you remember me, my Lord? I and two of my friends, we once journeyed…" He trailed off. Of course Jesus knew.

"You brought that deathly unguent as your gift. Perhaps instead of asking me why you did so, Balthasar, as you were thinking of doing, you should ask yourself."

"My Lord…I still do not know."

"Why should you?" Jesus shifted his crouch on the temple steps, hooking his thin arms around his even thinner legs as the flies danced around him in a humming cloud. "Any more than you should know why you chose to return. After all, you are only a man."

Balthasar was conscious of the murmurs of the watching crowd— *He is Here. It is as they say. Sometimes He comes in pitiable disguise*— and the knowledge that Jesus already understood far more about his thoughts than he was capable of expressing. "I returned, my Lord, simply because I am a man. And because you are a god."

"*The* God."

"Yes." Balthasar bowed. His voice trembled. "The God."

"So...Why do you doubt?"

"I do not—"

"Do not try to lie to me!" Suddenly, Jesus the Christ's voice was like the rumble of rocks. The sky briefly darkened. The circling angels moaned. "You doubt, Balthasar of Persia. Do not ask me why, but you *doubt*. You look at Me in awe but you cannot see what I am, for if you did, if all was revealed, your mind would be destroyed...Yet, even then, I wonder if you would believe in that instant of knowing? Or even after a million eternities lived amid glories which would make this city seem squalid as the stables in which I was born. Would you believe then?"

"I am sorry, Lord. I simply do not know." Balthasar blinked. His eyes stung. Terrible though it was, he knew that everything Jesus had said was true. Without this accursed doubt which even now would not leave him, he could not be Balthasar at all.

"I came to this world to bring eternal peace and salvation," Jesus was saying. "Not just for the Jews, but for all humanity. I was born as you witnessed. My parents fled Herod's wrath, and I was raised almost as any human child, waiting for the time of my ministry arrive. And when that time came..." He brushed the regathering flies from around his eyes. "When it came, I sought knowledge and solace in the wilderness for forty days, just any penitent would...

"I fasted. I prayed. I knew I could bring down the walls of this world, rip the stars from the heavens—indeed, just as you have imagined, Balthasar, in your wilder dreams. Or I could have entered this city as pitiably as you see me now, or as some holy buffoon riding on an ass. I could have done all these things and many others. If, that was, I wished to discover how little compassion the men and women who populate this earth possess. Or perhaps...I could..." The flies were buzzing thicker. The stench seemed to have grown. A different emotion, which might almost have been interpreted as fear, played across the crawling blackness of Jesus's face. "I could, perhaps, have gathered a small band of followers, performed small deeds, and declared myself in ways which the priests would have found easy to challenge. I could have allowed them to bring about my death. All of these things I could have done so that men such as you, Balthasar, might ultimately choose be redeemed. I could have died in an agony of unheeded screams, Balthasar…" Jesus smiled a sad, bitter smile. "If that was how your gift to me was intended…"

"But you cannot die, my Lord."

"No…" Jesus picked at a fly from his lips and squashed it between ruined nails. "But I can feel pain. I could have passed through this world as lightly as the wind passes over a field of barley. And human life would have continued almost as you know it now—and worse. Armies would march. People would suffer and starve and doubt my existence whilst others fought over the meaning of my words. Cities of stone and glass even more extraordinary than this one you see around you would rise and fall. Clever men like you, Balthasar, would learn how to fly just as you see these angels flying. Yes, yes, it's true, although I know it sounds extraordinary. Men would even learn how to pass even beyond the walls of this earth, and how to the poison the air, and the kill the living waters of the oceans. And all for what, Balthasar? What would be accomplished, other than many more lifetimes of pointless striving?"

"I do not know, my Lord."

"Indeed." Jesus shook his head. Then he laughed. It was a terrible, empty sound, and the flies stirred from him in a howling cloud. "Neither did I, Balthasar. Neither did I. And I was hungry in that wilderness, and I was afraid. There were snakes and there were scorpions…And there were other things…" Jesus shuddered. "Far worse. It was in those last days of my torment when it seemed that the very rocks taunted me to transform them into bread, that I finally understood the choice I had to make. I saw all the kingdoms of this earth spread below me, and I knew that I could take dominion of them. All I had to do was to show myself, cast myself from a high point of a temple so that all the angels in the heavens might rescue me. After all…" Jesus shrugged. "I had to make my decision. And this…" He looked along the marble steps at the awestruck crowd, then at the incredible spires and domes, then up at the heavenly skies. "…is the world I have made."

Even as Jesus the Christ spoke these last words, Balthasar and the crowd around him could see that he was fading. With him departed the droning flies, and the pestilential stink was replaced by the heady, sacred scents of the temple. He would be somewhere else, or had been in many other places already. Appearing as glowing vision on some hillside, or leading with a tongue of swords at the front of one of his many armies. All that was left of the Christ now was what Balthasar had once feared he might be—just a trick of the light, a baseless hope turned from nothing more than shadow, and a last few droning flies.

Balthasar pushed his way down the steps and out of the crowd. He walked the golden streets of Jerusalem alone. He'd been thinking before of sleep, but now he knew that he would never find sleep, or any other kind of rest, within this city. It was all too much. It was too glorious. And he was still just a man. Perhaps he would just crumble to dust when all the rest of the believing, undoubting multitudes were resurrected. Sacrilegious though the thought was, it felt welcoming. He passed out through one of the city's twelve great gates almost without realising, and found his way through the encamped battalions as they joined with choirs of angels in celebration of their inevitable victory. Looking back at the city as the land finally darkened and rose, he wondered once again why an all-powerful God should feel the need to protect it with such large and elaborate defences. Still questions, Balthasar...Pointless doubts and questions...Walking on and away from the blazing light, he realised that what he needed was solitude, silence, clarity.

He was almost sure that it was night now, for his tired eyes caught something resembling the glint of stars in a blessedly black firmament. The ground was rough and dry and dusty. He began to stumble. He grew dizzy. He fell, and lost track of time until light came over him, and he winced and cried out and covered his face in awe, only to discover that it was merely the harsh blaze of the sun. This place truly was a wasteland, and in its way it was terrible. But it was beautiful as well, in the deathless heat-shimmer of its emptiness.

Balthasar walked on through places of stones and dry bones. Then, as evening came, he sought shelter from the sudden cold in a decayed hole at the edge of the mountains. Others had been in this cave before him. There was a sour stench, and there were carvings on the rocks. Squatting on the dark hard ground inside after willing a few sticks to make a fire, Balthasar traced these marks with his fingers. A babble of symbols in different alphabets honouring different gods, all of which he now knew almost for certain to be misguided. Still, he found these leavings of other seekers after truth oddly comforting.

Some of the most recent markings, he noticed, were written by one hand, and in Aramaic. Studying these scratches more closely in the firelight, he saw that they mimicked the words of the old prophecies which Melchior had once shown him, and he looked around at this squalid place in which he had sought shelter with a different gaze. Somehow, and for all that he had witnessed, it seemed beyond incredible that this decayed hole was the very place in which Jesus Christ had sought shelter in his time in the wilderness. Yet how could he doubt it, after all that he had heard and seen? The writing was loose and ill-composed—you could sense the writer's anguish—and terminated in crude series of crosses.

The fire died. Balthasar sat alone in the dark, waiting for the return of the sun, and perhaps for an end to his own torment. He remembered again that first journey he had taken to this land with his two friends, and the subsequent slaughter of the innocents. Jesus had survived to fulfil the prophecies scrawled on these walls, yes. But what of all the others? Was *that* what his gift of myrrh had foretold, the pointless death of hundreds of children? And why—the question came back to him, although left unasked in Jesus's presence—had an all-powerful God permitted such a thing to happen? Why had pain and suffering been allowed into this world at all?

In the darkness, Balthasar shook his head. *Always the same with you,* he heard the Gaspar's voice saying. *You have too many doubts, too many questions.* Yet everything he had seen in New Jerusalem had left him unsatisfied.

A slow dawn was coming, rising from the east in gaunt, hot shadow. A cur dog howled. The wind hissed. Looking out across this landscape, Balthasar thought of Jesus squatting in this same cave, and wondered about his last days of torment, and about how he must have felt, and what he had seen. Then, as heat rose and the sky whitened, Balthasar took a stick of charcoal from the remnants of his fire and began to make his own marks across the rough stone. It had been a long time since he had engaged in the practice of serious magic, but the shapes to make the necessary spell of summoning came to him with astonishing ease.